The Kingdom

Rescue

Flames of Spring

K.L. Blake

KBlake

Contents

Dedication

Never let anyone extinguish your flame.

Map of Nedona

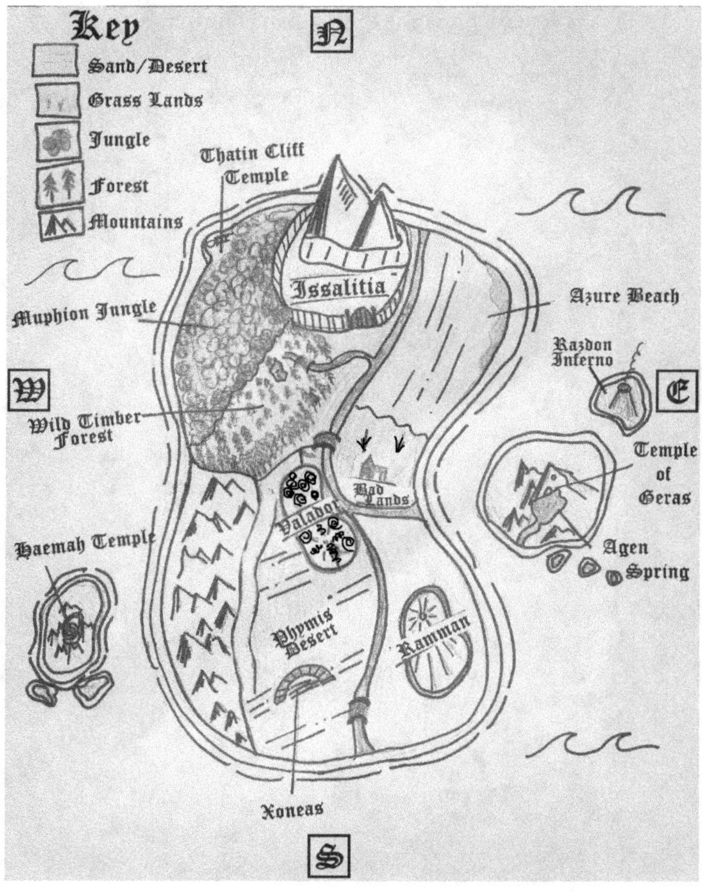

Prologue

Five hundred years ago

ON THE PLANET XANDELAR, in the continent of Nedona, there was a kingdom called Issalitia. The kingdom boasted tall, white stone walls, beautifully crafted buildings, and cobblestone streets. It was an incredibly safe and prosperous kingdom, and as in every kingdom, there was an heir who would one day inherit the throne. In Issalitia, that heir was a fae princess who controlled the magic of spring, creating greenery, ancient floral poisons, and beautiful gardens, along with a gift passed down by the Goddess of Spring.

The princess was in love with her childhood friend, the son of a nobleman. Their love was just out of reach as the princess was only ever meant to marry a prince. She loved the nobleman's son with all her heart; he carried water magic in his veins. Besides, what would be more perfect than a love between spring and water?

Over time, the princess and her nobleman's son grew closer. One evening, in her sixteenth year, she met him beneath the stars along Azur Beach, where he confessed his undying love for her. He vowed to be by her side, whether she married a prince or decided to leave the kingdom to start a life anew. Following this heartfelt confession, he made gentle love to her.

The following day, a messenger delivered a letter from King Brontos of Ramman, requesting a marriage match between the princess and his son. The King of Ramman was gentle and honest; he'd lost his beloved queen in childbirth of that very son. So deeply cherished was Queen Phoebe Illumae Brontos that the kingdom fell into a deep depression for a decade.

With the letter came a realization: the young princess's love affair had come to an end. Over the next nine months, the princess would marry the distant prince and prepare to ascend the throne of her kingdom.

The princess's parents died ten years before, and this day was inevitable.

They had tried for years to conceive an heir. It was only after they made a voyage to the Temple of Geras, praying that the waters of the Agen Spring would give them the gift they wished for, that they succeeded. Ten months later, the fae queen finally gave birth to her beautiful daughter, Zandra Isla Creighton. After the birth, the queen never truly recovered. She was exhausted, frail, and weak. The toll it took on her body was tremendous; when she inevitably succumbed to her fate, Zandra was only six years old.

One full day after the loss of her mother, Zandra lost her father. The mighty King of Issalitia had died of a broken heart. Zandra had only heard it in stories, myths, and legends, but never expected to be left to be queen of a kingdom at six years old. She was raised by servants and the wives of noblemen, which is how she met Jerix, the only man she would ever truly love. Jerix Rane Branisalva was the son of a member of the Queen's Guard. He was training to become one himself, to guard and honor his new queen. Convenient, considering the Kingdom of Issalitia was about to change, for better or for worse...

Part
One

Chapter
I

Present Day

Arysalia

"SAM, PLEASE, WE MUST get out of this castle!" I whine.

"Arysa, please. I want to sleep."

"We won't get caught, I promise."

"We *can't* get caught again. Your father will never let you leave your room," she says.

She has a point. My father's anger has worsened over the last few hundred years. Especially now that I'm older. As fae, we reach our mature age at twenty, and after that, we stop aging so quickly. Our lifespan varies depending on bloodline; it is said that royal fae can live between seven hundred years and top out at close to a millennium.

I am two hundred and one years old, and my father, the Mad King, is five hundred and sixteen. We have been trapped in this kingdom our entire lives. Samarra and I would love to be free enough to get out of here and enjoy what Nedona has to offer. All we have is the library, filled with books and illustrations of the continent we live on. We can't get out of this kingdom without getting caught by the guards at the only gate we have. I know this because I've tried. A lot.

"Fine," I say, defeated. "But if I die of boredom, it is all your fault. Maybe we can just stay in the courtyard and pretend we are out in the world?"

I can see my pleading chipping away at Samarra's resolve. I've only ask this of her because I know she can't resist the pull; the courtyard and our imaginations are our only escape.

"Fine, but we must get back before it's too late. You may not have to work tomorrow, but I do," she says with a note of finality.

I smile in mock surprise, as if I didn't already know she'd agree.

Samarra works at the castle bakery. Although I don't have to work, I do anyway. I'd rather work alongside my best friend than be anywhere else in this blasted castle.

The royal bakery is extensive, with its own wing off the massive kitchen to serve the entire castle. The castle is not only home to the monarchs, but also to most of the noble families.

We change out of our flour-dusted clothes. It is the end of winter and the beginning of spring now, but it is not yet warm enough for sundresses, so we dress in wool trousers and flowy tunics instead. Thankfully, within the castle walls of Issalitia, I don't have to don a dress, gloves, or hood.

We grab a book and head out into the secluded courtyard, where vines climb the walls and the flowers are just now beginning to bloom.

The castle is primarily constructed from the white stone of Issalitia Mountain that rises skyward behind it. Small courtyards were built into the walls of the entire kingdom. This courtyard is private, situated along the outer edge of the castle at the base of the tower, where my rooms are located.

I have an entire tower to myself, but I hate it. It's almost as much of a prison as this whole kingdom is.

I lie across the stone bench, my head in Samarra's lap as she braids and unbraids my hair while I read a story we have read countless times before.

"This is the story of a princess from a distant land who fell in love with a farm boy. That boy turned out to be a king in his own right, but he did not want to win her heart that way. He charmed her with his wit and knowledge of the world. She was a princess of spring, and he was a boy who knew how to coax water out of any nook and cranny."

"But the princess had a secret; she was cursed to live in a human form during the day, and by night, she turned into the wild willow tree within the kingdom walls."

As I turn the pages, I can almost recite it from memory.

"She had to return to the kingdom before the sun completely set. The farm boy didn't want her to go; he wanted to be with her forever. They promised to meet in this exact spot by the river every day, three hours before sunset. Every day for five years, they met and lay beneath the trees until the king became suspicious of the princess's whereabouts. He found her with the farm boy and banned her from ever visiting again. If she disobeyed, she would be forbidden from ever leaving the kingdom again."

Samarra's breathing becomes slower the longer I speak. She carries a lot of anxiety that I don't understand, but when I read, it disappears.

"After a moon cycle passed, the princess fell into a deep depression. If she couldn't see the love of her life, there was no point in living. She contemplated everything she could do to fix it, but it always led back to the curse of the willow. There was some correspondence for the king the next day, requesting the princess's hand in marriage. The princess declined, but the king accepted."

I will likely never have a choice in my union, I think, as I come to the best part of the story.

"Their wedding day came quickly. When she reached the end of the aisle, head down, eyes filled with tears beneath her veil, she finally lifted her head. She looked up into the eyes of the man she had loved for over five years. The king had no idea the poor, ill-suited farm boy she loved stood under all the princely garbs; he was the man who could save her from her father."

As the sun sets below the walls of our kingdom, I read on.

"When the noonday bells tolled twelve times, they kissed, sealing their marriage and undoing the curse of the willow. The willow curse had kept the princess confined to her kingdom, but it was broken with her marriage to a person of royal blood."

I finish the last page and snap the book closed, discarding it on my chest. Looking up into my beloved friend's face, I realize I don't need to find love if I have Samarra by my side.

"I adore that tale; it rings with truth in so many ways," Sam whispers to me, quiet joy in her tone.

"I wonder how I will ever find a love like that if I am trapped within these walls. If I marry outside this kingdom, could I leave? Would I be able to take you with me?" It is something I have contemplated every day for the last century.

"I believe anything could happen, Arysa. You know that, and I know that. Maybe there is a book in the library that can help us break our curse."

We have talked about this before; escaping, that is. We've searched the library high and low many times. The Enchanted Dagger of Rythorin is stored in a runed and cloaked area of the castle, a location known only to the king. His decision to close the kingdom was made five centuries ago. His people have been imprisoned ever since.

"You're right, but where else do we look?" I ask.

Samarra swirls my hair around her finger, humming a tune she has hummed our entire lives, an old fire sprite hymn meant to keep evil away, taught to her by her father.

"Hmm... maybe it will just come to us," she says.

"Maybe you're right. We never truly know what destiny has planned for us, do we?"

"No, Arysa," Samarra says, looking off in the distance. "No, we do not."

Chapter 2

Two hundred years earlier

Queen of Spring

"YOU CANNOT DO THIS, Maggard. He has been my guard my entire life. Please don't take him from me now," I plead.

My husband, the Mad King, plans to kill Jerix, after everything we've been through. Jerix has served as the head of the Queen's Guard for the last three hundred years, and now that I am with child, Maggard wants to kill him.

"You did this, Zandra. You have kept that water magic guard as your pet for long enough. He will not be around when my child is brought into this world," he bellows.

I can almost taste his foul breath as he spits. "I will end him and whatever has been going on between you two for the last three centuries."

"Please don't do this. He is the closest thing I have to family. Please don't take him from me."

"Zandra! Do not make me lock you in the dungeon!" he shouts.

He wouldn't, couldn't. Could he? This is my kingdom. He can't do this.

"Please…" I whisper into my hands as tears run down my face. "Please don't do this. I'll do anything."

"Yes, you will. You will get the fuck over it! You will choose a new guard, and you will raise our child!" He grabs my wrist when I attempt to escape his orbit. "You will not fight this. You have one night to say goodbye, and that is where my mercy ends," he whispers through gritted teeth.

My stomach roils. He drops my hand and pushes his way out of the room. I am unable to move, and my lungs refuse to take in air.

I can't do this. I won't survive if I lose the man I love; not now, after all this time.

I get to my feet. I must get to Jerix before Maggard does. I must warn him. Resolute in my decision, I make my way to the guard quarters on this floor of the castle, three floors above the ground throne room. Jerix is already there waiting. He stands and rushes to me, tears running down his face.

He knows.

"Please, Jerix, I tried to reason with him," I admit to him through my tears.

"I know, my queen," he whispers into my hair. He rubs my back in soothing circles. "I know, my darling flower."

"I cannot lose you. I won't be able to survive in this world without you." I cry harder now.

"You will. You must raise our child," he whispers. "Raise our bloom to know who I am, who her true father is. I will be waiting for you over the stars, my flower."

"Please, run away, get out of here. I cannot live in a world where you do not breathe, my darling," I sob.

He pulls away, holding me gently by the shoulders. "I cannot. You know as well as I do that this kingdom is a cage. I will go, I will die, and I will be so proud of the child we created. When it is your time, we will be together again, my queen," he whispers, choking on tears of his own. "I will love you forever. Now let's spend this last night together, alone in each other's arms."

Jerix carries me to my quarters, which are nowhere near Maggard's quarters. We may be married, but only in name, and that name is mine.

This is my kingdom.

"Kiss me, my darling," I whisper into his mouth, soaking up every breath he has, one last time.

Chapter 3

Present Day

Finox

"**Y**OU NEED TO FIND a new hobby, Finox. We can't keep breaking into other kingdoms and expecting not to get ourselves killed," Goren grumbles as we walk unseen along the cobblestones of Issalitia.

"Goren, you know that my illusions will keep us safe, they always do," I whisper–shout to my best friend.

"Do not start with me. When we decided it was a good idea to try making it through the Muphion Jungle, that jungle lady almost ate us for dinner," he mumbles as we make our way around the outskirts of the castle.

I take in the expanse of the castle's walls, the way I do every time I come here. The sheer height of the white stone is unnerving.

I know it won't collapse, but what if it did?

There are very narrow shafts of light glowing from the edges of embrasures in the wall. I know it well, just as I know they will be here too.

We scale the wall with ease, just like we have for the past five years, ever since discovering the impenetrable kingdom is, in fact, penetrable. We peer through the narrow slats to see two of the most beautiful creatures we have ever seen.

Lying on a stone bench is a young woman who must be about our age. She's holding a book above her head, reading aloud. Her hair, the color of the richest obsidian I've ever seen, shimmers almost blue in the torchlight. Her eyes are the lightest shade of emerald. Her delicate features suggest she is fae, like the rest of the continent. Her head rests on the lap of a taller woman with light pink hair, a shade you only see in paintings. The shiny pink strands sparkle around her face as she braids her companion's hair, listening to her read.

"You know this is really creepy," Goren whispers beside me.

"It is not creepy; they can't see or hear us." I chuckle. "It's like watching a play at the theater."

He rolls his eyes. "That is the definition of creepy, my lord," he whispers.

"Fine, I just wanted to see her," I tell him. He knows the reasons.

"I know you do. Now you've seen her. Let's go," he says as he tries to usher me away from the shaft of light. A shadow moves from under the stone bench. Glowing green eyes, massive and round, peek out from under it. I look over at Goren, whose face has been drained of all semblance of color. He knows exactly what I'm thinking, and the creature can see us.

Chapter 4

Arysalia

FEELING UNSETTLED, I LOOK over the edge of the bench. There she is, Umbra, the stray oracat we found on the streets when we snuck out last week. She's deep in a crouch and eyeing the slashes of night along the courtyard's edges. She moves out from under the bench and into the courtyard, plopping down in front of me. She cocks her head to the side. Her silky tail whips from side to side.

I wonder what it is that she sees.

"Are you seeing this?" I whisper to Samarra, whose eyes have gone wide.

Samarra nods slowly. "There is something out there." She shrinks into herself as Umbra stalks toward whatever is lurking in the shadows.

"Umbra," I hiss quietly to the feline. "What do you see?" She crouches down even lower, looking up, and clicks her tongue. The shadows in the darkness disappear, and two sets of eyes peer back at us from the dark.

"Who's there?" I shout.

There is shuffling and mumbling.

"They can see us, Fin," a gruff male voice echoes beyond the way.

"I see that," comes a reluctant response.

I look back at Samarra; she has shrunk even further into herself, eyes flickering between ice blue and magenta. I jump up from my seat and pick up Umbra.

"Who are you? I am Princess Arysalia Beck Creighton!" I try my hardest to sound as much like my queen mother as possible. With another click of Umbra's tongue, the voices we heard transform as two figures appear before us, no longer hidden behind the wall of stone.

"Hello, Princess," says the first man.

His hair is swept back into a knot at the back of his head, and his eyes glow like fresh amber. He is dressed as a commoner, but all in black. The massive man next to him stands a few inches taller. His hair is bright vermilion, with a shock of white over the corner of his eye, marred by a brutal scar. The scar extends from his forehead to his upper lip. One of his eyes is a burning silver that looks almost unseeing, the other a moss green that could put any forest to shame.

I ponder aloud, "You know me, but I still do not know you."

"I am no one of consequence," he says with a curt bow.

I look at the taller man and see that he cannot take his eyes off my Samarra. She stares back at him as if she can see into his soul. Her body is quivering, and the skin along her arms is standing on end.

"No one of consequence? Lovely..." I say, rolling my eyes. "And who is your companion?"

"I am Goren Chinook Clode, wielder of the wind," the larger man says. The first man stares at him, as though planning to murder him where he stands. Goren still does not take his eyes off Samarra.

"Well, Goren Chinook Clode, stop looking at my companion!" I growl. My free hand closes into a fist as I direct all my frustration at the massive man.

"Who is she?" Goren tilts his head to the side.

"No one of consequence," I say with a curt laugh. I take a step back.

"Fine," the first man says. "I am Finox Ralis Vimmaglyn."

I gasp. The King of the Middle Kingdom is in our courtyard... inside the locked kingdom.

"You claim to be the king of another kingdom, hiding in the shadows of *my* courtyard in *my* kingdom. Well, I highly doubt that. You're probably an assassin of the Forsaken Legion, here to find a way to get my king's dagger."

Am I trying to keep the atmosphere light because I am terrified of the truth?

"Oh no, Princess. I am indeed Finox of the Middle Kingdom, but I do not work for the Dark King. I am here for you," he says nonchalantly. The wink that accompanies his declaration makes me jerk my head back in shock. I grasp Sam's hand, holding it tightly.

The man who calls himself Goren speaks. "We have frightened you." He looks at me for a moment, then back at Sam. "It was never our intention. We did not know you had an oracat, or that they had the power to not only dismantle the illusion my king has created but to bring us through the wall itself."

Goren is speaking not to me but to Samarra. She sits still, holding my hand in a death grip.

"Well, your majesty," I say, with a growl, turning my attention to Finox. "Please explain why you have entered this locked kingdom and how you have made it past the front gate."

"Princess, if I told you all of my tricks, how would I return here to see you again?" he jests, eyes twinkling in the moonlight.

"You will tell me, or I will scream and let the guards have their way with you. King or not," I say with the calm elegance my mother taught me.

"Fine." He places his hands in his pockets and paces. "I will place an illusion around the courtyard, so we are not seen or heard."

He looks at Umbra. She stares unmoving, as though she's looking right through him.

"Good," I growl at the presumptive kingling.

He removes his hand from his pocket, waving it across the sky in an arc. I see the signet ring on his right hand now, with the swirl and star that tells me he is indeed of the Middle Kingdom of Valador.

I can almost taste the magic around me, like cherries and citrus. The scent floods my senses with a hint of sweetness but is inherently sour. If I didn't know there was an illusion around us, I'd think we were standing in a citrus grove.

"There," he says, as he and Goren move to the other bench in the courtyard.

They could be brothers, considering their similar coloring and the hint of red in both their hair. Goren's a head taller and a bit broader than Finox, though Finox looks strong, given the way his tunic and trousers strain over his chest and thighs.

"We have been trying to find a way into your castle for a long time, trying to find out why this kingdom is closed off. It still receives correspondence from other kingdoms, but it never accepts visitors. And no one ever leaves willingly, or alive for that matter," he says, crossing his arms in front of him. "First, it was just out of curiosity. But then, with everything happening in the desert to the south, I had to know how we could end the curse and fix the unease on the continent, and hopefully trap the Xoneas Kingdom instead."

"The Dark Kingdom in the south? What's happening down there?" I ask, my brow furrowing. "How do you plan to trap them?"

"That's why we have been watching you. We need to get the dagger out and find a way to destroy it or use it against King Morbious." He pauses and looks at Goren, who is busy looking at Samarra. "I believe it is only a matter of time before Morbious comes for the dagger."

I take a deep, centering breath. How could the King of the Dark Kingdom make it in here with his Forsaken Legion? It should be impossible... But then again, Finox is in here, so maybe it's not so impossible after all.

Chapter 5

Arysalia

"**H**OW LONG?" I ASK. All my stubbornness and anger boil beneath my skin as I contemplate Finox's presence in my kingdom.

"How long is what?"

I grind my teeth together. *This insolent—*

"How long have you been sneaking into my kingdom and spying on us?" I say as my lips curl into a sneer.

"For a while," he shrugs. "I never expected we'd get caught. My spells and illusions are almost imp—"

"We need to find a way to stop this from happening," Goren interrupts, "or the entire continent will be under Morbious's control." He sounds quite shaken. His eyes are still glued to my friend.

"What do you suppose we do?" I ask. "We have never left this kingdom. Assuming I can leave, I am not leaving without Samarra." Goren's eyes light up, and I realize my mistake too late.

"Samarra," Goren repeats, his voice soft and gentle. His eyes soften as he looks at my companion. "A beautiful name for a beautiful girl."

Samarra blushes and squeezes my hand harder.

"That is enough," I hiss. "This isn't a date. We need to decide what we are going to do. What we need to do."

"Precisely," Finox nods.

"The king keeps the dagger hidden away, locked and guarded. How do you suppose we get the dagger?"

"We could illusion it out, trick the guards into believing what they are seeing," Finox says. "With the curse in place, it shouldn't matter *where* the dagger is, but" he pauses, "I still need to do some research on the dagger."

"I thought we didn't have a lot of time?" I wonder out loud. "How do you expect to gain information on the dagger without tipping anyone off? And where would someone even find the information?"

"I also have a library, Princess; I can do research," he growls. "But maybe you could do some research of your own?" He looks at me with eyes that twinkle in the torchlight. "Ask your king about the dagger. See if you can find out more about what it would take to get someone out of the kingdom without the curse killing them at daybreak." *The curse was placed long before I was born. We were all under the impression that no one could ever leave, and if they did, they wouldn't make it back in time... Their life was forfeit, so no one left, no one attempted to enter in fear they would be trapped and never leave the locked kingdom. What I didn't know was that nothing was stopping people from coming in; we only have one way in and out.* I think, giving the kingling a look of utter dismay. *He didn't get seen by the guards, so no one could stop him in his quest for answers.*

"You have got to be kidding. You want me to ask the man we plan to steal from about the thing we are going to steal?" I say incredulously. "Absolutely not."

"Do you have a sorcerer or sorceress?" Finox questions.

"Besides my mother, the Queen of Spring? She has great power and knows many things about elemental magic—" I start to explain.

"No, not of elemental magic, the Dagger of Rythorin was not made of elements. It was forged by dragon fire millennia ago, and it is almost impossible to destroy. Depending on the rune magic it contains, we need a loophole. We cannot destroy it here in this kingdom, of that I am certain." Finox divulges this information as if I am a complete idiot.

"I am not an idiot. I know how magic works," I say, growing increasingly irritated with his beautiful face and stupid mouth.

"I never said you were. How am I to know of your magical prowess, Princess? I have only just met you," he quips.

I growl immediately in response. I feel the tightness in my hand loosen, and Samarra stands abruptly.

"I–I know how to get out of the kingdom without being killed," she whispers to Goren. All our heads turn toward her. She is staring at Goren, and the corner of his mouth quirks up. Her eyes shift from fearful pink back to the ice blue that is usually hers.

"Tell us, Samarra, of the pink flame." My eyes widen at Goren's assertion.

"Excuse me, who the fuck do you think you are?" I hiss. "She is not a pink flame!"

Sweat runs down between my shoulder blades. *How could he know my darling best friend has the rarest magic on the continent?*

My thoughts race. The consequences of this knowledge could be dangerous.

The king raises his hands on behalf of the wind wielder general. "My apologies, Princess, but I want to hear what she has to say," Finox coaxes.

I want to drown him where he stands.

I am on the verge of telling him that when Samarra starts speaking.

"If I carry the dagger, the pink flame will protect me from harm." She turns, looking down at me now. "I have known for a long time that a curse or magic cannot kill me, but it can harm me. If the pink flame makes contact with the dagger, it will act like a shackle. It will keep the magic from harming me without destroying the king's beloved runes." She looks away from me, her shoulders shaking even in the warmth of the night.

I quickly realize that this means we could have left this godforsaken kingdom a century ago. We tell each other everything. How could she have kept this a secret from me all this time?

My mouth falls open, but nothing comes out. As if sensing the betrayal I feel, Samarra says, "Arysa, I am so sorry. I wanted to tell you, but my father didn't want to risk the king knowing anything about the pink flame or the fact that I could, in a way, dismantle the runes he put in place to keep us all enslaved."

"Well," Finox coughs, severing the awkward moment, "Now we just need to plan for how we will achieve—"

"We are not doing anything until I know the facts and have time to think about this. Come back in two nights' time when the moon is at its fullest. We will decide on a plan then," I command.

"Two nights? Why not right now?" the kingling asks.

"Because I need to talk to Samarra without your brooding male staring at her like he wants to wear her like a tunic." I tilt my head in his direction. *Yup, he is still staring at her.*

"Fine," Finox grinds out. "We will return in two nights' time under the illusion. Make sure you have that beast with you to suck us through the wall again."

"Fine," I say.

With that, Umbra clicks her tongue without warning, and the men disappear from view.

***

"Good girl," I coo at Umbra, scratching below her chin. "Are you okay, Sam?" I question lightly.

"I– I'm fine, Arysa. I am sorry I lied to you. I didn't want to put your life at risk," she says shakily. "I love you and never want anything to happen to you." A single tear falls from her blue eyes, running down her porcelain skin. She looks at me, her eyes brimming with sorrow. "Can we go to bed now? I need sleep."

"Yes, we can go to bed. Would you like to sleep in my chambers tonight?" I ask, knowing she will likely tell me no. She hasn't slept in my chamber since we were tiny.

"Yes, Arysa, I would like to be in the tower tonight." She hooks an arm through mine, turning us toward the entrance.

"Of course. I can have the cook make us hot chocolate?" I offer.

"I just need to tell my father where I will be, then I'll meet you at the tower door."

I nod, and we make our way to the courtyard's heavy iron door.

Chapter 6

"**W**ELL, WE ARE GOOD and fucked, I'd say," I say to my longest-living friend as we fly to a safe area to rest and ponder how to get the dagger out of the kingdom and destroy it.

"Yes, Sire, we are," he shouts over the gusts of wind blowing past us while we soar over Nedona on our hippogriffs. Hippogriffs are not a common beast on Nedona; they are a hybrid mix of a griffin and a horse. The two we are flying were born in a twin litter, which is incredibly uncommon in hybrid creature breeding. Most hybrid beasts conceive and deliver one foal per cycle. They are almost identical, but mine, Sasha, has a red tuft of feathers on the crown of her head, and Goren's girl, Greta, doesn't have that iconic crown. It is almost as if the universe knew we'd have these two beautiful creatures for ourselves.

We visit the locked kingdom every month, without fail, since I have been able to enter using my illusions. We have been collecting information and evidence on how to disable the curse that plagues the once-great kingdom, but we have never been caught until now.

We finally land within the Wild Timber Forest that lies between both our kingdoms. This is a neutral zone, probably because Issalitian's haven't left their kingdom in five hundred years, but who's counting?

This forest isn't without its dangers. Creatures lurk that could kill and eat us both. Some of those beings, like spinspiders, are the size of a large child and will spin an adult in threads while they sleep and eat them on the spot, while pumars, enormous cat beasts, are known to play with their food before eating.

There are so many monsters here, but I have something most travelers don't. "Illusion is up, Goren. Let's get some sleep and work out a plan in the morning."

"I need to ask you something before we rest our heads for the night, Fin." His face betrays his worry; it is paler than usual, and there's a hunch to his shoulders that isn't normally present.

"What is it, Goren? Is everything okay?" I ask tentatively, not wanting to upset him further.

"She is the pink flame from my dreams."

He doesn't need to say more. I know exactly what he's talking about. The pink flame, who has been living in his dreams his entire life. He knows what she can do, the devastation she can cause. We share a look.

Her pink flame can devastate entire cities, not just a dagger.

"I know, but does she know that she can shift? Because you and I both know an unpracticed shifter can be dangerous, but a—"

"I know!" he exclaims, then pauses to collect himself. "I am sorry. I know she could be dangerous, but she is the key to saving the entire continent." He lowers his eyes to the forest floor. "There is something else, though."

Suddenly, he can't meet my eyes. I lean in to hear him better.

"I am in love with her."

Chapter 7

Samarra

"ARYSALIA! WAKE UP!" I pull the blankets off my very stubborn princess, then continue to get ready for the sun to rise.

"Sam, we were up late. Let me be," she half groans.

"You don't have to come, but how else are we going to figure out a plan for how to find you-know-what and what to do next?"

I don't know how else to get her out of bed. She is a princess, but she is also very stubborn.

"Yes. Yes, I'm getting up," she says, reluctantly rolling out of bed and barely getting a leg out of the fluffy duvet before crashing to the floor. Jumping upright, she exclaims, "I need a grog draft first. You know I'm not me without the boost."

"You can have it while we bake," I say, giving her an exaggerated, "Your Highness" as we get dressed and make our way down to the kitchen. It is time to bake, scheme, and figure out how the fuck we are going to handle this mess we're in.

***

Finox

The morning sun shines through the limbs of this terrifying forest. We survived the night with the illusion intact, but we need to plan. "Goren," I whisper, "are you awake?"

"Yes, Fin," he responds, rolling over on his bedding mat.

"What the fuck are we going to do? They weren't supposed to see us. I feel as if our plan went from collecting information to a full-fledged war."

"That oracat did, somehow." He pauses thoughtfully. "When I laid eyes on Samarra the first few times we visited, I had a feeling." He looks down. "The only issue was that her eyes were wrong. The fire goddess in my dreams had eyes of dusty pink skies, not azure blue.

Her terror at our appearance must have temporarily removed the runed magic that was disguising her eyes."

"That's how you figured it out?" I ask.

"The prophecy in my dreams shows so much destruction, but she is so unassuming and delicate," he explains. "I mean, you saw her. I want to wrap her in my arms as if she were my sole reason for breathing."

"Well then, Goren, we have to figure this out quickly. We only have two nights, and we can't make it back to my library in that amount of time."

If we hadn't been caught, we would have had much more time to plan this, but no, that annoying feline forced us to give up our advantage.

"We could always try to find the Dryad witch. She is likely watching us as we speak," Goren suggests.

He isn't wrong. The old witch is likely watching from the tree limbs.

"The illusion should have blocked us from both her foresight and actual sight."

The snap of a whip rings through the air.

"You spoke too soon..." Goren whispers as we watch the edges of my illusion dissipate, revealing not what, but who, is standing at the edge of the woods: the Dryad witch herself. The air turns cold, and the sweat at the base of my spine cools. A shiver rolls up my back.

This is not going to be good.

Chapter 8

Finox

A PETITE YOUNG FEMALE stands before us, dressed in shades of brown and green that easily camouflage her in the forest. Her hair is tied into a braided crown with sticks, twigs, and vines wrapped intricately around the strands. She is stunning, but this, too, is an illusion of her own making.

The Dryad witch of the forest is, in fact, very, very old—older than all the kings and possibly the forest itself.

"Kingling," she rasps. The sound sends a feeling of dread through my body.

Her voice gives away her age; its cadence is one that echoes a life lived long and hard.

"Dryad." Her beautiful façade is unsettling; it's almost too gorgeous for someone who dwells in the forest.

"It isn't polite to talk about someone when they aren't around to hear it," she grates. "I have heard from the trees that you have a problem."

"Yes, Dryad," Goren speaks up, interrupting my thoughts.

I look over, and he shrugs. He's never afraid of conversation or confrontation; his fierce mother and foreboding father raised him. They raised me as well, but I wasn't their kin. I was their king.

"Goren Chinook Clode, wind wielder to the King of Illusions." She tilts her head as a predator would, as if she can hear his thoughts or even taste his fear. I fight the urge to run.

"Dryad, witch of the forest," he replies.

"I have come to help you with your problem." She looks back at me. "Kingling, you have a dilemma, and I have answers."

There is always a price, I remind myself. *Information, like any good, comes at a cost.*

"What's your price, witch?" I question, trying to restrain my anger and fear.

"I request only one thing." She steps closer. "I request one favor, whatever I need, whenever I need it."

"I can't do that, witch. You know I am a king. I cannot owe favors to anyone." I try to sound like a monarch.

I know I cannot make this deal. Kings should only be beholden to their kingdom.

"This wouldn't be a favor of cruelty or malice. What I need will not be needed for ages," she explains. "When the time comes, I will whisper your name into the forest three times, and you will return to me and help me with a task."

"We promise," Goren responds.

He's decided for us both, apparently.

He looks over at me sheepishly. "Sorry, Fin, I need this information."

I pinch the bridge of my nose in annoyance.

"Fine," I breathe.

"It is a deal then," the Dryad says. "For the flame to be freed, the creature must be freed. The flame must no longer hide but be alive."

"What the fuck does that mean?" I shout. Her riddle makes no sense. "How do you expect us to do that?"

"The flame has been hidden for centuries and centuries, wasting away. Someone must ignite the flame and bring it back to the continent." She says it as if this morsel of information means nothing of consequence.

"How do you expect us to find this dead flame?" I ask the witch.

"Goren Chinook Clode knows the way. He has been shown."

I look over to my friend, who looks just as puzzled. I look back at the woods, and the witch is gone. There is no trace of her anywhere, as if she has turned into the trees themselves.

Chapter 9

Arysalia

SAMARRA AND I HAVE been baking all morning. The fresh air is blowing through the open windows, and flour is getting everywhere.

"Sam, please explain why you've never told me," I plead. "How did I not know that you could be tethered to the dagger? That we could escape?" My best friend, my confidant, the girl I would give my life to save, didn't tell me.

"It was a secret meant to be kept for our safety, but there is more." Her eyes close, and she takes a deep breath. "My mother did not die in the way you have been told, and my father is not truly my father."

"What?" I am stunned. I know her father. I love her father. He speaks so highly of her mother. "I don't understand."

"My mother and father prayed to all the gods and goddesses of our realm for a child of their own. The only one to answer their prayer was the fire goddess, Seraphina Zinnia," Sam explains quietly, not meeting my gaze. "One spring morning, a storm destroyed part of the kingdom; lightning burned homes and trees, but also brought me." She looks up at me now. "The daughter my parents had always wanted was lying in the courtyard of their estate. I was wrapped in pink linen with eyes shining like magenta flames, and my hair was already pink."

"They adopted you and raised you as their own?" I ask, knowing the answer.

"Yes, my mother and father kept me a secret for a long time. They runed my eyes to hide the flame and came up with a story about how they had me." She went on, "Unfortunately, on my second birthday, my mother fell ill from Nedonarian Influenza, which was rampant at the time, leaving my father to care for me."

I remember we lost a large majority of our kingdom during that bout of illness. I thought Maggard would surely do something to bring in healers from other kingdoms or at least send the sick to receive treatment. He did neither. He let families lose their loved ones while the kingdom lost valued members.

"My parents and I worked in the bakery the entire time as I was growing up," Samarra continued. "That's when I met you. I was delivering bread to the castle when I heard you crying in the hall. I was not like the other kids in the kingdom, and neither were you." Her gaze is wistful.

I smile, thinking back to that day. "I remember you had a basket with rolls. They smelled like heaven. You gave me one and asked if we could be friends." I think back to that day fondly, the day I met my twin flame, my best friend.

"I do, too. That is why keeping this from you has been so hard." She looks at me with shame and sadness. "There is something else I need to tell you, but I've been too afraid."

The frustration I felt earlier builds inside me again. "There is more. What could it poss—"

"I have been having these dreams." She gestures to her temples with trembling fingers. Closing her eyes, she rubs them gently. "I have had glimpses of him."

"Glimpses of *who*?"

"Goren." She takes a deep breath, and I struggle not to do the same. "It first started with a glimpse of a man with vermilion hair, then I saw his eye; his unseeing silver eye." She drops her hands. "Most recently, though, I have been seeing his green eye, full of warmth and longing. As if he, too, had seen me before, or was seeing me in that moment."

"That's why you were terrified when they appeared in our courtyard?" That explains her unease.

"Yes. He looked at me, and I knew he was the man who had been living in my dreams for years."

"Years? You have kept this from me for *years*?"

"It has been happening for five years now."

She looks so ashamed. I grab her and hold her tight to my chest, the one person I have loved and confided in. It may have been a mistake not to tell me the truth, but she had her reasons.

Shortly after her confession, Samarra retreats to spend the evening with her father while I scour the castle's main library. The castle has several smaller libraries that do not hold the kingdom's records or older tomes. The information I am looking for is more than a few centuries old.

I open the ornate doors that lead into the grand hall, which serves as the entrance to the library. This library has multiple wings, mezzanine balconies, and more librarians than I can care to count. Unfortunately, they are incredibly notorious for being gossips and will inform the king if I investigate topics that I have no business looking into.

It's up to me to find the tome or scroll in the vast expanse of shelves. I need more information on Seraphina Zinnia. After what feels like a lifetime of searching, I'm in the part of the library with sections on everything throughout our kingdom and beyond. Some ancient texts detail the history of our planet, continent, and neighboring kingdoms. The only issue is that most of my information is from hundreds of years ago. This library hasn't been updated adequately since the kingdom was isolated from the continent and our sister kingdoms.

I scan through scrolls that cover the many gods in our history. Our continent, Nedona, was named after the God of Birth, who created our continent, perhaps even the world in which we live. The God of Geras brings gifts to those who are worthy of them. The gifts come in different forms, but the most common is a miracle. One that the holder has been desperate for. The God of Muphion is the god of the insane, the keeper of the crazies. The list goes on and on. When Xandelar, our planet, was an infant, the only beings to live here were the gods themselves.

Finally, I find the texts I have been searching for. One is a dusty scroll that appears to have remained untouched for decades. Along the wooden seam that connects the ends of the scroll to its innards is an engraving: *The Last Fire Goddess, Seraphina Zinnia.* The other resembles a map, and it is of much greater importance.

Scrawled into the corner of each of the large schematic papers are "dungeon," "first floor," "throne room," and so on.

I make my way over to the large table in the center of the library and set them and a candelabra on the table. The smell of worn cloth emanating from the scroll makes it hard to breathe. The urge to sneeze all over this ancient thing is too tempting, so I stifle it. When I manage to get the edge of the scroll rolled out far enough, an image catches my eye.

There is a tall, lithe woman with long, flowing hair. She has scales running down her shoulders, along the sides of her arms, extending to her back. The scales wrap around the front of her body beneath her breasts. That's not even the part that surprises me the most. I already know Seraphina has dragon scales from the depictions of her in other mythology texts, but what is truly astounding are the flames that grow out from her shoulder blades and into large wings. A flaming whip protrudes from behind her like a fire tail.

A fire whip, maybe?

It makes me wonder if Samarra has the same abilities.

Chapter 10

Xoneas

King Kedron Krel Morbious

"CAPTAIN, WHERE DO WE stand on securing the dagger?" The king's voice carries a sense of urgency as he gazes at the captain of his Forsaken Legion.

"Your Majesty, we have scouts following leads across the continent. We have received word that King Finox of Valador has arrived in Issalitia and is currently in the Wild Timber Forest. There was a sighting of the Dryad witch." The captain bows his head, waiting for a response from the unpredictable Death King.

"Good, let them do our work for us. We will obtain the dagger once it leaves the locked kingdom," he sneers, cracking each of his knuckles in succession. "Until then, keep our Forsaken Legion hidden. Keep watch and kill whatever gets in their way."

"Yes, Your Majesty." With that, he leaves King Kedron to rest.

The king is centuries old, and this will be his last chance to obtain the dagger, conquer the continent, and find a way to live forever.

***

The Queen's Chamber

Arysalia

I knock quietly. It has been a long day, and I've found more information than I ever could have imagined. I need to find a way to get us out of the castle without relying on the two men who have been dropped into our lives.

"Yes, come in." I hear the soft tone of my mother's voice coming from behind the large wooden door.

"It's me, Mother. I need to talk to you," I whisper to stop the guards from intercepting my words. There are so many different types of fae guards in the castle, some can play back memories, like my head guard, Brandon, but others have a keen sense of hearing. It's very inconvenient.

"What's the matter?" The queen stands from her desk and meets me at the door.

I need to tell her everything. I know she won't try to talk me out of it. It's high time the kingdom was freed.

"We have a plan to destroy the dagger, but I don't know the best way to get it out of the castle without the Mad King finding out."

She nods. She understands.

"Why now?" The questioning in her green eyes, so similar to mine, has the words catching in my chest.

"Apparently, his curse isn't entirely bound to outsiders. The guards may guard the one entry into the kingdom, but if they don't *see* the people entering, how can they truly stop them?" All at once, it's almost as if a candle has lit behind her eyes.

"Someone used magic to hide themselves to get into the kingdom. Who? How? Where did you find them?" Her questions come so fast, I don't know which one to answer first.

"Yes, they got in. I'm terrified to tell you who. As for *how*...he has illusion magic. Umbra sensed their presence, and the oracat snapped their illusion and teleported them into the courtyard," I whisper loudly. Her eyes grow wide, and her mouth falls open.

"The young King of Valador came into our castle unseen and unheard," she quietly declares.

"I didn't tell you that. How did you figure it out?"

"Darling flower, his kingdom is known for its mischievous illusion magic. In fact, some even say his parents aren't actually gone and that they have created an illusionary life off the continent."

"Oh, well, that does make sense," I admit, sighing heavily. I move from her grasp and flop onto her massive bed. "Now you see why I need to find the dagger. I need to protect our kingdom. If anyone else finds out that, as long as you stay unseen, you can get into the locked kingdom, our people won't truly be safe anymore."

"Well, I am proud of you, my darling. You are thinking like a queen," she admits with a smile. "I think we need to come up with a mischievous plan, just like that king of yours."

"I was hoping we could find a way to avoid involving him in the retrieval. This is our kingdom. I have the schematics of the castle, and I have a plan for the dagger's removal. We just need to keep the guards out of the way. He and his companion have been breaking into the kingdom and spying on us for *five years*." The words rush out of me too fast to stop.

"Excuse me?" My mother's eyes, once a calm meadow green, are now bright and angry. "He has been in my kingdom that often without tipping off any of the guards?!"

I realize now that I probably should have kept that fact to myself.

She collects herself, sighing, "Well, then you're right. You and Samarra need to do this on your own, and I have the perfect idea."

"Yes, tell me."

She leaves me where I am and turns to scan her miniature herbalist library. She pulls out a few hefty tomes with ornate leaves on their covers and spines.

"We need to put that bastard to sleep, though it is likely the blood magic. He has used it periodically through his many years in my castle. If he did use it on the dagger, it will awaken him if it is disturbed in any way."

She flips through the tomes page by page, finally stopping on a page decorated with tiny bunches of small white flowers. At the top of the page, the letters spell out "Valerian Root." The next page displays a description that I have difficulty reading from where I'm standing. "Here it is!"

"Here, what is?" I ask. I know what valerian root can do, but it is just a mild sleeping tonic herb.

"It is a tonic that mixes valerian root and henbane, and if we add a bit of garlic and ginger, we will be able to hide it in some food quite easily." She looks so mischievous. "Lucky for us, Samarra is in the bakery. I'm sure she could spare you so you can help Sharize in the kitchen with soup preparation." Her motherly tone has disappeared.

"But won't Sharize know what I am up to?" I am a little frightened by her confidence in this tonic.

"I will speak to Sharize now. She is my chef, not the Mad King's; she'll happily make my favorite soup," she says with a wink. She stands with a flourish, puts her tomes back on their shelf, and sweeps out of the chamber.

I knew my mother would know what to do.

I turn to take my leave and realize too late that she never said whether the mischievous King of the Middle Kingdom could be trusted. I suppose I'll have to decide on my own.

Chapter
II

Earlier that evening

Arysalia

"A RYSA, WE SHOULD WAIT. Finox can use his illusions to get us into the chamber," Sam whispers as we quietly stalk toward the unnamed chamber I found on the map. I am positive it holds the dagger that keeps this kingdom locked away.

"Stop worrying, we've got this! You can use your flames to break the runes and get us inside," I chastise. She didn't trust me with her secrets, but I trust her with my life. I wish she could trust me now. I worry my lower lip as we continue our trek.

"That's the thing, Arysa, I have had very little practice with my fire magic, remember?" she scolds me, warmth coming off her in waves. "You only knew I could heat things up, not use a massive magenta flame to burn the door to the ground!"

"I'm sorry. Let me try again. Can you blow this shit up so we can get in there?" I ask with just a hint of sarcasm.

Sam throws her hood back and removes the protective runes from her eyes, which change from blue to magenta. "Watch this!" She takes off toward the door.

We had already neutralized the guards with the sleeping tonic. Thanks to my mother's expertise in herbology and our affinity for plants, we devised a plan to "poison" everyone into a deep sleep, and it worked! Everyone in the castle ate some sleepy-time soup except the two of us.

"Be careful! I'm right behind you." I watch with rapt attention as my quiet best friend lifts her hands out in front of her chest, and bright pink magic flows luminously down her arms and out of her palms. It crackles around us, and I'm in awe.

I have never seen anything like this. Samarra usually just uses her flame as a sort of oven.

The bright pink light transitions into magenta flames. I watch as they lick up the door panels, feeling for their weaknesses and dismantling the runes protecting the chamber. The door melts off its hinges with a loud crash, and we're in.

"See, I told you," Samarra says as she looks back over her shoulder at me.

"Yes, you did! Now let's get this dagger and get the fuck out of here!" I shout over the sound of the crackling flames.

We stalk into the chamber and see a single case in the middle of the room. The room is void of any other furniture or drapery. Since we are practically in the dungeon right now, that makes sense. The case itself has a levitating black dagger with dragon scales etched along its hilt and an onyx stone embedded at its end. The blade is thick and sharp, and the runes meant to hold it up magically wave and twinkle.

"God, what's that disgusting smell?" I cover my nose and mouth, searching for the source.

"Yuck." Sam covers her face with her cloak. "He did use blood magic to create this curse, then..."

My brows shoot up. *Blood magic is still forbidden in Issalitia. But really, so is locking your kingdom up tight, keeping your citizens prisoners and slaves. I'm not surprised he did this; I am surprised however at the disgusting stench coming from the spells.*

I search the room for booby traps or tricks.

"Well, I don't care what he used; it fucking stinks in here, like the butcher's alley after the harvest. We need to move," I tell her. "Use that incredibly stunning but terrifying flame you used on the door and destroy the runes holding this thing."

Sam doesn't hesitate, immediately dismantling the runes. When the smoke dissipates, the glass melts away from around the dagger. She reaches in tentatively, grabbing the dagger quickly and turning to me with an expression of utter terror mixed with delight. We turn on our heels and make a run for the courtyard.

Goddess, please let us make it there. I pray to any of them, hells to all of them.

"The men should be waiting outside the wall. We just need Umbra!" I yell, trying to breathe and run simultaneously.

I need to run more; this is torture.

"Call out to her! She will come to you!" Sam tries to shout through her ragged breathing.

"Umbra! Umbra!" My shouts echo off the walls of the long hallway. There is the sound of a whip cracking, and a roar shakes the walls. Sam grabs my arm, stopping us dead in our tracks. "What the fuck was that?" I whisper.

As we move to the edge of the hall, we don't see anything coming. The only sound is a mix of whooshing and flapping. We both look up toward the hall's ceiling, and there she is. Umbra has grown like a weed and is the size of a large jungle cat with large obsidian wings beating the air as she hovers above us.

Sam shoots me a grin. "Well, hello, beautiful," she croons to the massive cat.

Oh, this is going to be marvelous, I think, as we high-tail it forward.

Chapter 12

Arysalia

WE HEAR COMMOTION COMING from the other end of the hall. Some of the king's guards must have woken from their soup nap.

"Stop, in the name of the king!" a guard shouts. Their suits of armor are too clunky, and they struggle to catch up to us.

"Your turn, Arysa! Show them what you have been hiding!" Samarra yells over the clatter of steel rattling. Umbra lands behind us, facing the guards, growling. The guards don't balk at her growl, to their credit, and continue toward us.

"I'm so sorry," I whisper. I unleash the torrent of water I have been holding hostage inside myself for years. I pull water from the air, the walls, the ground, and deep inside myself. The deluge of water rips down the hall. The guards do not stand a chance.

"Run!" I shout as we continue toward the courtyard, the water flowing down the halls like a river.

Umbra knocks down every guard in sight, protecting us from their sharp swords. The torrent of water that trails us effectively neutralizes their attempt to follow us out.

When we reach the iron gate at the courtyard entrance, Umbra rears back onto her powerful haunches and slams her front paws into the gate, ripping it from its hinges, and it clatters to the ground. Samarra hurls herself through the opening while I continue checking behind us to make sure we are safe.

With another terrifying roar from our fully grown oracat, we blink onto the other side of the wall. *I never imagined Umbra would grow into such an incredible beast, and teleporting through walls now makes complete sense in how she got into the kingdom in the first place.* I think.

"Good girl!" I yell to the massive feline. She looks toward the slits in the courtyard wall and releases a menacing growl.

Goren and Finox must be there, awaiting our arrival.

"Gods! Okay! We get it!" Finox yells from his invisible perch, next to whom I can only assume is Goren.

"Come down. We need to get the fuck out of here!" I demand. The illusion and smell of cherries and citrus fills my nose immediately.

"They cannot see us. I have created an illusion that makes us invisible. However, you must stay close to me to stay within the illusion."

"How fucking close?" I spit, unimpressed.

"Such a vulgar tongue on such a beautiful princess," he says.

I snort. "I'll act however I please, thank you very much! Now, how close?" I grind out through my teeth.

"Within ten paces or so," he explains. "Once we are out of the kingdom, blending into nature will be much easier." He looks into my eyes; there's a sparkle behind the amber spheres. "Trying to create an ongoing, changing illusion to match these buildings and gardens takes more energy than you can imagine."

"Fine," is all I say as we descend the winding stone streets. Alarms are being blown from the castle, informing the entire kingdom we're under attack.

We make it out of the kingdom, stealthily avoiding guards, citizens, and the gates, to the edge of the forest.

"Holy fuck!" I exclaim. Finox's cherry citrus scent is no longer filling my nostrils. I have never seen trees so tall. The canopy of limbs and leaves blocks out the sky. "Holy fuck," I say again.

Finox looks at me quizzically, as if I were a child or a lost animal. "You've never been to the Wild Timber Forest?" he asks, amused.

"What do you not understand? Is it the locked part or the two words in a row? We have never left the Locked Kingdom of Issalitia." I glare at him, wondering how a king could be so clueless.

Finox puts his hands up in surrender. "Hey, I don't know what you have or haven't seen," he says, looking over at Goren. "Let's go."

Goren grunts and shoves his thumb and forefinger into his mouth. With a deep exhale, he blows out not breath, but wind; a haunting whistle rings through the air. Umbra does not appreciate the sound and growls, moving in front of Samarra and me protectively. After a few beats, we hear the sound of whooshing and flapping again, similar to what we heard in the castle halls when Umbra made her entrance.

Looking up at the sky, I see them. Two enormous beasts with golden feathers, hind legs with hooves, and front legs with talons. They have the body of a lion with the face and neck of an eagle, and they're nearly identical. The only difference is that one has a large streak of red feathers on top of its head.

My mind goes through the codex of all the creatures Samarra and I have studied, when finally, my mind latches onto it. "Hippogriffs. Real Hippogriffs!"

I feel a warm hand intertwine with mine. Sam has moved in close, not out of fear but more out of protectiveness.

She is usually the one who hides herself away, but this time, it's me.

"Sasha," Finox croons as the massive beasts land next to them.

Goren grabs his hippogriff by its halter and runs his hands down its neck. Comforting the creature, he whispers lovingly, "Greta, such a good girl."

Judging by her growls, Umbra doesn't seem impressed. I can only imagine what she would do to protect us. Hopefully, it's not whipping us back into that castle. I reach out and touch her dark, muscular shoulder. Her skin ripples beneath my contact as she looks back and into my eyes. She sees straight into my soul with those eyes. "It's okay, Umbra," I say, and she begins to relax as we watch the men interact with their creatures.

Chapter 13

Queen Zandra

I WAKE IN MY chamber, dazed. I knew that eating the soup the girls concocted was risky, but it had to be just right. The king had to believe I was not involved in the plan for it to be effective. A chill runs down my spine, and a prickle of awareness takes over.

"Good morning, Sleeping Beauty," a voice growls out from the far side of my chamber.

Fucking hell.

"Maggard, hello," I say in the most placating tone I can muster. "Why are you in my chambers? Is there something you need?"

"Bah," he spits, "you're telling me you have no idea what our daughter has done?" He rises from where he has been sitting. He moves across the room like a wraith. He has always had an air of darkness lurking in his light magic, but now the darkness has completely taken over. I look up at his fury-filled expression.

"What? Where is she? Is Arysalia alright?" I ask, panic bleeding into my tone. I jump up from the bed and move toward the door. I am dressed only in my sleep slip, but nothing will stop me from getting to her.

Gods, please let her have made it out of the kingdom.

"No, you stupid woman. She has fled the castle with Samarra, that idiot peasant you let her cavort around with." He is standing between me and the door. "She has stolen my dagger and has fled." He stares into my eyes, searching for a lie or a hint of knowing.

"Gods! Why would she do such a thing? Where has she gone?" I try to move past him.

"She is gone, Zandra; fled. Left a mess of water in her wake." That comment freezes me solid. All the blood in my body feels like it has stopped moving, leaving me feeling cold.

He knows.

The room goes dark as a searing pain spreads across my cheek.

***

Arysalia

Now what?

We have the creatures with us, and we are making our way through the terrifying forest. I shiver slightly with wariness.

Should we make for Valador?

My mind is racing as we move slowly through the forest. I hear Goren whispering to Samarra, who has shifted from fear to bashfulness.

"Finox, why are we walking through this terrible forest when we can fly to Valador? Isn't that where we need to go?" I ask, unable to hide my annoyance.

"Princess, it *is* safer for us to fly, but only at night." He rolls his eyes at me like a petulant child.

"Well, *sorry,* Your Majesty," I say, my voice echoing through the trees. "I guess we will fly at night then!" A rough, overly warm hand covers my mouth, effectively silencing me.

"Quiet!" Finox whispers in my ear. I feel pinpricks of awareness where his hand rests, electricity thrumming between us. *Fuck this,* I think before licking the king's hand.

"What the fuck, Arysa?" he groans while wiping his hand down the front of his tunic.

"Next time you touch my mouth, I'll bite your hand off," I say with all seriousness. Never again do I want to feel that awareness and how my body reacted to the *good* King of Valador.

A noise stops the winged creatures in their tracks. I swivel around, but I don't see anything coming our way until a flash of green catches my eye. Umbra crouches low. With almost no sound at all, she pounces into the trees. A loud shriek sounds, and her head pops up from the ferns. Sitting atop her head is what I can only describe as the cutest furball creature I have ever seen.

The green and brown creature has a small head, large front teeth, and a fern-shaped tail with small, leaf-like protrusions poking out from its tan fur. "Oh! It's a shrubble!" Goren says, delighted.

"It is quite cute," Samarra says, looking up at him with adoration.

The unexpected pang of jealousy is almost overwhelming. I need to get my best friend away from that man. I look at the tiny creature, which has now made itself very comfortable on Umbra's head.

"What exactly is it?" I am ignorant of anything that was not published in the library in our kingdom.

"A shrubble is a creature that blends into its surroundings by camouflaging itself with the foliage," Finox says. "There are many different kinds. Their species is part of the rodent family, but they can be bred and changed to look and hide within any shrub in the Wild Timber Forest." His voice shifts to one of whimsy, and I find that I quite like his teaching tone.

Chapter 14

Arysalia

THE SUN HAS DIPPED below the horizon. We have already consumed about half of our supplies for the two-day journey. Tonight, we plan to fly until dawn and then rest for a few hours. Once night falls, we'll make our final stretch of the journey into the heart of the Kingdom of Valador, the first kingdom I will ever have visited.

Since leaving our kingdom, Samarra and I have had many new experiences. For starters, the attention of men we did not grow up with, the creatures we hear but cannot see, and lastly, the flying. I must fly with Finox, and Sam flies with Goren. We use Umbra as our scout, making sure the areas we land in are safe. She relies on her instincts of the unnatural world and her environment to keep a watchful eye. Finox enjoys calling her the "flying death cat." I do believe he is still sour that she caught him spying.

I have been daydreaming and thinking for much of the flight, but I have a horrible feeling in the pit of my stomach.

Later, when sleep finally overtakes me, I can smell the scent of cherries and citrus in my dreams and feel Finox's warmth. I have never slept this close to a man in my life.

***

Queen Zandra

Waking up on the cold, damp ground in my kingdom feels ridiculous.

Well, you did marry the Mad King.

I have no idea how long I have been knocked out for. There are two plates of food in my cell that are untouched. We only feed our prisoners once a day, not that we usually have any. I eye the disgusting meals in front of me.

"Guard," I shout, but there is no reply. It is silent down here in the dungeons of Issalitia.

I realize I will have to sit here and wait until the Mad King deigns to speak to this kingdom's true monarch. I should never have married that disgusting man. I lay my head back onto the ground and fall back to sleep.

Chapter 15

Arysalia

A S THE SUN FINALLY begins to rise, we make our way down to the forest below. As Sasha heads toward a clearing, making her landing, I hold onto Finox's waist tightly. He never needs to speak or yell; Sasha seems to know the way. We land gently in the clearing, which is a meadow filled with delicate wildflowers. Nearby, a stream flows lazily through it. I can only assume we'll wash ourselves or take a nap, probably both. The hippogriffs don't smell per se, but they don't *not* smell.

There is a crop of hazel trees, which I have only ever read about; they're trees of wisdom and healing, and their sap can be used as an antibiotic.

"We'll make camp here." Finox's voice cuts through the haze of my thoughts. I agree that we need rest and food. Also, the beasts need to sleep more than we do. As a passenger all night, my sleep was jostled, but it was sleep, nonetheless.

"Sounds good to me." I make my way over to Samarra.

It's as if I'm seeing her for the first time. Gone are the runes that once covered her eyes, gone is her mistrust and delicate nature. She is beautiful, and I am so lucky to have her here with me. At her waist, she wears a belt from which the ominous dagger hangs. That dagger has ruined the lives of my people for longer than I care to admit. I move closer. "Sam?" Her dusty eyes rise to meet mine.

"Hey," she exclaims wistfully. "Do you want to go down to the stream?"

She knows I need to feel the water. I must bend it to my will and let it flow through my body. I need to feel one with water again.

After the escape, I feel completely drained. I once felt cool, content, and relaxed, but that has morphed into anxiety, dryness, and a sense of confusion. "Yes, please. You knew I needed it?" Our eyes lock, and there is a knowing glimmer in her eyes.

We can speak without words and understand without sound; she is my twin flame, and I hers. Fire and water, who would have guessed it?

***

Finox

Goren and I watch as the girls amble down to the water's edge.

"You are so tremendously fucked." I emphasize my meaning by raising both my eyebrows in the girls' direction.

"I would disagree. I think we are saved," Goren responds solemnly.

This is the girl he has been dreaming about for years, the one who is to be our savior and our demise all in one. Of course, he is fucked. Samarra has him wrapped around her tiny finger, and he won't admit it, not even to me.

I don't argue. "Whatever you say. Let's get Sasha and Greta settled in. Where the hell did that midnight hellcat go off to?" I scout the area where the meadow meets the trees, but the beast is nowhere to be seen.

"She's probably eating and getting out of the sun; they are midnight creatures, not sunbathers like the hippogriffs," he explains, as if I am ignorant about these things. "How far away from the kingdom do you think we are?"

"At least half a night's flight, probably five or six hours at least, if we don't come under attack or lose the stars that guide us."

"I cannot wait to be back in my bed," Goren sighs as he takes a seat on a boulder, resting his elbows on his knees, chin in hand.

"Oh man, I know. Sleeping on the ground is not for the faint of heart," I agree. "We need to prepare better before our next journey. Once the princess figures out exactly what we must do with the dagger."

"I have a feeling that Samarra is going to be the key, but how, exactly, is what I am most afraid of."

I watch as genuine fear washes over his face, then vanishes in an instant. I sit down next to him in the grass, lie back, and stretch out under the morning sun.

I can smell the difference in the air; the closer we get to Valadar, the closer we get to the desert. I can feel the twinge of dry and stale air whenever the wind blows in from the south. The Southern Kingdom has been a blight on this land for centuries. The king is determined to take over the continent at all costs. He creates creatures even the gods would be disgusted with. Being this close to his kingdom sends chills up my spine.

We must be cautious, the closer we get to my kingdom, the closer we get to the Kingdom of Xoneas, and more to the point, Kedron Morbious.

I contemplate, worry creeping in and attempting to take control of my actions.

As if reading my mind, Goren looks down at me. "Are we worried about the king beneath the sands?"

"Yes, my friend. Yes, we are," I manage to say before we fall silent. In the distance, laughter drifts from the water.

Chapter 16

Arysalia

SAMARRA SEEMS LIKE A different person out here in the light of Nedona. There's a sparkle in her that was dulled within the walls of Issalitia. The magenta of her eyes glimmers in the sunlight as we wash. I wish I'd shared this light with her sooner. I wonder what our life might have been like if we hadn't been trapped inside that kingdom for so long.

As I lie next to the enchanted stream, I soon find myself lost in thought. I've heard so many scary bedtime stories about the Wild Timber Forest; the Dryad witch and pumars would steal you from your bed and hold you hostage in the woods. But as I sit here, I see the most incredible creatures.

There is a group of tiny green furry creatures, no bigger than my hand, bouncing around on the banks of the stream. Wildflowers were sprouting everywhere from them, tangled in the green of their fluffy fur. I'm not even sure what they are called, but they are captivating. "Sam, look at these little darlings." I point at the cluster of bouncing green.

"What darlings?" Sam looks confused, looking in the direction I'm pointing, as if she isn't seeing them.

"Those little green flower-topped fluffs."

"I don't see anything, Arysa. What are they?" Her tone is unsettled.

Can she not see them?

"The small green fluffy creatures with little wildflowers sprouting out of their heads. They are bouncing around over there, along the bank. Do you not see them?"

How can she not see what is right before her?

"Arysa, I only see green grass and wildflowers. There are no creatures playing over there." She looks between me and the bank. "Are you feeling, okay?"

"I'm fine, Sam. I'm telling you they are right there. Never mind," I say, pushing myself up from where I've been lounging and getting dressed in the extra clothes we packed.

"Oh. Okay, I'm sorry." Sam's sparkle dims, and she returns to washing in the stream, no longer meeting my eyes.

"Don't be sorry, Samarra. I am sorry I snapped at you." I shrug. "I guess there are things in the world I don't yet understand, and our magic is untested. Maybe it has something to do with that," I suggest.

"Maybe we do have a lot to learn about this continent," she reminds me. "We have never left the walls of Issalitia, and we have far to travel."

She leaves the stream and begins to dress. We packed lightly when we left the castle, so we have only a few outfits between us. We are both wearing darker tunics and trousers. Thank the goddess, because wearing a dress on the back of a hippogriff would not be a pleasant experience.

I take one last look at the edge of the stream, and the little green fluffs stop and watch us as we leave. I feel unsettled.

Are they real or a figment of my imagination?

Chapter 17

Xoneas

King Kedron Krel Morbious

"**W**HAT HAVE YOU GATHERED?" I ask sharply.

The small group from my Forsaken Legion of assassins exchange glances. They are the most ruthless assassins on our continent, skilled in intelligence gathering, murder, and torture.

"Your Majesty, we have been tracking the group through the Wild Timber Forest. But, Sire, they have an oracat," the captain says. "We are unable to get very close. The cat can sense when we are near."

"Then I suggest you dispatch the beast and collect the dagger!" I shout. "How hard can it be to bring me what is mine?"

"We can't. The feline will teleport us into its mouth and kill us all," the sniveling assassin claims.

"So, you failed your mission?"

"No, Your Majesty! We will retrieve the dagger. We will."

He sounds terrified, as he should. I am the Death King beneath the desert for a reason. The shadows around the room begin to creep closer to the captain. His face pales, and I can see the sweat running down his temple. I can feel his pulse quicken, and the terror in his eyes fills me with such glee.

"Please, your majesty, we will get it." He drops to his knees, but doing so only tempts my shadows more.

With a snap of my finger, the shadows completely engulf the captain, leaving only a pile of black sand where he once stood. The rest of my legion stands straighter. No one speaks.

"Does anyone else want to tell me how they failed? Or are you going to get the mission done?" I am as cool as the southern breeze off the Branera Tempest. A few moments pass, and no one utters a word. "Good. Dismissed."

***

Finox

The princess and the flame come back from the stream. Something seems off, but I can't put my finger on it. They are no longer arm in arm, and the princess looks angrier than usual. "How was the stream, ladies?"

"Fine," the princess huffs as they walk right past me.

I have been watching her for years, and she has always seemed to have an underlying anger, but her beautiful smile always covers it. Now it's as though nothing will make her smile. The princess takes a seat next to the fire.

"Okay..."

Samarra steps closer. "She just needs some time."

I nod, and she moves off to be near Goren. I have never seen him like this before. He has been disobeying me, making decisions without discussing with me first. He has been my best friend since we were little; he has never gone against me. But this feels different, like he doesn't seem to have a choice in the matter. Part of me wonders if the Pink Flame, Samarra, and my best friend are fated mates, bound, and unknowingly so.

We need to get ourselves up in the air soon if we want to get above the trees before whatever lurks in the shadows decides to pay us a visit. Before I can inform the group that we should leave, I hear a very angry growl. The hippogriffs are stomping, swaying their heads side to side, and clacking their beaks.

The girls jump into a battle stance, with Arysa more protective of Samarra than the other way around. Goren moves closer to them as we scan the tree line and listen for sounds.

In a flash, Umbra hurls through the forest's edge with a deafening roar. The oracat is a fearsome beast, but there are creatures in this forest that I'm sure frighten even her. Her eyes are wild as she searches for the princess. She takes off into the air just as a massive blast comes from where she jumped.

Shooting up into the air, she banks sharply and is just nearly taken into the mouth of a giant desert soul-eater worm. "Run!"

We sprint into action. The black worm doesn't have a face, only a mouth with fangs that could make meat sticks out of our entire group. The worm originates from the Kingdom Beneath the Sand. Morbious has been tracking us, and the closer we get to Valador, the closer we get to him. He has creatures of death, destruction, and terror that he uses as enforcers, partially starved to keep their hunger heightened, and this is no exception. The soul-eater's mouth drips with black, inky saliva.

"Sasha!" I shout. She bows to me as I grab Arysa by her waist. Her eyes go wide, but we don't have time for bickering. I toss her straight up, and she lands on Sasha's back. I put her in front so I can hold on to her this time, we don't need the heir of Issalitia sliding off the back.

Goren does the same with Samarra before taking off into the night. The dagger is still secured to her side as we bound off into the sky. Umbra is circling, distracting the soul-eater.

The sun has not dropped low enough beneath the horizon. I craft a careful illusion to mimic the thin clouds, purple-hued sky, and slowly emerging stars as we make our way to Valador.

A loud roar sounds from far below, and I can feel Arysa stiffen in front of me. I look back, and it isn't Umbra but the worm. Umbra is making her way closer to us, flying as hard as she can.

The roar came from the ground where another terrifying creature joined the soul-eater. It paces back and forth in anger. A shiver runs up my spine. I have never had to face a zorag, but I know the death they bring is quick. My instincts are screaming at me to keep flying until we can land in the courtyard of my home.

The zorag is controlled by Morbious; they are bonded. The zorag is a creature he created in one of his disgusting laboratories. Part wolf, creature, and part succubus, the beast won't just tear you apart; it will feed on your fear. The chase, the hunt, and the terror you emit only make the zorag stronger.

"What the fuck is that thing?" I hear the princess yelling back at me, pulling me from my thoughts.

"A zorag," I shout back, still feeling incredibly uneasy.

"What is a zorag?" I glimpse her lips when her head turns, and I almost forget to respond.

"One of King Morbious's lab experiments, his version of a hellhound," I yell over the whipping wind. "It is bound to the king and only does what he wishes."

"So, the Dark King wants to kill us and feed us to his creatures?" she yells, her face grim.

"It seems that way."

She faces forward again. Umbra has made it back to us and enters my illusion. It is incredibly unsettling how she can rip it open and fly right in, but she's safe, and that's all that matters.

I look over at Goren, who is holding onto Samarra tightly. She is hunched into him, her eyes wider than usual. It seems like she is taking in every detail.

We give each other a nod without speaking. We are safe, they are safe, we are almost home. But we both know that this is just the beginning.

Chapter 18

Arysalia

WE HAVE BEEN FLYING for what feels like forever, and the King of Valador has had his arms wrapped around me the entire time. My first flight on Sasha, I rode at his back, which felt safe and comfortable. This, however... This feels too intimate.

He was just trying to protect you from the desert soul-eater creature and that zorag beast. Don't read too much into it.

I can smell his cherries and citrus magic all around me. I can feel his warmth at my back, the strength of his arms around me. *Stop,* I tell myself. *He is the king of another kingdom.*

"We're not far off," he says into my ear. I can feel his breath on my neck, and it sends an involuntary shiver down my body. I feel him stiffen behind me. I don't say anything, just look to the horizon. Something is sprouting up out there. No longer surrounded by trees, I can see a massive river to the east. It must be the Issalitia River, named after our kingdom. I have never seen it, and I have never felt its water or drifted in its currents.

As we fly closer, I can see the spires of a castle. The stone walls are tall and light brown. They look as though they have been kissed by the sun. To the south, there is a large and expansive desert. We must be in Valador now. The moon gives us much-needed light; it is bright enough that I can see almost everything.

"Are we here?" I shout without looking back, too nervous to allow myself the temptation of looking at Finox's angelic face.

"Yes, Princess. Welcome to Valador. My kingdom is nestled between the Wild Timber Forest, Issalitia River, and the Phymis Desert," he shouts back, not as close to my neck this time. "The Phymis desert is where the Kingdom of Xoneas is. It's almost entirely underground. The sands close and open only for its people."

"That's terrifying."

"There are disadvantages, it being this close to us, but the river is a stone's throw away, and it connects to the Ynos Delta, which takes us east to the Branera Tempest," Finox relays as we get closer and closer.

We fly over the side of the kingdom's walls. The guards mounted along the top must know Gretta and Sasha, apparently, or they can't see us at all. We glide into the castle itself. I can still smell his citrus scent, so the illusion must still be intact.

On our right, Umbra is flying next to us, head swiveling, always looking for trouble. To our left, I see Goren speaking with Sam, pointing at things and smiling.

I long for a connection so much, but then again, it is a distraction.

I shake all thoughts unrelated to our mission as we finally begin our descent; down, down, down to the courtyard below.

***

Finox

We land Sasha and Greta near the hippogriff stables, where we are met by grooms. The grooms take care of them while we are within the castle, though I long to be with Sasha as much as I can. The bond between rider and hippogriff is strong, and we are almost connected mind to mind. Sasha can read my intentions while we're in the sky, as if she and I are one.

It makes me wonder if Arysa is able to connect with Umbra. In reality, little is known about the oracat, their origins, their true nature, or why they can do the things they do.

Looking over, I see Samarra and Arysa with their heads together, gripping each other's forearms. The grip does not look angry or forced; it's almost as if they are grounding each other.

They have never left their kingdom or their family.

Not that I'd know what that is like. My parents died two hundred and fifty years ago, when I was only a year old.

"Ready, Your Majesty?" Goren's voice brings me back to the present.

The girls turn to us, hand in hand. They are leaning more on each other after our long journey through the darkened skies. My kingdom is drier and more secluded, while Issalitia is dewy and flourishing with green. The lands surrounding Valador are different on all sides: the desert lies to the southwest, the river flows to the east, Arysalia's home kingdom stretches to the southeast, and to the north; from whence we came, the Wild Timbers.

"Yes, let's go and take them to their rooms."

"Rooms?" Arysa asks almost instantly.

There is movement at her waist, and I see they are holding hands even tighter now, as if glued together.

"Yes, rooms. Is that a problem?" I question.

"Yes," the quiet, beautiful flame says. "We would like to share a room."

That is interesting, indeed. I guess I never really thought about their friendship. Goren and I can go kingdoms apart, and our friendship stays the same.

"Don't look at us like that, Kingling," Arysa says, frustration marring her expression. "We haven't been separated since we were children, and this is not our home."

"Not even in the castle?" I interject, lifting a brow.

"No, we slept separately in the castle, but we did sleep together a lot of the time as we grew up," Samarra tells me. "We are far from home, and we are each other's only piece of home left." Her face is challenging to read.

"We can make that work. The castle has many rooms!" I brighten my tone, hoping I can break the tension. I look to Goren for agreement, and all I receive in return is a nod.

"Right this way, Princess." Goren guides us all into the castle of slate stone walls, flickering torches, and the scent of home.

Chapter 19

The Dungeon of Issalitia

Queen Zandra

UNCERTAIN OF THE TIME, day, or even how long my beloved daughter has been gone from the kingdom, I drift in and out of consciousness. I've only managed to eat small amounts of bread and drink very little water. The water tastes strange, as if it has something in it. Before I can stop myself, thirst overtakes me, and I swallow mouthful after mouthful. I set the chalice down, wipe my mouth, and lie back on the cold, wet stones.

"Zandra, my darling flower, you must stay strong for our girl."

I open my eyes immediately, and I am no longer in the disgusting dungeon. I am in a place I have not seen in over two centuries.

The sound of waves crashing onto the shore, the smell of salt in the air, and him. Oh, he smells so perfect; the scent of the sea and the sky, as if they were one. Cool and crisp, like drinking the air. I spot him lounging in the sand, the crystal blue water lapping up and touching his toes.

Jerix, my Jerix. He has not aged a day, looking every bit the beautiful knight I lost all those years ago.

"Jerix, you're here...but how?"

"I am here, but I am not. You are fading, my flower. Your bloom has wilted, and we need you to stay strong, like the majestic goddess that I know you are."

All I can do is move closer and closer to him.

I hear him, but I see him and smell him more. This has been a dream of mine for so long. I have had snippets of dreams and moments where I can smell his crisp scent. Jerix Rane Branisalva smells of the sea salty but fresh, pure male.

"Jerix, you're here."

"Yes, my queen. I am here."

He stands and moves toward me. I'm not sure what comes over me, but I break into a run. As I sprint down the expanse of the beach between us, he matches my speed. When we meet in the middle, he lifts me into his arms and raises me into the sky. Our lips meet and I can taste him, feel him, smell him. Tears run down both of our faces. This can't be real. Because this can't be...the Mad King took him from me.

"How are you here?" I whisper into his mouth, not wanting to break contact, worried he would disappear completely.

"You are in danger, my darling. He may have taken my body, but he could never take my soul. I have been here the whole time. I have watched you raise our beautiful daughter."

His eyes look deeply into mine. I know he has been here. I've sensed him, smelled him in the wind.

"It has been so hard without you here. I have never let her forget you, but she has made a grave mistake."

"I know, Zandra. I know she used her water magic on the guards to free the kingdom of the dagger."

My mouth opens in surprise as he tells me what I already know is true. "I watched as she used the water to create rapids down the kingdom halls to stop the knights and guards. She was magnificent, Zandra."

"She really was. This was her backup plan, but we hadn't thought it through. The Mad King now knows the truth and will never let her destroy the dagger or free the kingdom. He will never let me see her again." Tears *flow steadily as the grief of never holding my beloved daughter again takes hold. She is the last piece of Jerix I have...*

"That is where you're wrong, my queen. She will free the kingdom, kill the king, and see you again. I have seen it." He kisses my forehead and holds me tight.

Something is wrong, though. The grip he has on me is slipping, and the crashing of the sea grows quiet. When I open my eyes, I see my true love fading away. "You must go back now, my darling flower. You must be strong for our girl," he whispers. I feel a chill where his once warm body held mine.

"I love you, Jerix. I will always love you." Large wet tears trail down my cheeks, and I can't breathe, a blessing and a curse. I had him, and now I am empty again.

"Be strong, flower." His words reverberate around my mind.

I know I must stay strong, but it is so hard when everything I love and hold dear has been ripped from me.

The clank of an ancient lock sounds, pulling me from the beautiful vision. I remain still. A small light orb floats above me. I can see its brightness from behind my eyelids. Before I saw his light, though, I felt his darkness. Maggard.

Maggard was once a kind and loving prince from the Kingdom of Ramman, which he left to come here and marry me. He is my king consort, but he believes that he rules this kingdom. I let him think that, because I had Jerix. After I lost him, I had only Arysalia, our little spring puddle. She became my only true purpose in life.

The darkness creeping around his orb grows stronger as he nears my still form in the dungeon. "Zandra, wake up." He drops down to his haunches next to me.

"What do you want, Maggard?" I spit without opening my eyes.

"Look at me." He gets right in my face. "You may be the queen of this kingdom, but I am the king! Your daughter has committed treason against the crown."

"She did no such thing!"

"Oh, she did. The guards that awoke saw her. She has fled the kingdom with that peasant, and you're going to tell me where she took my dagger." His voice echoes throughout the cell. "How did she get my dagger?"

"I don't know. I was asleep the entire time." I feign ignorance, though in truth, I honestly didn't know much beyond the fact that they were leaving with the dagger.

My daughter is going to save this kingdom. I know it.

Chapter 20

Arysalia

DARK GREY STONE STRETCHES as far as the eye can see, a stunning contrast to the pure white stone of Issalitia. Each stone is stacked in a way that looks like you could climb the walls. This must be one of the kingdom's famous illusions. As I run my hand along the cool stone, there are no points or even jagged edges. Our steps echo through the halls. We take one of the torches from its sconce and make our way further into the castle. It really is magnificent. Occasionally, we pass the most extravagant stained-glass windows. I know very little about the history of Valador, but these windows tell a story.

"Finox, what are these?" I'm unable to hide my wonder at the illustrations.

"Um, windows?" he quips. It takes everything inside of me not to slap him upside the head.

"Yes, genius. I am aware of their use. I am asking about the ornate stained glass," I corrected. There is a beautiful red-haired woman in this window. She is holding a small bundle in her arms. Her yellow eyes meet those of a very tall man adorned with a crown, his wild brown hair flowing around the gold and gemstones. His arms are wrapped lovingly around the two of them.

"It's my family." That is all he says as we keep walking; he doesn't even look up at the window. Samarra catches my eye, and I know now what I was missing before. I'm not sure how I overlooked or suppressed the fact that this young man is the king of this kingdom. He isn't an heir like I am, he is their king, King Finox Ralis Vimmaglyn.

"Oh, I'm sorry." I do not say another word as he leads us to the chambers where Sam and I are to stay. "Thank you," I whisper.

"It's not a problem, Princess. I will send someone up to retrieve your clothes for washing and get you something comfortable to wear. There is no need for formalities here." He turns on his heel and walks away. His tall shadow follows him after one last look back at Sam.

"Let's check it out, then?" I ask my best friend. She grasps my hand, and we walk into the grandest chamber I have ever seen.

***

Finox

"That was a bit harsh," Goren says as we enter my study. "She was just asking what the stained glass meant."

He isn't wrong. I was harsh, but she doesn't need to know anything about my kingdom.

"What business is it of the Princess of Issalitia?" I huff.

I don't know why I am so angry. It was so long ago that I have no living memories of them.

"One, she is here because you brought her here, and two, you like her." He raises his good eyebrow at me, not both, but a single eyebrow. "I am not the only one with feelings for our new companions."

"I feel nothing for the princess. She is just helping me free the enslaved kingdom. We have been without their products, fabrics, produce, and people for far too long," I explain. "She is a means to an end."

Not even I believe the words that are tumbling out of my mouth. He knows when I'm lying. I may have loved her since I first heard her reading aloud the story of the cursed willow princess.

"Whatever you say, Your Majesty." Goren nods and turns for the large, ornate black walnut doors.

"Wait, will you make sure our guests have everything they need? I need to make sure everything has been running smoothly in my absence." But really, I need to be alone with my thoughts. He does not speak again, only nods, and closes the doors behind himself.

This study was once my father's and is now Goren's mother's while I am away. I leaf through the reports she left for me. Alizée is the mother I didn't have growing up, and she also acts as Regent when I am away. Her husband, Caelus, is the head of the guard, responsible for the kingdom's security; the two make a formidable pair. It is why they are trusted with my kingdom in my stead.

The longing I feel is like sitting alone at that dark wooden desk, thinking of the father I never truly knew, and it is all–consuming at times. This room was once filled with stories and laughter. The walls are made of stone, but they are entirely covered with large bookcases, stuffed to the edges and overflowing. There are books on Xandelar and Nedona; all the kingdoms, all the lore, and lastly, magic.

I need to find the book about the Dagger of Rythorin. Its origin is poorly documented, except that it was forged by dragon fire. Forged in the flame of the dragon bringers themselves, we call them "flames" now because they are so rare that they were thought to be extinct. That was, until Samarra. From what I have gathered, her magic descends from Seraphina Zinnia, the last of the fire goddesses, the *Last Flame*.

Hours of research later, I think I have finally found it. There is no system to the madness that is my father's shelves, but I have discovered an ancient text. It was created centuries ago, and the worn, dark leather has a texture that resembles what I think could be dragon scales. The text is in an old language that Goren's mother knows well. She made a point of teaching us everything she knew; she wanted me to be king of the people.

The Dagger of Rythorin was forged in dragon fire.

The dagger was created to harness the power of anything or anyone the holder wishes.

The dagger can also be warded to prevent theft or destruction.

~ Like can only destroy like. ~

~ Created from, destroyed by. ~

If one possesses the Flame, they are able to destroy the

dragon blade.

There is only one flaw: the Flame must be temple-blessed.

A temple blessing can only be performed at the Temple of

the Geras – Temple of the Gifts

BE WARY – IF BLOOD MAGIC IS USED ON THE

DAGGER OF RYTHORIN

– THE DONOR WILL DIE.

Chapter 21

Arysalia

"THANK YOU," I TELL the quiet maid.

She is my height, maybe even my age, and she has angular features, a small nose and large, ice-blue eyes that are like the shards of ice that crystallize over the ponds of Issalitia. She brought clothing, including wool trousers, warm tunics, sleepwear, and undergarments.

The best part of this journey so far is that this castle has running water. The previous king charmed the castle itself, but just because he died, his magic lived on. This kingdom seems to have an affinity for making things out of nothing, the illusionists that they are.

There are two massive standing tubs set up beside one another, so I am able to bathe next to my best friend. I know it sounds weird even to myself, but Samarra is so much more to me than a best friend. Samarra Yurdo, I now know, isn't biologically her father's, but I am not biologically my own "father's" either. She lost her mother; I lost my father. Jerix was my mother's one and only true love, and they created me. I don't know where I'd be without Sam.

I can't help but think of our lives, how there are so many secrets we have both kept from each other and for each other.

"I love you, Samarra Yurdo." I look over to her magenta flame eyes, which sparkle in the candlelight.

My best friend is finally free from the confines of runes.

"Arysalia Beck Creighton, Princess of Issalitia, I love you, too." She smirks at me. "Why so sentimental today?"

It is a fair question, but I don't actually know.

"I'm not being sentimental. We're far from home, and we don't know what the next day or even the next moment will bring. I want you to know that you are loved, and we are free."

"We are not free until our kingdom is free, Arysa, you know that," she says sternly, a furrow appearing between her brows.

"Well, I am trying to say that we don't have to do this. We could leave the kingdom, leave the continent, find somewhere new," I breathe, my voice shaking. "What if something happens? What if I lose you?"

"Oh, Arysa..." she croons, reaching her hand across the tubs to grasp mine again. "Even if I leave this plane, I will be waiting for you in the next one. Death won't keep you from being my best friend," she admits quietly.

She is right, we will be friends again in another life. We are twin flames, one and the same. She is the flame to my water.

But I can't get rid of this uneasy feeling.

"Just be careful. Let us take care of you," I confide. "I have had the training that will protect you, all those days I was grounded from the bakery, I was learning."

"Ah, yes, well, we also have two large men in our convoy now; they will also protect us," Sam shrugs. "If they weren't such creeps, we wouldn't have known it was possible."

"Well, let's hope that is true. If not, I am not opposed to—" I drag my hand across my throat, then let my head loll dramatically to one side.

Samarra blanches.

"What? I'm kidding," I say, incredulous.

"We don't need to kill anyone," she says solemnly. "I won't."

"No one asked you to, Sam. I was only kidding. I will behave." I'm confused... Samarra usually knows when I am joking.

***

Finox

Goren comes back to the study with cured meat, cheese, and bread. He sits down in front of me, his face utterly calm. "Have you found anything?" he asks without a change in his expression. I'm not sure how to respond.

"Well... I think I have, but I need to discuss it with the ladies to find out what they think. Have they settled in, okay?"

"Yes, they are clean, clothed, and getting food now. They will be here soon." As if on cue, there is a knock on the door.

"The princess and her companion, Your Majesty." The servant opens the door, bows, then lets them enter, shutting it behind him.

"Well, hello, Princess." I look her in the eyes, then my gaze roams down her body. She is wearing dark wool trousers that fit her legs magnificently and a tunic that ties at the front. Showing just a hint of skin, I meet her eyes again. Her cheeks are now a shade of pink.

"Like what you see, Kingling?" she quips. I have been caught gawking.

"Oh, I'm sorry." I might be red, but I am not at all sorry. "You look lovely."

Goren stands and makes room for them. Two chairs are set in front of the large desk. He comes around the desk, as if standing sentry behind me.

"Have you found anything?" Arysalia asks. "Was your library extensive enough?" She gestures at the walls of books and scrolls.

"Actually, I have." I turn the hefty dragon-scale tome around so she can read it and look at the inscriptions. Her eyebrows knit together in confusion; Samarra is wearing a matching expression.

"You can read that?" Arysa asks. "It is another language; we have never seen this dialect before."

Huh, I guess I didn't think of that.

I grab a piece of parchment and a quill and begin to translate.

"Yes, Your Majesty." Goren isn't speaking to me but to Arysa, drawing their attention while I work. "My mother raised us together, you see, this language was a common tongue when she was young, and she wanted to make sure we were well versed in all the languages of our kingdom." I look up for a moment and see that Samarra is beaming at my friend, her eyes have a magenta hue that unsettles me.

She is dangerous, I think, once more.

Chapter 22

Xoneas

King Kedron Krel Morbious

"**W**HAT DO YOU MEAN they got away from the soul–eater *and* the zorag?" I spit. "You didn't go after them yourselves? What imbeciles!"

"Sire, we did get intel…"

I envision decapitating and hanging him behind my throne. I raise my brows, giving him the cue to continue before I lose my patience. "Well, they had hippogriffs, Sire, two golden hippogriffs. They were fast!"

That is interesting. The King of Valador keeps hippogriffs, and there is also the Princess of Issalitia.

"What else?"

"Uh, Sire... That was it. We had trouble finding them." He looks pained as he shares this last piece of information with me.

I make eye contact with the eager lieutenant behind him and nod. Moments later, the captain's head is rolling across the floor, and I have promoted the lieutenant.

"Find the girl and that child king! Get me the dagger! Do not disappoint me again, or this will be your fate." I gesture lazily at the disembodied head and dismiss my Forsaken Legion, who can't even seem to do the simplest of tasks.

***

Arysalia

Finox has translated the text from the tome.

"So, you're telling me we must get Samarra blessed at the Temple of the Geras?" I say, visibly unimpressed with this new development.

"Yes," he says. He gives no reaction to my tone at all.

"The Temple of the Gifts?" I say in layman's translation of "Geras."

"Yes."

"The temple where the Mad King's brother is the head priest?" Now that gets the reaction I was looking for. "The second eldest brother, who I'm sure would send some correspondence to my kingdom immediately *and* deny our request."

"Well, that is a bit of a snag. Maybe we could use a different priest?" he asks. "He doesn't even know what you look like, does he? He has never met you?"

"That is true. He doesn't know what I look like, but still, he has met my mother. I have her face and eyes."

"Arysa, we need to try at least." I'm surprised to hear my best friend supporting this plan.

"I mean, is it worth your life? My life? The kingling's?" I question pointedly when Goren steps in, ever the gentleman when it comes to Samarra.

"Your Majesty," he says calmly. "I believe we need to let Samarra make her own decisions. If she wants to take the chance, we need to allow her to make that decision."

I know I radiate my anger.

"She is of my kingdom, not yours. She is my companion, and I say no."

I cross my arms stubbornly.

They will not risk my best friend's life for this dagger. She is free of the kingdom. We can leave this continent behind and start anew.

Finox is very quiet. I shift my gaze to him, and he is looking between Samarra and Goren with concern in his eyes as well.

"Arysa, we are no longer in your kingdom," Samarra tells me. "I will go to the temple with or without your permission. I want to free my father and my kingdom." She looks down at her hands.

"Fine." I stand and walk out of the study. I have no idea where I am going, but I need to get out of this suffocating room before I drown everyone in there.

When I close my eyes, I can see all three of them drowning from the inside. I need the images to leave my mind. This happens when my anger bubbles over into my water magic. When my spring magic is involved, I kill every plant in my vicinity.

I follow the hallway back toward where I think our chambers are, but I end up outside, walking past a passage that smells like water. My fingers tingle with the urge to release the anger inside. There is a small path that leads to another stone building within the courtyard. There is a gate, but as I get closer, I find it isn't locked.

The set of dark stone stairs leads downward, and the coolness of the water in the air draws me closer to the source. I begin with uncertain steps; down, down, down; until I draw in a deep breath. At the bottom of the stairs is a hot spring. Some candles are lit, but they don't seem to be melting; an illusion, though they look and glow like real flames.

I look around the chamber and see that I am alone. I immediately remove my leather boots, untying the complicated knots. The tunic and trousers come off easily. My underthings are small, consisting of a cropped silk top and pants that end just below my bottom. The waistband is high, but the silk makes me feel as though my entire body is naked.

Even though I just had a bath, this is different. The feel of elemental water, straight from the ground, has a stronger pull on the magic that runs in my veins. As I step one toe into the water, it seems to move out of the way for me, creating a path to the other side of the chamber. The water leads me to a smooth ledge that acts as a seat. As I take my seat, the water releases and smooths over my submerged body.

I can feel it in every pore and every breath, winding around me as if welcoming me home. I have never seen a hot spring like this one, and it makes me never want to leave this pool.

Chapter 23

Samarra

ARYSA LEFT THE STUDY, and I was so angry with her. She may be the princess and heir to the kingdom, but she cannot keep me from saving anyone. I clench my hands into fists.

Finox left after telling me that he would take care of it, it being Arysa's stubbornness and anger.

So, for the first time, I let him try, let him find a way to calm the anger that was so close to exploding in my best friend. My twin flame has so much anxiety about everything; she wants to explore and see the world, but only on her terms. This was not part of the plan she had envisioned for us.

Goren still stands behind the desk where Finox left him. "We should keep looking to see what we can find here. Fin is more of a translator than I am, but I will give it my best."

"I am sure we will find something. Where did he leave off?" I ask, leaning over the tome and notes placed beside it.

"I can't read this line here, but I think it has something to do with the Muphion Jungle."

A tremor climbs up my spine. According to the stories, there is nothing in that jungle but death. People venture into the jungle, believing they can unlock the ancient magic that lies within, but they are never heard from again.

"I really hope not. The temple I can handle, but I don't know about the jungle," I reply hesitantly.

"I will not let anything happen to you, my flame." My cheeks heat at his forwardness and the possessiveness in his tone.

"I am your flame now, am I?" I ask quietly, almost hoping he couldn't hear me.

"You have been mine since I saw fragments of your beautiful face, haunting my dreams with your beauty," he admits, his cheeks now flushed a shade of pink that mirrors my own.

"Well, all right then. Let's take a break. You could show me around the castle?" If I am alone with him much longer, I don't know if I'll be able to stop myself from letting him touch me.

"I'll leave a note, and we can get right on that tour." He smiles and then begins to write on a piece of parchment he's ripped from the bin.

Taking my hand in his callused one, he places my arm in the crook of his. We walk, holding onto each other while we stroll through the dimmed, fire-lit halls of the Kingdom of Valador. And for the first time, I feel seen for who I truly am, for I am no longer hiding.

***

Finox

After Arysalia stormed out of the study, I decided it was time I had a chat with her about what this curse means for the entire continent, not just Issalitia. As I head toward her chambers, not knowing what to say to her, I look up and see a palace guard at the entrance to the massive courtyard. He comes to attention.

"Your Majesty, the princess entered the hot spring chamber. I did not wish to intrude, but I am here to guard the entrance."

"Thank you, that's very good. I'll go down and find out if she's all right."

"Yes, Sire. She looked incredibly angry on her way here," he tells me, a strange shine appearing in his eyes. "But then she stopped in her tracks." He gestures toward the path.

"I'm not sure how she knew about the chamber in the courtyard. I've never seen someone's demeanor change so suddenly." He looks toward the courtyard. "It was as if it called to her, Your Majesty."

"Thank you, yes," I nod, knowing that the water in the springs must have indeed called to her.

Without another word, I stride through the courtyard and head straight for the iron gate. Placing an illusion around myself to hide my footsteps, I head down the stairs.

Chapter 24

Arysalia

I AM LOST IN my own thoughts about everything that has happened in the last few days: the rapids that appeared in the halls of my castle, Umbra growing so quickly, the king of another kingdom being in our locked kingdom. So much has happened, and I can't stop the journey we are on. It's as if Finox unearthed a secret, a secret we can no longer control.

The unknown of what's to come may be the end of us.

Suddenly, the scent of cherries and citrus coats the damp air. I don't open my eyes.

I'm going to let this play out.

I can't see him or hear his footsteps, so he must have placed an illusion on himself to match the walls and dampen his sounds.

I wonder if he knows that I can smell him coming. Suddenly, the silence is broken, not by Finox, but by a loud growl and click of a tongue.

As if on cue, it is Umbra. She must have been stalking him and followed him in here.

My sneaky girl is always here for me.

Once Umbra clicks her tongue, I see him. Finox is standing stock-still near the edge of the water, his eyes wild.

My eyes are open now and locked on his. "Hello, Kingling," I purr, smoldering with anger at the sight of him.

Why can I have no peace?

"Hello, Princess. This isn't what it looks like." He is as white as a sheet as he stammers out his flimsy response.

"I'm positive you being here is exactly what I think it looks like," I reply sternly. "Looking for a show?"

"No, that isn't it!" he snaps, looking away. "Why are you like this? Everyone isn't out to hurt you." He crosses his arms and turns entirely around toward the stairs, where Umbra blocks the only exit. Her feathered fur stands on end as she releases a low growl at the king.

"I'm not like anything?! I came in here alone, to be alone." I growl through my clenched teeth.

Why can I not calm this anger inside me?

He spins to face me and stalks toward me, not bothering to remove his leathers. His boots are still laced, his tunic clinging to him as he steps into the water.

But the hot springs do not part for him; the water's surface stays undisturbed as he makes his descent.

"I only wish to speak with you. There is no reason for you to get so angry at me."

"Speak from over there. Do not come closer," I growl, using my water magic to cause a current against him. He cannot move any closer to me.

"Fine," he spits, looking irritated. "I want to talk to you about the kingdom and what it would mean to free your people."

"What do you actually know about my people?"

"Well, for one, your kingdom thrived on its extensive exports. Other kingdoms loved your produce, florals, and magic herbs. The livestock raised in your kingdom is like no other on Nedona. The entire continent benefits from the resources your kingdom creates and tends," he says. "Five hundred years, Arysa."

"I am aware how long the Mad King has enslaved my kingdom," I whisper. "Unless you are over five hundred years old, you weren't here when my kingdom was a prosperous nation. You never tasted our crops, our livestock, or used our magic herbs."

"No, I did not, but I have the journals my father left behind," he states matter-of-factly.

"Journals?" I brush my hair back from where it sticks to my forehead from the steam.

"Journals, yes. They detail our kingdom's decline without those resources, and the importation of your goods to the only other safe kingdom, Ramman. It may be the Kingdom of Light, but it does not grow crops and herbs as well as the Kingdom of Spring," he tells me.

"I understand, but what if we release the kingdom and all hell breaks loose?" I whine. "What if the continent knows our kingdom is free and thinks they can take it for themselves?" I meet his eyes now, tears welling in my eyes. "What if Samarra di—" I cannot even complete the sentence because she can't.

I cannot risk the life of my only true friend, soulmate, best friend, for the possibility that the world might end anyway. I can't be the cause of her death.

"Arysa, she does not need to die for this to work." His eyes jump back and forth between mine, trying to make me understand. The resolve in me to hold him at arm's length releases, and the tears come in full force now.

"You don't know that!" I sob. I sound like a dying woodland creature sucking in the air, trying to quell my tears. Finox acts immediately, and Umbra growls and moves toward us. Finox grabs my shoulders firmly and meets my eyes.

"Breathe, Princess," he commands. The scent of citrus and cherries fills the air once more. "Look up."

I do as I am told, tears streaming down my cheeks, landing with soft plops into the hot springs around us. We are standing too close, but I don't care. Deep underground, Finox has created the night sky above us. I can see all the constellations, belts, and small galaxies that normally dance across the sky above ground.

My heart immediately slows down, and I catch my breath. "It's beautiful," I whisper into the darkness. He is less than a foot from me now. Our chins almost graze as we gaze up. "Thank you." I look down and pull from his grasp.

He drops his hands into the water immediately. His expression reveals nothing, and a look of pure boredom appears on all his features once again.

"You're welcome, Princess," he says quietly and steps back from me. Umbra has already disappeared into the night, no longer seeing danger in Finox's presence.

"Arysalia, my name is Arysalia," I correct. Just because I am a princess doesn't mean I want to be reminded every time someone speaks to me.

"Arysalia," he says resignedly. "Enjoy your soak, think about what I said." With a curt nod, he moves to leave the chamber. With a flash of light, his once–damp clothes are instantly dry. They even show new designs, colors, and fabrics. I shake my head. *His illusions are wild.*

Chapter 25

Finox

I AM FLUSTERED AFTER trying to make Arysalia understand why this is so important. I can still feel her warm skin on my palms and fingers. Her scent of the sea and flowers fills my nostrils even though I am no longer near her. She is such an angry woman. I don't know why I even try. I just can't seem to stay away from her. I walk back to my study in a daze.

It is empty now. I am unsure where Goren and Samarra have run off to, but it's getting dark. The study is cast in shadows, and I see something written on parchment left on my desk.

Finox,

I am taking the flame on a tour of the castle and getting her some food. We have read more words tonight than I think I have read in an entire turn of the year.

We agree that the temple is the only way to ensure the blade's destruction.

Now, where do we destroy it? There are a few words I cannot translate, but here is a skull similar to the one on the maps that represents the Muphion Jungle.

Goren of the Wind

I'm not the only one who can't seem to stay away. I set the note aside and begin to translate.

***

Arysalia

What the fuck was that? The Kingling could calm the panic and anxiety that was welling up and ready to blast out in a way of uncontrolled elemental magic.

How did he know the stars calm me? The stars have always calmed me, which is why the courtyard in Issalitia's castle is built the way it is: open with a clear view and quiet. Maybe those tranquil moments, when I lay on the courtyard's bench, weren't true silence but an illusion.

Once I have soaked long enough, I exit the pool. Using my magic, I wring my slick clothing and completely dry my hair. The water runs off my body and down into the hot spring behind me. Once dressed, I decide it's time to find Samarra. I owe her an apology.

When I get to the chambers, she isn't there, and the sun has receded below the horizon. Confused, I put on a warm coat and head back into the hallway. This place is a complete maze, the only one who could possibly help me navigate through it is Umbra.

I let out a low whistle and shout, "Umbra, come!" Within minutes, I hear the whooshing of her large wings and finally the clatter of claws on the cool stone floor.

She approaches me, purring. She passes by, rubbing her head along my hands, up my arm, and along my chest. Spinning in place, she starts again, as if she is a nine-pound barn cat instead of the hulking feline she has become. Her inquisitive eyes meet mine; they are enchanting and could probably draw me into my own demise.

We don't really know how dangerous you are, do we, love? I continue to pet her gently.

"I need you to help me find Samarra," I request. This is returned with a huff, then she plops her butt down on the floor. "Umbra, seriously, I need to find her to apologize."

She is ignoring me, licking her paws one by one while I stand staring at her. I growl a bit and grind out as gently as I can, "Umbra, I need Sam. Now."

Her final foot flops to the floor, and she spins around to strut down the hall.

Thank you, you sassy cat.

After a lot of searching, Umbra is unsuccessful in finding Samarra, and I'm over it. We turn down another few halls and end up at the ornate door I recognize as our chamber.

"I'm fine now. Go find something to eat." I shove Umbra away; she doesn't listen. Plopping down next to me, she looks at me knowingly. "I will be fine, I promise. I just need some sleep."

Growling, she stands and pounces into the air of the towering hallway; instantly, she disappears into the shadows. The only way to tell she was here was the whoosh and flap of her wings echoing down the halls.

I just need to calm down and sleep. I open the chamber door and find it empty, again.

Part
Two

Chapter 26

Arysalia

WE ARE TO MEET again in the overcrowded study. Samarra hasn't spoken to me much since she came late to our chambers two days ago. The next day consisted of packing and finding supplies for our voyage. With a vote of three to one, I was overruled, and now we are trekking to the temple. My uncle, a man I have never met or heard from in my entire life, will be there, and I am not sure how to feel. If my uncle is loyal to the Mad King, our journey will be over before it even begins.

Now I listen to Goren and Finox work together to translate the last bit of text, telling us what and where we need to be in order to destroy the blade.

"Goren, it's either the Muphion Jungle where the jungle meets the sea or the Orcus Avala Mountains,"

Finox tries to explain as they look at the map of our continent on the wall.

Finox points toward the jungle, then drags his finger down the west coast. From what I have read about the west coast, it is covered with cliffs, mountain ranges and snow murderers. The snow murderers are fae sprites that dwell within the snow-capped cliffs of Orcus Avala. The people are locally known as the Oreads. It is undocumented if the Oreads kill for sport or for food, but I don't want to find out.

"Sire, I think it is the jungle," Goren responds, trying hard not to raise his voice. "There is a temple on the cliff over the sea once you pass through the jungle. There is no such temple in the Orcus Avala ranges; the only thing over there is the island off the coast." He isn't wrong; a name is scrawled along the edge of the jungle that meets the sea: Thatin Cliff, The Cliff of Miracles.

My eyes have been all over the map today, and I didn't even notice the small land formation off the west coast that seems to be surrounded by cliffs. Haemah Temple, there is no name for the mysterious island, just the temple on it.

Pointing at the island, I say, "What is this temple? I have never heard of it. What does Haemah translate to?" I am perplexed. I thought I knew all the land formations related to Nedona, but I have never heard of that temple.

"Oh, that is the Haemah Temple. Translated in its roughest form, it means blood," Finox says with a straight face, as if I should have known. "This is the island where the dagger was created. Did you not know?"

My cheeks heat up because I didn't know that tasty tidbit. "So wouldn't the Orcus Avala Mountains make more sense than the Cliff of Miracles for the destruction of the dagger?" I slowly inhale the stuffy air of the study and exhale just as slowly.

"The jungle is safer than the mountain range," Goren explains. "If we are unsure, surviving the jungle will be easier. If we are wrong, then we simply move along the coast to avoid the desert and reach the mountain range. We do not want to cross the desert or run into the King of the Kingdom Below the Sands."

I look over, Samarra is nodding at Finox, and he is doing the same. Three to one again. I must survive the deadliest jungle in Nedona. That is, only if we survive the visit with Lucis Spirus Brontos, The Light Bringer Priest of the Temple of Geras.

Along the eastern side of the kingdom, there are a few secret tunnels we can take that, according to Finox, will lead us to the River of Issalitia. I am not pleased that we are making this trek on foot, instead of flying with Sasha and Greta. "How much further? I can smell the river, but I'd much rather see it from the sky!"

"I've already told you! The girls are too well known in the kingdoms, and we will be spotted, shot down, and murdered," he yells back, unamused.

Get over it, Kingling.

"Ugh," I sigh audibly.

Samarra is ahead of me with Goren by her side. We resemble a diamond. I'm holding up the rear, and Finox is leading the way. I don't particularly enjoy being in the back of this caravan, though I do feel better hearing Umbra's clicks every once in a while, when she sees something in the shadows.

"Here we are!" Finox shouts from the front, as streams of light come in through the grate at the end of the tunnel. Passing through the illusion with ease, I hear Samarra gasp with surprise. It is stunning. I can feel the water thrumming, ebbing, and flowing, begging for me to join it.

Chapter 27

Arysalia

I HAVE NEVER SEEN anything so beautiful in my entire life. The images of the River of Issalitia do it no justice. The bright ball of light gleaming down onto the azure blue surface is a sight I could never have imagined. The river is calling me; I want to submerge myself in it and breathe it into all my pores.

"Your mouth is hanging open, Princess." I glance at the Kingling and almost growl. He put his hands up. "Sorry, Arysalia. I promise it wasn't intentional."

I close my mouth shut and move toward the river; its siren's call is intoxicating. I have never been this close to a large body of water before. The water and spring inside me are warring. I look down at where I am standing along the edge of the flowing river and see that patches of wildflowers are blooming all around me.

Their colors range from all over the rainbow: pinks, yellows, blues, and greens bloom everywhere. This has never happened before; I usually have enormous control of both my water and spring sides. It was how I hid my water magic from the Mad King for so long, but being this close to the river and the sea is making it incredibly hard to control.

"I've never seen your magic do that," I hear Samarra say beside me.

I look over at her from where I am standing. They are all staring at me. Their expressions range from surprise to awe to confusion. "I didn't realize you sprout flowers," Finox says.

"I don't!" I shout. "This is new, I have never been so close to a water source of this magnitude before." *I've only ever been around ponds and streams within the kingdom... This is so vast and unending.*

Samarra is immediately at my side, hand in mine. "I am here, Arysalia. I am with you," she whispers as she places her forehead against mine. "We will figure everything out. We will always have each other."

I try my best to believe her when she speaks, but part of me already knows there is a farce behind her well-meant words.

"Thank you, Samarra." Leaning away from my friend, I drop her hand and turn to the men. "How the fuck are we getting to that gods awful temple?"

"Right this way, Arysalia." Finox gestures with his hand, sweeping it along the riverbank. In the reeds, there is a large canoe. There is no mast, only large oars, which we won't need if I can control my water magic.

Goren and Finox lead me and Samarra through the reeds, and they help us settle into the canoe. It isn't an ordinary canoe, though; at least not one I have ever seen, that is. It can hold about six people and our supplies. I daydream as Goren pushes us out of the reeds and into the open river.

"Be careful, everyone; stay alert and watch the surroundings," Goren instructs as we start paddling toward the Ynos Delta.

It's just a river, what is there to be afraid of?

Just as I am about to turn my focus toward the delta and the river, a song, a sort of call, plays in my head, a call I thought was the river telling me to come in and play. But this siren call is eerily different. It is no longer playfully asking me to go in and swim; it is demanding that I do.

"*The water is cool, the water is quick, come play with me, we'll make it quick.*" A siren sings. "*The water is fun, the water is grand, come play with me, and find a new land."*

I think I might be losing my mind. Am I the only one hearing this right now? I look around at the three people sitting in the canoe with me. A shiver runs down the back of my neck.

"The water is cool, the water is quick, come play with me, we'll make it quick. The water is fun, the water is grand, come play with me, and find a new land."

"Arysa, you look very pale," Finox says. He is seated in front of me, looking back over his shoulder. I can read his lips, but it's hard to hear him over the song now playing on repeat. It is begging me to get into the water.

When I don't respond, he says, "Princess, what is wrong?"

"The water is cool, the water is quick, come play with me, we'll make it quick. The water is fun, the water is grand, come play with me, and find a new land."

I don't know if I can hold out any longer. I stand with the grace of a woodland creature, freshly born.

"Arysa!" Goren shouts from behind me. Samarra is seated somewhere behind him. "Sit down, you're going to fall in!" He reaches for me as I fall in slow motion toward the azure blue beauty that is the River of Issalitia.

I crash through the water headfirst, falling and falling. The water is pulling me deeper into its depths. I don't know if I am dying or if I am coming alive. I hear the siren shift from singing to squealing with joy.

"*Yes, yes, yes! The princess has come! The princess is here! Come play with us, come play with me, my dear!*"

It is so dark down here. I look up toward the surface. Sunbeams shine through the water, creating a breathtaking sight.

If I am to die, this is as good as it will ever get.

A shadow passes over the sun's beams, and I am being yanked from the lovely death I was waiting to be given.

The siren is dismayed.

"*No, my pretty. No, my dear. You must stay with me, down here.*" The water wants to keep me, pulling me further into its depths.

A rough hand clamps around my wrist, and suddenly I am being yanked through the water. A shadowed form surrounds me, the light above dimming, my lungs burning. I am almost out of time.

"*The water is fun, the water is grand, come play with me, and find a new land.*"

I believe the land she sings of is the land beyond the veil of existence, life itself.

As my head gets closer to the surface, the edges of my vision blur completely, and the dark takes me.

"Breathe, Princess, breathe," is the last thing I hear before the sky goes dark.

Chapter 28

Finox

"FOR FUCK'S SAKE! BREATHE, Princess!" I take in another deep breath and wrap my lips around the lifeless mouth of Arysalia. "Breathe, damn it!" I yell, and Goren grabs me and pulls me back.

"Give her a minute, Fin. You've been filling her full of air," he grinds out. "Let her come back to us."

Overhead, Umbra is circling and screeching. She is as upset as I am with what is happening. Once I let go, though, that is when something changes.

With a click of her tongue, Umbra has Arysalia. She teleports her to the banks of the river, circling her beloved master. "Get me to the shore now!" I shout at my best friend.

"I'm trying!" He uses his wind to guide us toward the shore.

Looking over, I see Samarra; her eyes are flaming magma. She is shaking, and her hair is whipping in the wind. If she wasn't so fucking terrifying right now, I'd say she looks magnificent. She hasn't spoken a word since Arysalia fell into the river.

Did she fall? I heard her grumbling about the canoe and rowing, and then she just fell utterly quiet, no more sassy retorts. She was so pale, as if all the blood had rushed out of her body.

Without thinking, I dive in after her. The need to keep her with me is stronger than I have ever felt.

We make it to shore, and Umbra has her massive black forehead resting against Arysalia's.

"Wake up, Arysalia!" I yell as I make my way closer. Umbra growls, lifting her head and glowering at me, a deep, low growl building in her chest. She whips her tail swiftly from side to side, making it impossible to get close to her.

"Umbra," I hear her name softly spoken. Looking down, I see pink hair whipping in the wind next to me as Samarra makes her way to Umbra and the princess.

"Umbra, my darling, please. Let me come to you," Samarra whispers, hand outstretched, as if Umbra is a wild thing that needs to be tamed. The massive cat with wings is a force to be reckoned with.

The oracat lifts her head from Arysalia and bows. She shuts her eyes as Samarra creeps closer on delicate feet, making no sound and without disturbing the earth beneath her ever-present heat.

What is she doing?

As I pace from side to side, Umbra whips her tail and growls again.

Samarra settles on her knees. The world stands still as she takes Arysalia's hand and gently places it on her chest. Resting her palm against her breastbone, she bows her head and begins to whisper. It is then that I remember the cuts she and Samarra had on the insides of their palms. I thought it was just girls playing witchcraft, like kids, but now I know. It was a blood oath.

As Samarra whispers, her hands glow bright pink. The color and light run down both their arms and encircle their bodies.

She's going to burn her.

But just as I have that thought, the princess's eyes burst open. The green in her eyes turns to pink before she sucks in the deepest breath I have ever seen. The whips and growls from Umbra cease, and Arysa is breathing again.

Samarra slumps down, dropping her hands to her lap. Goren bolts ahead before I can get my footing, before I can even think to run to Arysalia.

She is alive, my gods, she is alive.

I don't think I have ever been more heartbroken and scared in my entire life.

Chapter 29

Arysalia

I JUST HAD THE most incredible dream. The rushing in my ears, the yelling, screaming, terror, and blinding fear went quiet. As I opened my eyes, I was lying on a sandy beach. The beach was so beautiful, its water was bluer than any I've ever seen. The sun was setting in the distance, painting the sky in the most gorgeous shades of purples and pinks.

The overwhelming scent of salty sea air permeates my senses, along with something I have never smelled before, though it smells like home. I look around the beach. I am alone, and the siren is right. I am in a new land.

A man clears his throat. I turn and am startled to my core. The man in front of me is tall, with dark hair the same shade as mine, freckles dusting his nose and neck.

His beauty marks carry down his arms to his hands. He looks at me with eyes a shade of gold. This man... I feel I know him completely.

"Darling flower," he says. It's the name Jerix gave my mother when they fell in love so long ago on the Azure Beaches of Nedona. "Oh, my flower, what are you doing here on such a beautiful day?"

"I am lost. I'm not sure how I got here. I heard the most terrifying song, and I couldn't stop myself." I look into his eyes. "I was down by the river, and I felt it calling and singing to me to come play, but we needed to start our journey."

He's listening with rapt attention.

"She sang, begging me to come. I had no choice." I take a shuddering breath, remembering all whom I left on the canoe. I stifle a cry. "I just want it all to go away. I want everything to just stop."

"My darling, you cannot just give up. You are too important to let go." His voice caresses me in a warmth that could only come from the most valid form of love. "Unfortunately, I know quite well the siren's song you speak of. It is both a blessing and a curse. The water we carry in our veins, which represents strength and power, can be both wonderful and dangerous. The siren lives within us."

"What siren?"

"It is a part of our magic that we must work hard to keep under control." He gestures to the sand, inviting me to sit next to him. We sit cross-legged on the warm sand, listening to the mysterious waves crashing against the coast. "I will tell you the story of the siren who gave her magic to save the man she loved."

"Before water magic was shared through the blood of water elemental fae, there was a clan of sirens. A queen, Queen Neryna of the Northern Tempest, led the sirens. Neryna was a notorious siren, known for drowning entire ships and their crew. She would sing them to the sea, and feed on the emotions they felt. Then, she would drown them."

"After hundreds of years and thousands of men sacrificed to the Northern Tempest, Neryna met her match. On a foggy summer morning, before the sun could truly clear the sea mist, she sang, *'Come to my captain, come play with me, the water is warm, come, my captain, come play with me, show me spirit, fill me with glee.'* Changing her chorus often, she would coax the crew off the deck, one by one. *'Hello, handsome, come play and see, come swim in the ocean, come show me your glee.'*"

"The sirens kept their distance from the ships to avoid being spotted. When the sun finally dispersed the low-hanging mist, Neryna noticed a man she had never seen before. He exuded strength, power, and beauty. He was tall, with dark flowing locks that curled and whipped in the wind. His arms were bare, showing his strength, and in his hand, she noticed a spyglass. After she had drowned his entire crew, the captain was on a hunt.

"Neryna was enamored for the first time in her life by this man, the only man she ever revealed herself to. He pulled away from the glass, then gazed into it again. He saw her, too. Neryna was a shade of blue that would make the sky jealous. The hue made her blend seamlessly into the surf and waves. Her hair was as black as night, helping her blend into the shadows and disguise her form, but her eyes shone with an unnatural light that could lure the blindest man to his death."

"Is she the siren who took all of his men?" I ask tentatively. Jerix is lost in his story.

"She had always been elusive with her truths," he continues. "When the man confronted her, accusing her of drowning his men, she gave him an answer in a voice that was not entirely her own. It was a lie, and they both knew it. But rather than lash out, the man, with calm determination, warned her of the price: if she had taken his men, he would be forced to return the favor with death."

"Still, she denied it. Still a lie. And when he called her closer with the promise of understanding or maybe something more, she refused him, not out of fear, but out of protection. Her instincts told her not to trust him, no matter how striking his features or how strong his voice was. He seemed sincere, even stranded and wounded by the loss of his crew, but she couldn't afford to risk her clan for the sake of one human. And so, she slipped beneath the water's surface, her apology trailing like foam on the waves.

"Months passed, then years, but the sea captain's face never left her memory. She survived, hoping that one day she would find him again and bring him into her world, even just for a day. On a stormy fall evening, Neryna was about to begin her siren song for a lone ship in the middle of the Northern Tempest when she recognized the man standing at the bow, spyglass to his eye, arms bare but now with a blue tattoo. His curly brown hair was a mess in the spray of the sea and unrelenting wind.

"She began her siren song anew, one that she never thought she'd be able to sing. She sang a song not of death but of love. '*Captain of the northern tempest, come here to me, come take away this lonely. I have searched for you for years, craved your tears, captain of the northern tempest, come to me. Come to me finally.*'

He saw her through his spyglass, dropped it to the deck, and dove into waves so dangerous even monsters didn't attempt to surface."

"However, Neryna wasn't a monster any longer. She had deprived herself. She had not taken another crew since that day years ago. She swam with the speed of a siren, slicing through the water, making her way to the man she had loved madly for so long. She did not even know his name, but he knew her heart, for that, she was certain.

"She reached him, but the waves had caused damage. He wasn't conscious, and he wasn't breathing. Neryna used what little magic she had left and breathed life into him, leaving a bit of herself behind. She gave what was left in her to the captain. Neryna, Queen of the Sirens, sacrificed her life to save the one she could never truly have.

"Edmond, Captain of the Siren's Song, was saved that day by Neryna. She transferred what was left of herself to him, creating a new line of human–siren hybrids. They could control the seas, waters, and rivers, but they could not control the siren who sang them back to the sea.

"He never wanted to hurt her that day. He only wanted to be near her. Her song cut so deeply that he fell instantly in love with her. He never stopped searching for her, and he even had her likeness tattooed on himself so he would never forget her. After she saved his life, he went on to name a ship for her and carry her line of water elementals that they created together.

"Edmond married, not his one true love, but someone who could bring him honor, children, and life. They settled on the continent of Nedona, along the Azure beaches to carry Neryna's magic into the ever-changing world of Xandelar. Edmond could not be too far from his tempest, but he also could not be too close. The siren's song that sang in his blood would be his demise if he stayed. The siren's gift of bringing the men of the seas in has had an ill effect on our ancestors. Now, we can no longer get too close to the seas or larger bodies of water, her song will not call to anyone except ourselves."

Jerix finishes his story. "My father is a descendant of Edmond, Captain of the Siren's Song. The elemental magic that called to me when I was close to bodies of water was my salvation and my curse. Do you now understand, my flower?" he asks gently.

"Yes, I do, the spring and water magic work together, but being so connected to the sea makes my water magic stronger. It pushes spring aside, almost wanting me to drown in its power." That is what it felt like, at least.

"Flower, I did not have the spring, but I know that the water in my veins made me feel that way. Too close to the edge, and my own siren song would have drowned me too," he explains, looking at me with pain in his eyes. "It is time to wake up, Arysalia."

"No, please, don't go," I cry. "Please, Father, don't go!"

Chapter 30

Finox

"**B**REATHE, PRINCESS!" I SHOUT to Arysalia. Samarra has just delivered a form of magic to her, and her eyes are now open. Flames of magenta now rim her once light green eyes, but she hasn't taken a full breath yet.

Umbra places her head on Arysalia's chest and purrs, a calming sound that seems to wake her more effectively than my apparent screaming. I was more scared in that moment than I had ever been.

She is okay. She is breathing now, and she is alive.

I hear her sniffle, as if she's crying. I can't see her face with the oracat comforting her and blocking my line of sight, but I can hear what sounds like weeping.

"*Arysalia*, are you... Are you alright?" I ask patiently, hoping for a snippy remark or her usual sass.

Unfortunately, she does not reply. She just weeps into Umbra's feathers. An agonizing sob leaves her, and my heart truly breaks in that moment.

Goren is huddled around Samarra, holding her close to his chest. It seems whatever magic she used on Arysalia sapped her of her energy. I'm not sure how far we've made it on this river, but the Ynos Delta is not in sight, and we need to set up camp for the night. I begin preparations to create an illusion around all of us. The magic acts as our protection from the elements and whatever creatures lurk in the shadows when the sun sets.

Once I retrieve all our belongings from the canoe, I will also cloak the vessel. I tether it to the shore, so if we need to make a quick escape, it is there. Looking over to the princess, I truly have no idea what to feel. She lies curled in a ball beside the fire that Goren built with some help from Samarra's flame. Umbra has not left her side since she awoke. Arysalia is no longer glowing pink, and her sobbing has subsided. Her eyes are rimmed red and puffy.

I want to wipe away her tears and hold her myself, but I can't. She does not wish for my touch.

✳✳✳

Arysalia

After waking up from my vision of my true father, I now see what my mother saw. The gentleman I met was very much like me if I were a man, tall of form with gentle speech, and incredibly kind. My heart broke. I was never able to meet Jerix, the man who sired me, who created my life with my mother, who gave his life to keep me safe.

The Mad King had no idea I wasn't truly his. My mother explained that they would have the heir-creating sex needed twice a month. Before each encounter, she would take her tonic to make sure she did not fall pregnant. She wanted to create life with Jerix and have her life with him for as long as possible.

I don't blame her at all.

Maggard grew impatient and wanted an heir; he had the kingdom he always wanted, and now he needed to secure his bloodline. Jerix and Zandra devised a plan to become pregnant before her next session with Maggard, during which she would skip her tonic. Doing so, there was no way to know if I would be his or Maggard's, but after my true father was murdered, my mother realized their plan had worked and that she had created a child, an heir of her own. I would carry on the siren's magic song in my blood alongside the spring.

Lying here next to the fire with Umbra cuddled close, I mourn his loss. I mourn him more than I ever thought possible. I have developed a newfound hatred for the Mad King. I am determined that we will break his curse, the curse that has kept my water magic hidden quite well on its own. It kept me locked in a castle, unable to awaken the siren song in my veins until I laid eyes on the River of Issalitia.

Rolling over and away from the flames, I catch his eye. The kingling has been hovering, and I am not quite sure how to feel about it. I have yet to forgive him for spying on us for so long. Though I must admit, there are sparks between us. Sparks that I have quashed with as much gusto as possible.

I close my eyes one last time tonight, the scent of his magic in the air lulling me to sleep. I hope I dream of my father, but I know I won't be that lucky.

***

The next morning, we wake up on the shore, and I have no idea how we will make our plan work. I can be near the river but not be upon it.

How the hell am I supposed to get to an island temple, surrounded by water?

Finox is sitting across the fire from me. He must have sensed me staring at him. His eyes open slowly, the flames making his amber eyes shine a shade of yellow that squeezes my heart. He is such a brat most of the time. *The Kingling makes me feel like an ignorant girl. Though he's right, I am ignorant. I know nothing outside the walls of my kingdom that was not written down and kept in our library.*

"Good morning, Arysalia." Finox pulls me from my constant overthinking.

"Good morning, Finox," I reply in a cordial tone. I want to be his friend, but I have so much frustration built up inside of me.

"What do you think we should do about the 'siren song' while we continue downstream?" He asks the question I have been thinking about all night.

"Well, I either need to fly there, or you'll need to sedate me or maybe even tie me down," I explain, not wanting to tell him about the vision I had of my father. I don't want him to know how much I know about my magic yet. It is still new to me, and my strain of the elemental magic could be different than Jerix's.

"Oh," Finox replies, making a visible O shape with his mouth. His face turns a light shade of red that creeps down his neck and into the collar of his shirt. "You want me to tie you down, and also drug you so you're asleep?" Embarrassment is written all over his face.

"Yes, Finox, I want you to drug me and tie me down while we are near any large waterway, sea, river, and so on." I give him a devilish look because I thoroughly enjoy his discomfort.

"Well, we have the herbs your mother gave us, the ones you used in the soup."

"I don't know how much we will need or if we will have enough for the return trip," Samarra interjects as she pulls the herbs from the pack she has been carrying. She carries the essentials for survival, and I carry the weapons.

"Perfect, let's do it," I say with a bit more pep.

The sooner we get this over with, the sooner we can save the kingdom.

Chapter 31

Finox

WE ARE BACK ON the river. I am in front of the massive canoe, with Arysalia secured between the benches and out cold. Her onyx blue–black hair has an entrancing shine. I find myself looking back at her still form. Samarra is sitting behind Goren, none the wiser, but Goren can practically read my thoughts.

Each day in her presence holds the possibility of growing affection. Learning of how we were stalking them in the cover of illusion and darkness has to be why she is so sour toward me. Now that I think about it, I would likely feel the same way.

I look over my shoulder again and see that Goren is distracted by something Samarra has told him. I envy my best friend. His attraction to Samarra seems to be reciprocated. She must have also been put off by our antics for a little while. Once she realized that they are both fated, and that they had first met in their dreams, she and Goren have been inseparable.

I am drifting through thoughts about the night we all first met, and the first night I saw Arysalia. She was alone when we made it into the kingdom. Goren did not want to come back after our first visit, but when Samarra had poked her head out to ask the princess to go inside with her, he was just as hooked as I was.

Unlike Goren and Samarra, Arysalia doesn't seem to have a deep connection with me. I feel defeated. My attraction for her was there the moment I set eyes on her. Back when I first saw her, she was adventurous and strong, but now she is consumed by anger.

***

Arysalia

I have no idea where I am. I remember taking the tonic, but I am blasting through memories, or moments in the future.

Samarra looks disheveled, and her skin has more scales than the last time I saw her. The pink hue against her pale skin is breathtaking. Her eyes shine brighter, but she looks exhausted. I don't know where we are. Goren is holding Sam, but I can't find Finox anywhere. I am unable to move in this state, as if I am tied to the spot. I watch the world go on without me. Flashes of pink flame, smoke, screams, growls, and darkness take over my vision.

✳✳✳

I feel warm hands on my arms and legs; it feels as though I am being carried. Samarra's hand is holding mine tightly, and I know I must be out of the sleep state. We have arrived at the Temple of Geras. I pray we are all safe. With the number of hands touching me, I can surmise everyone survived our trip down the River of Issalitia, the Ynos Delta, and into the Branera Tempest.

I finally open my eyes and see the sun descending toward the horizon. The sea surrounds us, and there is water in every direction. The siren inside me is quiet, thankfully. This must be a sacred enough place that she doesn't want me to kill myself here. I remember the way it felt when the darkness took over. I shiver, even though it was still warm from the day.

"She's awake," Goren's deep voice murmurs.

"Arysalia?" Finox's voice cuts through my haze.

We are still walking up the incline. I am still in his arms.

"How do you feel?" he asks, holding my shoulders.

And my gods, he is above me.

When I first opened my eyes, my head had lolled to the side; I'd seen water, cliffs, the blur of distance. But now I'm staring straight up at him.

Oh, his eyes are beautiful. The shadow of amber in them places them a few shades away from brilliant yellow.

"Princess," he says sternly.

I twist, attempting to escape his gaze. "Don't call me that," I growl. Which apparently was not the right thing to say because his jaw tightens. "I said I'm fine. Can you both please put me down now?" It's uncomfortable being carried like dead weight up a cliffside.

"When we get to the top," Sam tells me. "I don't want you to get dizzy before we get there."

It makes sense, but everywhere Finox touches me feels like it's on fire.

"Fine," I say, and shut my eyes tight. I can feel his eyes on me again, but I refuse to look. I can't. His beautiful eyes will be my undoing.

After what feels like a century, we make it to the temple, and the men put me down. I feel quite dizzy, and I am incredibly anxious.

We are committing treason against the crown of Issalitia.

Perhaps we could use fake names and pretend to be from another kingdom, learning about dragon fire daggers, tools, and how to destroy runes. *Have my companions thought about any of this?*

A tall man with greying blonde hair and cobalt-colored eyes walks out from the entrance of the large temple. His features look soft, calm, and eerily similar to the Mad King's. But his eyes are gentle and kind, as opposed to Maggard's, which are purely evil. Maggard possesses light magic, but it must be nothing compared to this man, whose aura is emanating it.

Before I can tell Finox precisely what we should say, I see the pain in my ass bending at his waist, bringing both of his hands in front of his chest, palms together. "Hello, sir, I am Finox."

Gods, I hope this man doesn't know which Finox he is being introduced to.

The man's eyes widen, and his mouth forms a flat line. He presses his palms together in a bow that looks much more graceful than Finox could manage. "Your Majesty, what a surprise."

Well, fuck.

Chapter 32

Finox

"I AM SORRY TO show up at the temple without notice."

I need to be wary of the priest. This man is related to the beast that has locked up a kingdom for five hundred years.

"Your Majesty, you are always welcome to visit the temple." He bows. "What can we do for you and your cohorts?"

"We are hoping you can help us find some information on enchanted daggers and weapons," I say to be as vague as possible.

"Ah, yes, we have an extensive library." He turns and gestures toward the temple.

Looking back at my friends, I see Goren in a stance that projects an air of protection, shielding us ladies from the priest's gaze. Samarra applied her runes to her eyes and dressed herself in a way that covered the new scales, which had become more visible on her shoulders and arms. Arysalia is quite recognizable, but not many know her face. She did not rune herself before she took the tonic. Samarra dressed her in a dark hood to hide her beautiful green eyes and onyx hair.

I find myself thinking about Arysalia more than I should. Looking back at her now, she looks like a different person. Her eyes and hair are hidden, and her posture is altered from her usual regal stance.

As we walk down the temple halls, the priest looks us over. He is not overtly staring, though; he just seems curious as to who the King of Valador has brought to the temple of gifts. "My name is Lucius. I am the high priest of this temple," he explains as we continue through the stone halls.

Unlike the castles I have been in, this temple is made entirely from the stone of the mountain on this island. Natural springs run along the path's edges, flowing through the halls and large windows that are left wide open to allow air and light to permeate.

Once we make it to the library, Lucius leaves us to look around the shelves and stacks that line the walls and take up most of the space. There are no windows. We must be deep within the mountain. There are light orbs scattered about, but no flame. There is no heat source of any kind that could harm the documents, tomes, and scrolls stored here.

I watch Arysa bounce from shelf to shelf, knowing precisely what she's after. Samarra and Goren are glued together, her permanent guard. I feel a twinge of sadness. I have never loved or cherished someone like Goren cherishes Samarra, let alone someone I have just met. Though I mentally correct myself, we've been around these women for five years... without their consent. And in that time, we've grown attached.

Arysa still hates me. I can tell she feels betrayed. I don't blame her; I just wish I could change everything about how we met. There are so many things I wish to explain, if only she could hear me.

"Have you found anything?" An angelic whisper pulls me from my thoughts.

"Not yet, Arysalia," I whisper back. Her hood is pulled back a bit, and her enchanting eyes are exposed. She smells like the sea and lilies. I thought it was just being near the Azure Beach while we were in Issalitia, *but it was her.* My heart starts to pound at her proximity to me.

"There." She points beyond my shoulder. It is an old-looking tome, with dark leather scales running along its spine. There is no name on the tome, but I have an eerie feeling that this could be it.

A chill runs down my spine as she reaches over me. "I'll get it."

Once the tome is retrieved, I gather Goren and Sam and find a table with a light orb. "Look at those scales," Samarra whispers as she runs a delicate finger down them.

"It's incredible; they look exactly like the scales on the dagger," the princess says. "Open it."

So, I do just that. It's ancient, and it isn't a large text, but it does share some specific information about many weapons that were forged in dragon fire, the last of which is the same dagger we wish to learn about. At the back of the text, there it is, etched in ink on the page: "The Dagger of Rythorin."

The last fire goddess, Seraphina Zinnia, created the Dagger of Rythorin. It was the last weapon to be forged in deadly fire. Her magic enabled the weapon to carry and conceal a great power; a power that has yet to be understood by anyone.

The previous dragon–forged weapons could only be destroyed in one way: by a temple blessed with flame. The weapon must be brought to the cliffs beyond the jungle. An ancient ruin holds the most potent magic on the continent. The Thatin Cliffs ruins are beyond the

Muphion Jungle. Known to the locals as the jungle of death. Few have ventured and returned to tell the tale. The jungle itself is inhabited by death and its creatures. The canopy blocks out the sun, leaving the land cloaked in shadows.

Below the text, there is a note scribbled in an almost unreadable script, with a dark line scratched through it: "~~The last goddess, the last flame, no one can stop me, oh, what a shame.~~"

"I have seen that scrawl before," Arysa hisses. "The Mad King has been here." She stands abruptly. "We must take this with us. We cannot leave it here for the priest to stumble upon." She isn't wrong. There is dust on this tome, indicating that it has been here for centuries.

"We cannot remove texts from the temple," Samarra explains. "We will have to hide it here or destroy it."

I'm not sure how I feel about this. If we leave the tome, the odds of it being discovered by a priestess or, gods forbid, Lucius, remain high. And if we are found stealing it...

Well, needless to say, the consequences would be significant.

Chapter 33

Arysalia

I TUCK THE TOME into my cloak as we make our way out of the library. We head back the way we came, looking for Lucius, the uncle I have never met and probably never will. I mean, I have met him, but he has never met me. Does he know how evil his brother is? How can I ask without raising suspicion?

We return to the path lined with springs, and the water in my veins is pounding. The siren is at bay for now, but I need to soak in the molecules of this pristine water. My siren wants to play in its depths, but I cannot give in to her. My true father would not want me to waste myself like that.

"Ah, Your Majesty. All finished with your research?" Lucius steps out of a corridor along the path we are on.

"Yes, we did have one last request."

This gives me pause because we did not discuss how to get Samarra to receive a blessing.

"What can I do for you?" he asks kindly.

"This is Goren and Samarra." Finox gestures to both our best friends. "They wish to be wed within this temple, as close to the gods and goddesses as they can be. They have seen much sadness and grief, and they hope to be blessed by the Temple of Geras and its enchanted springs."

I feel heat filling my face; no one can see it, of course, but I am enraged. The siren is awake now, and she wants to kill. She wants to drown everyone who dares to touch her twin flame, her best friend.

How dare he suggest Samarra marry a stranger!

"I see. Is that what you wish?" Lucius looks at my best friend, whose eyes are glowing blue. She has a smile across her face as she holds the hands of the wind wielder, Goren.

She does love him. I am going to lose her to him. My best friend is going to wed someone for our cause.

Samarra looks longingly into Goren's eyes. "Yes, priest."

They take each other's hands and bow in unison.

"It will be done. Come this way. I will begin preparations immediately." He looks back at Finox. "Will you be staying the night?"

Without a beat, Finox replies, "Yes, we only require two rooms, please." I am about to growl when he takes my hand. "This is my darling fiancé. We are to be wed next year, and she has been permitted to accompany me on our marriage quest."

Lucius looks a bit confused but does not question the King of Valador. We turn and follow him to the suites that have been prepared for travelers who need a place to stay. The king and I receive less modest rooms. There is gold and marble in areas that I did not expect to see within a mountain temple.

I watch as Lucius escorts Samarra and Goren down the corridor... Without me.

Finox reaches around me, grazing my arm as he does. The smell of cherries and citrus engulfs my nose, and I know he has illusioned us. No one can hear us.

"What the fuck did you just do?!" I rush to the king. He is ready for me, though.

He must have sensed the siren in me when he spoke to the priest. I pound my fists against his chest as he gasps. "I had to, it was the only way."

I don't stop. I pound and pound until he grabs my wrists. The tears will not stop now. "How could you?" Those are the only words I can get out as he releases my wrists and wraps his arms around me.

"Breathe, princess. You need to breathe," he whispers delicately into my hair.

I can't breathe. I am going to lose her. The only person who has ever had my back other than my mother...

His voice cuts into my scattered thoughts. "I've got you, Arysa. I've got you." He does have me. He is holding me tighter than he has ever held me before.

Every place his body meets mine buzzes. I could die right here. "She is going to leave me. She is going to leave me, just like everyone else," I whisper. "She can't leave me."

"Princess, she isn't going to leave you. There is something I need to talk to you about, though." He mumbles into my hair as he lifts me into the air. He wraps his arms under my legs and behind my back, cradling me like a babe.

"What could you possibly need to tell me? I apparently know nothing of this plan," I growl, wiggling in his arms.

He is far too near.

He walks us to the chaise and puts me down delicately. I immediately right myself. "Tell me, Finox."

He sits at the edge of the bed, resting his elbows on his knees. I see him now, he looks exhausted. "We all talked while you slept."

I furrow my brow at him. *When I slept?*

"While you were unconscious during the boat ride. We were unsure what was to come."

"So, you devised a plan to have them married?!" I am trying very hard not to yell at this man, this king...

"No, not exactly," he tries to explain before I bite his head off more than I already have. "If something needed to be done, something where Samarra had to be blessed, spill blood, make an oath of any kind..." He trails off, his face tinged with a shade of pink, and takes a deep breath. "We could not risk exposing you to the temple so that she would be the sacrifice for the quest. She'd do whatever was required, marry, bond, bleed; anything she needed to do. And she would do it with Goren as her mate."

Mate.

My mind goes blank.

"Goren is her mate," I say slowly. I can't breathe and gasp for air. This cannot be happening. How the fuck did Goren become Samarra's mate?

I am going to kill him. Darkness circles my thoughts.

Chapter 34

Finox

MY HEART RACES, AND my stomach hurts. I'm in physical pain as I watch Arysalia sobbing in my arms. I had no other choice; we had no other choice. Samarra and Goren knew going into the temple that this was a possibility, but they also knew Arysa would never let it happen. The love she has for Samarra is that of a sister, a twin flame. I knew she would not take it well, but watching the strong princess crumble in front of me is awful.

When we were in the corridor and I told the priest our needs, I could sense and smell a change in her. I wasn't sure if anyone else noticed, but I could smell the sea and lilies stronger than I ever have before. The water in the springs was bubbling, but no one else seemed to notice.

We sit like this until her tears slow. The scent of the sea and flowers has dissipated, and I feel her breathing regulate. I almost believe she may have fallen asleep when one eye pops open.

"Did you know when you use your magic, you smell like a cherry orchard and a citrus plant had a baby?" she asks without an ounce of humor.

Laughing harder than I have laughed before, I say, "No, princess. I did not know I smelled that way when I used my magic."

"Well, you do. It's quite irritating." Her eyebrows knit together. "It is how I knew I could yell at you and pound on you once the door was shut behind us." This time, she smirks.

Gods, she may only have one eye open, but that one eye forces a shiver down my spine. I am all too aware of where she is currently, in my arms.

"Well, you smell too," I say once I finish laughing. This seems to get her attention more than my laughter.

She sits up straight. "Excuse me? I smell?"

She has both eyes open now, and both are filled with fury. I could kiss her. She has never looked so beautiful. Her sea and lilies scent has awakened again. The siren that lives in her magic has an anger issue. She was always a bit angry with me for everything, but these bursts of anger began after she found out about her siren.

"Yes, Princess," I say as I lean in closer, "you smell." She raises a dark eyebrow at me. "You smell like the sea on a windy day. The salt mixes with the air, and it's as if I have walked through a meadow of lilies and wildflowers. Your magic smells incredible."

Her once-pale cheeks have flushed to a bright pink, the color running down her neck.

"My siren can be very forceful with my magic. I assume my magic is indeed what you are smelling," she confides. "No one has ever mentioned they could smell it before."

"Well, it smells divine. I could smell it for the rest of my life and never grow tired of it," I confess.

I may have said too much, but it is my turn to feel happiness.

"Well, I enjoy the scent of your magic as well."

It wasn't the response I was looking for, but it will do. She has not growled at me for calling her princess yet today, either.

***

Arysalia

I have finally calmed down. I have no idea what to do or think, but I cannot change it. "Fin, do I have to go to the blessing?" I ask, sounding smaller than I usually do.

"No, Arysa, you don't need to come. I will go in your place and stand in for our friends. We don't know if the siren in your magic will respond well to the union," he explains kindly.

I wish I weren't so afraid to let my true feelings show. I could kiss this man. He has protected me at every step of this journey, but I'm unsure if I can trust him with my heart.

"Thank you. I think I should rest. I have not fully recovered from the near-drowning." I give him a shy smile.

He helps me take off my cloak and pulls the covers back. I remove my boots and crawl between the sheets. He covers me and places a chaste kiss on my brow.

"I will return soon. The blessing should take no time at all," he whispers and leaves the chambers. The scent of his magic lingers in the air, he must be keeping the room disguised.

I am safe with him, is my last thought before the darkness takes me.

Chapter 35

Finox

I LEAVE ARYSA IN the chamber and cast another illusion, one to keep people from being curious about my chambers, and then I lock her inside. She will likely scold me for my impertinence, but I can't let anything happen to her. I will likely regret kissing her, but I couldn't help myself.

I traverse the halls until I find Lucius speaking with a priestess.

"Your Majesty, we are almost ready for the ceremony. Will your betrothed be accompanying you?" he asks, with no noticeable malice in his tone.

"Unfortunately, no, she is ill from the river. She doesn't fare well in boats." I make a squeamish expression. "If you know what I infer."

"Ah, yes. I, too, do not handle boat rides well." He nods. "Here, let me show you to the Sealing Chamber and Blessing Pool. We can discuss what you'd like to happen."

This confuses me because this isn't my wedding.

"I don't need to make any decisions, Goren and Samarra are capable—"

"Your Majesty, we do not hold just any ceremony here. You have requested the union and blessing, which means you must help us determine a few things. It is tradition." He is firm but calm when he explains. "A blessing isn't usually required for a wedding ceremony; we need to discuss *why*."

"Ah, I see. Well, the two have a family history of tragedy. I love them both dearly and would like their union to be as blessed as possible. This temple grants gifts to those who are worthy, and this couple is more worthy than the gods and goddesses themselves." My explanation seems to be enough.

We continue down the hall and into the Blessing Pool chamber. There is a large, steaming pool of crystal–clear water at its center, and benches of stone line the walls. It looks very similar to the chamber in my castle. There are statues of gods and goddesses that have come before us. One small window makes it feel as if the sky is gleaming down into the chamber. The window is a large hole in the ceiling, a light to the sky. A channel of light lands in the pool's center, and it looks incredibly magical.

There is a scuff of footsteps behind me. I turn and see Goren and Samarra walking toward me. Her eyes are still runed with blue, and a beautiful white robe covers her arms, legs, and chest.

"Finox," Goren says as he claps his hand onto my shoulder.

"Are you ready, my friends?" I ask, looking at Samarra. She is smiling from ear to ear, and her eyes glimmer with happiness. I wish Arysalia could see how happy her friend is right now.

"Where is Ary..." she asks, not continuing to finish her name. "Where is she?"

"She isn't feeling well. The siren in her magic has been wreaking havoc on her emotions. I didn't know if the water in this chamber would harm her or help, and I didn't want to risk it."

She nods in response, but the sparkle in her eye has dwindled.

"She wanted me to tell you she loves you and that she understands why it has to be this way."

"Thank you, Finox. It means a lot that you can calm her. I have been the only one who has ever understood her anger," she explains. "She has felt lost for a long time. I was her only anchor to life in the castle. Now I can only imagine how she feels."

"Your Majesty," Lucius's voice cuts in from behind us. "Are you all ready?" he asks as the priest and priestesses enter the chamber.

"We are," Goren confirms as he holds Samarra's hand and walks to the steps leading into the pool.

"You may both stay clothed if you wish, or you may undress," a petite priestess tells them. Samarra's face turns a shade of pink closer to her normal eye color.

"No, thank you. We will stay in these lovely robes." Samarra bows her head to the priestess, and they sink into the water.

I feel a little uncomfortable. I know that this is necessary for the success of our mission, but it also feels very intimate. The priests and priestesses begin to speak their blessing. They chant in unison in the ancient language of the gods. I don't understand a lot of it, but the word "geras" is spoken, which I know means gifts. The entire speaking portion of the ceremony lasts only a few minutes.

Lucius speaks now. "The Temple of Geras grants you a blessing and a gift. If you could please submerge yourselves completely into the water." I look down. Samarra is holding onto Goren as tightly as she can.

They are facing each other and slowly begin to sink into the water. "Deep breath, my children."

I watch as they disappear into the crystal water. There is a moment when the blue light turns pink. The blue light fights back against the pink and disappears.

I hold my breath. I hope her runes have held.

Goren and Samarra emerge from the pool, smiling. I can't see her eyes, but he shows no concern on his face. They exit the water, and Goren blows a warm breeze around them. All the priests and priestesses exit the chamber.

Lucius, walking ahead of us, shouts over his shoulder, "We will convene in the Sealing Chamber when you're ready."

"Well, that was exciting," I tell my best friend. He and Samarra are now dry from the wind he blew around them.

"I thought my runes were going to go, but the rune magic fought off my dragon under there," Samarra says.

"You're telling me. I saw the flashes of light in the water. Everyone else in the room had their heads bowed for the ceremony, so I don't think they saw." I run my hands through my hair.

"Are you ready to get married?" I hear Goren ask Samarra behind me as we walk toward the Sealing Chamber.

"I have been ready since I saw you in my dreams. Your presence has been a feeling of safety for me for a long time. It is incredible that I have found you."

I feel a pang of sadness and jealousy at her words. I feel that way for Arysalia, but I doubt she will ever feel that way toward me. We rule two separate kingdoms; we could never truly work.

I attempt to ignore their conversation as we walk into the chamber. People flank the walls, and orbs of light are floating around. There is a large skylight illuminating the end of the aisle.

"Come, my children, you may stand here." Lucius gestures toward the end of the aisle. "Your Majesty, please be seated wherever is most comfortable."

With that, I hug my friend and kiss his bride on the cheek, leaving them at the head of the aisle, then sit down in the first row. Lucius has donned a new robe, this one a light shade of blue, almost the same color as the waters that surround this incredible place.

A flute begins to sound, playing an enchanting ancient hymn.

Looking over my shoulder, I see my friends walking hand in hand down the aisle. They look delighted together, smiling like no one else in the world exists except one another.

Once they reach the end of the aisle, Lucius instructs, "Please open your left hand, palm to the stars."

They do as they are told. He then pulls a blade from his robes. "With this dagger, I will seal their love before the gods and goddesses of our realm."

He takes Samarra's hand first, and a small prick on her palm soon pools with blood. He repeats the process with Goren, then turns and places his hand onto her outstretched palm.

"With this blending of two, I unite this couple." He looks both in their eyes, then says, "You have been sealed beneath the Temple of Geras, a union so holy so as to last a lifetime and beyond."

Once he has completed his declaration, he wraps their hands with a turquoise scarf representing the completion of the sealing ceremony.

I feel another twinge of jealousy for the closeness they now share. I have loved Goren as a brother since we were infants, and I have now truly lost him to another. I wonder how Arysa will deal with this development. The siren within her is not impressed, but does the girl within feel the same?

"That was..." I pause, my eyebrows furrowed. I have never seen a union within the Temple of Geras. "Unique."

"It was amazing." Samarra glows as she looks at Goren. "I have never felt this close to anyone, ever." Goren nods and places a kiss upon her head.

"Well, let's get you back to your chamber. I need to go check on Arysa," I say with false happiness and a smile that doesn't reach my eyes. A pit lodges deep in my belly.

I am not jealous of my best friend.

Chapter 36

Samarra

GOREN PICKS ME UP by my waist and spins me around. He begins to make love to me, the kind of love that he's been harboring for five years. It is incredible, terrifying, and hot. He takes his time with me, torturing me thoroughly with kisses, licks, and bites. He starts at my head and makes his way down. I have never experienced anything so intense in my life.

Back in Issalitia, Arysa and I have separately fooled around with the boys in the kingdom, but nothing like this. Goren is a man, an incredibly sexy and strong one. I can feel how his scarred hands roam over me, touching every inch of my soul. When I am alone with Goren, I can be myself. My magenta eyes are in full flame, my scales uncovered. I am no longer hiding who and what I am. He has always known, has always loved me.

Lying me down onto the bed, he takes my nipple into his mouth, causing the flames under my skin to ignite. Moving from one to the other, he kisses down the plains of my stomach, down the V-shape along my groin. Kissing the inside of my thighs, he hovers over my entrance.

"May I worship you, my queen?" he whispers at my entrance. I can feel the heat of his breath when he speaks. I nod in response, and that's all he needs to proceed.

He dives down, licking me thoroughly. Swirling his tongue around my swollen clit and driving me wild, I feel the flames dance in my irises as I watch him, mesmerized.

"Please, my love, do not torture me. I need all of you," I beg. I'm completely at his mercy.

"Shh..." he whispers into my dripping wet center. He continues to worship every square inch of my body; licking, sucking, and teasing pleasure out of me. My body begins to build flames and energy deep in my belly. I am on the verge of imploding when...

"No!" I squeak out before he pulls me down the bed and underneath him, capturing my mouth. He's covered in my scent, and I can taste myself on his lips and tongue.

This is the most erotic thing I have ever experienced in my entire life.

"Let me taste you, Goren, please." I can see his expanse straining against his trousers.

"No, my love, this is all for you tonight," he tells me gently between kisses. I pull my head back and give him my best impression of a pouty lip. It does not deter the man. He bites my lip and sucks it into his mouth. I was already on the edge, but that, right there, nearly pushes me over.

"Please, just a taste, then you can have all of me," I say dramatically and sprawl out on my back like a star.

"No," he says. "I am going to make you come all over my cock, my flame. I will not allow you to come any other way tonight."

"That's not fair. Are you going to keep teasing me, then?" I raise an eyebrow in challenge.

"Hmm... Why are you in such a hurry? Do you not want the pleasure to last?"

I scoff. "We have a lifetime for you to tease me." I raise my hands around his neck and lace my fingers through his vermilion hair. Pulling his lips down to mine, I kiss him and wrap my legs around his hard, muscular body. I rub myself up and down along the bulge that so wishes to be freed for me.

Goren wraps his arms around me and pulls me up into his lap, my legs draped around his body as he kisses me deeply. The world seems to stop as he tastes all of me. Then, all at once, he releases me. I can feel the cool air where his warmth once was.

He tosses me onto my back in the center of the bed. He stands up from where he was on the bed and begins to undress.

Finally. My fucking god, I could come right now.

He slowly unties the lace at the neck of his tunic, lifting it straight over his head and revealing a body covered in scars. His tanned skin bears beige marks, some of which are almost white and old, while others are new and an angry shade of pink. Scars or not, this man is a masterpiece. His torso distracts me so much that I almost miss the best part. He unlaces his trousers and slowly edges them down his muscular waist, then thighs.

"My gods!" I throw my hand up to cover my mouth. *That was meant to be an inside thought.*

"I can be anything you want me to be, my flame. I can be your god, your king, your husband, or Goren. Do with me as you wish." He releases his grip, and his trousers fall the rest of the way to his ankles. His cock has been released and springs to life. The hard, thick, almost juicy appendage is begging me to touch it.

He fists it in his hand, gliding his hand up and down himself until a tiny bead of precum drips out. My mouth goes completely dry. The only thing that could quench my thirst is this man.

I am on my knees in front of him in moments. The feather-soft bed gives way, making it difficult to maintain my balance.

I grip his perfect ass for balance with one hand, while the other wraps around his base, guiding him into my mouth. I lick his tip and die a little at the taste of him. *He is absolute perfection.* His hands, once on his hips are now lost in my hair, pulling me closer, then pushing me away along the length of his cock.

When he has had enough of me playing with his magnificence, he grabs me under my arms and lifts me straight to his mouth, kissing me fully as we maneuver across the bed.

Gently, he lowers me back down, laying me flat on my back with my legs spread wide for him. I tremble with anticipation. He pauses to gaze at me deeply, from my pink hair to my tiny feet. Licking his lips, he moves toward me, leaning in to kiss my center, over my mound, across my stomach, between my breasts, up my neck, and finally on my lips.

"Are you ready for me, my love?" he asks. I spread my legs wider and lift my pelvis to him in response, grazing his tip with my soaking wet center. I bite my bottom lip between my teeth.

He nudges my entrance, adding small amounts of pressure with each small thrust, allowing my body to stretch for him. He has the most enormous cock I have ever had; its fit is a painful pleasure that I never want to end. As he becomes fully seated inside of me, his pace changes, and he adjusts me into a position that allows him even more access. He lifts my leg and bends it so he can fill me to his hilt.

I reach between us to rub my swollen clit, and he bats my hand away. He shakes his head and replaces my hand with his, circling and pulling pleasure out of me as he fucks me harder. The mixture of his cock filling me and fingers teasing my clit makes me unravel. The flames are building, higher and higher.

I feel like I am on fire, and Goren is sweating above me from my flames. He blows a breath across the front of me, which makes the pleasure even more intense. My flames are eating up his oxygen. He begins to pump inside me harder and harder. I am almost there. Stars begin to fill my vision when he yells my name. I can't take it anymore. I explode beneath him, coming harder than I have ever come in my entire life. He fills me to the brim, chest heaving.

"Never stop doing that to me," I whisper.

He chuckles in response and falls on top of me.
I could lie beneath this man for eternity.

194

Chapter 37

Arysalia

I WAKE TO THE sound of the chamber door clicking shut. In his absence, the scent of Finox's magic has been all around me. Now that he has returned, the scent grows stronger and does something to my insides that I am not sure I could ever admit out loud.

"You're awake." His voice breaks my thoughts, quenching a bit of the desire I feel for him.

With an exaggerated yawn and stretch, I reply, "Well, you did wake me."

"I did no such thing! I was incredibly quiet," he says in his defense, with a smirk that I could quite literally kiss off his face.

Arysa, calm down. What is happening to me?

"They will be bringing up whatever stew they have for the priests and priestesses for dinner, and some fae wine." He removes his cloak, unties his tunic, and removes his leather boots. I watch him, entranced. He proceeds to remove all his weapons from his belt and cuirass. Each blade comes out closer than the last, twinkling in the firelight from the massive fireplace.

He doesn't make eye contact with me, and I can't tell if he can even feel my stare.

Why does he look so unbearably attractive sometimes, while other times, I'd gladly lop his head off if given the chance?

It would most definitely cause an international alarm, but it would feel lovely, nonetheless. Movement pulls me out of my inner monologue, and I see he has gone into the bathing chamber.

He left the door ajar, just wide enough for me to see his toned body.

Oh, my gods.

He steps down into the massive tub built into the stone floor. It is filled with water from the springs within the mountain, no doubt. I watch his muscular form slowly descend into its depths. He has two distinct dimples above his perfectly sculpted ass.

Yum.

The tub is small enough that the siren does not call for me to drown myself, thank the Gods. I really wasn't ready to give up on hot springs.

"Care to join me, Princess?"

I have been caught.

***

Finox

Silly princess.

She has been staring at me unabashedly. I don't think she knows I'm aware of her gaze. I am always aware of Arysalia, the princess of the locked-up kingdom. Her movements, her moods, her hunger, her strength, her magic. The smell of her as she wields water and spring, as though the ocean is kissing my senses with lilies and peonies for lips.

Arysalia looks bewildered. She is just staring silently.

"Princess?" I repeat, hoping to get a response from her.

She shivers and her beautiful brows furrow, making the light green of her eyes sparkle in the firelight.

"What did I tell you about calling me princess?" She grits her teeth.

"I thought maybe you'd forgotten?" I joke.

Her cheeks burn red. She stands abruptly. I am half expecting her to come in and drown me, but she doesn't.

"It's Arysalia to you," she spits out and then slams the door.

Well, that could have gone better.

As I look at the darkly stained door, I wonder if she is playing games or if she truly hates me this much.

I don't take long to wash up and get ready for bed. I wrap myself in the dark blue dressing gown with silvery blue stitching, and then I open the door to the chambers.

I see a beautiful mess of onyx hair draped over a pillow, and I cannot wait to sleep next to her.

Making my way around the bed, I see that she has wholly disrobed, and all her clothes are in a pile on the floor at the foot of the bed. She must also be wearing a dressing gown. Lifting the covers gently, I slide in, hoping not to wake her. Small snores come from her side of the bed, sounds so delicate they could easily be missed.

But I can't miss anything about this woman. She lives at the forefront of my mind, always.

Chapter 38

Arysalia

WHERE AM I?

I lie in what feels like tall grass. I am alone. There is no one around me. I smell the acrid scent of burnt flesh and smoke. The sun has set, and the stars have made their appearance.

I take stock of my body. I am dressed head to toe in my leather armor. I must have been in a battle because I am bleeding, or I have someone else's blood all over me.

"Sam!" I shout, but no one responds. I am too frightened to stand. I don't know where I am.

"Umbra," I whisper into the night. Hoping my loyal companion is nearby, I whisper again. "Umbra." A loud flapping and whooshing fills the night.

She lands and wraps her large wings around me, purring deeply into the crook of my neck. It feels like it's been a very long time since I last held her.

She was once so small and delicate. Now, she is my giant protector, my oracat.

"Umbra, where is everyone? What happened here?" I ask, knowing she cannot give me the answers I need, but then she does something impossible.

Umbra places her brow, covered in onyx feathers, against my forehead. Shutting her eyes, she purrs deeply, and everything goes completely dark.

The darkness clears, and I am in the air, gliding through the sky, looking down on… Oh gods, there is a massive battle. The Forsaken Legion has attacked, and disgusting creatures have surrounded me and my friends. There isn't anything that can be done from these heights.

"Umbra, we have to go down there," I shout through the air. She does not respond, just watches and waits.

Before I can get out another word, a giant man is attacking me, not me right now, but me down on the ground. I can see myself on the ground. He pulls away from me, and Finox charges in with magic, pulsing and tearing at the giant. There's no time to thank him. I need to keep fighting. I can smell the citrus and cherries in the air. He must be shielding me because no one has come after me again.

A loud, earth-shattering shriek cuts through the air. Samarra is standing over Goren. He is bleeding... There is so much blood.

"Arysa!" It's Finox. He sounds far away, and I can't see what is happening. I dive down, down toward the earth. Umbra is making her way to Goren.

"Arysa!" Finox is screaming my name.

He sounds closer. I can feel his hands on me, feel the way he held me as he carried me up through the temple.

I hear my name being called one last time, and now I am the one screaming. I can hear my screams in my ears, but they don't feel like mine. I open my eyes, terrified.

What the fuck is happening?

"Princess, you're okay! Stop screaming. I've got you," I hear Finox croon against my neck. He is holding me tightly against his chest.

I inhale his scent, and he is right; I am okay. Taking stock of my body, I realize I am still in the temple. I'm drenched in sweat and shivering.

"Arysa, it's okay. I've got you," he repeats.

I don't have enough energy to thank him. I just sob uncontrollably in his arms and fall back into a deep and dreamless sleep.

***

Finox

I have no fucking idea what just happened. Arysa was sleeping soundly beside me until her magic stirred awake. The scent of the ocean and lilies filled the air, intoxicating me. Then, the screaming would not stop. If I didn't have my illusions up surrounding the chamber and blocking out all sound, inside and out, the entire temple would have thought I was murdering her.

The agony in her screams was so disturbing...

All I could do was wake her, which took more effort than my groggy sleep-filled mind could handle. Once she finally realized she was safe, she passed out again, snoring in my arms.

She is drenched in sweat and shaking, but I would be lying if I said I hated this. I absolutely adore the feeling of her in my arms. She is a medium-height woman, the top of her head comes up to my chest. She is always looking up into my face and eyes, her eyes a light green color that could put the grasses of the Bad Lands to shame.

The Bad Lands are an area of the continent where those without a kingdom live. They don't want to be part of a monarchy, living underground in the sand, or hidden in the woods and jungles. The Bad Lands are a grassy area with straw buildings and small villages spread throughout. They have a reputation for being filled with thieves and bad people, but they just want to be free. If I could be free, that's where I'd be.

Arysa has stopped shaking and has slid down onto my chest, where she seems quite cozy. I am positive she will wake up incredibly angry that she's in my arms, but I'll take what I can get.

I place a kiss on the top of her glorious onyx hair and drift off to sleep myself.

Chapter 39

Arysalia

I POP BOTH EYES open. I know exactly where I am this time. With a stirring of irritation and what can only be lust, I realize I am in the arms of none other than the King of Valador. Finox is cocooned around me.

How did we end up like this?

I remember waking up screaming, and him calming me down. But I don't recall falling back asleep in his arms. I think to myself, trying not to breathe or move. I'm torn between liking how this feels and wanting to kill him where he lies.

I decide the king can live...today.

"Finox, get off me!" I shout, startling the man awake. The heat he was providing immediately dissipates as he pulls his arms out from around me and moves to stand next to the bed; he reacts as if I have scalded him with flames.

"Oh, I am so sorry!" he replies, pulling his dressing gown around himself tightly. "You had a night terror. I must have fallen asleep after," he affirms. "I am sorry."

I'm unsure of how to respond. He has never been so sincere with an apology before.

"Well, thank you for waking me from my dream, but don't snuggle me again, please. Just drop me on my side next time," I say sweetly, with a little tiny bit of bite.

He doesn't reply. He simply salutes me and saunters off into the bathing chamber. I get dressed, unsure of how much time I have. I use the magic in my veins to draw water from the air and wash my face, underthings, and body. I pull up my pants, with my back turned to the chamber, when the door opens.

"Oh! I am so sorry!" Fin apologizes, yet again.

I look over my shoulder and see he is bright red and still in his dressing gown. I am naked from the waist up. My breasts tighten, and my nipples pebble into hard peaks.

"It's... It's fine. Can you give me one more minute, and we can switch?" I ask, squeezing my thighs together while I stand awkwardly.

"Yes, yes, of course. I'll close my eyes!" he shouts, placing both hands over his eyes. Doing so lets the ties of his dressing gown slide open just a little. I can see the stiff muscles of his body. My mouth immediately goes dry.

"Thanks," I say tersely, grabbing the rest of my clothes and sprinting to the bathing chamber.

Shutting the door behind me, I place my ear against the cool panel of wood. I can hear Fin muttering, "Gods, what the fuck is wrong with you, Finox. You're over two hundred years old; get it together. She will never see you the way you see her. Just—"

Before he can finish his sentence, I swing the door open, unable to stop myself from interrupting his tirade.

Chapter 40

Finox

I AM IN THE middle of quietly berating myself when the bathing chamber door slams open against the wall.

"How do you see me?" Arysalia asks.

I don't have the words. She stands before me in her leather pants, with her boots unlaced and without a tunic. There is nothing to cover the blush pink of her nipples. Her creamy skin is on full display.

"Oh, you heard that?" I say.

Gods.

"I did. Now tell me what you're talking about," she says firmly, the black of her eyes growing larger with desire. I can feel my length stiffen again. I just got it to go away.

"I–I don't know," I lie. I care for her deeply, and I desire her. I wish I knew how to tell her this...

"You just said, and I quote, 'She is never going to see you the way you see her.' What does that mean?"

She takes a step toward me, wringing her hands. I have never seen her act this way.

Is she nervous?

This has caught me off guard. I don't know what to say.

"You desire me then?" she asks.

"I..." I take a deep breath because, gods, she looks stunning. "I do."

I feel a flush rising up my chest and neck as I watch her skin bloom with color; her chest blotchy, her cheeks beginning to blush.

She smiles a devilish grin and starts to reach for me. She touches the scruff that has been growing on my chin since we began this adventure. I savor the touch that does not occur often.

Looking down, I see her nipples are as sharp as razors, pert and ready to be placed in my mouth. I lean in, but before I can, she breaks the silence.

"Good," she squeaks, turns on her heel, and slams the bathing chamber door behind her.

"Okay." It was the only word I could seem to get out. I am as hard as a proverbial rock. The woman I want more than anything just bared herself to me, caressed my cheek, and slammed the door in my face for the second time this morning.

It's going to be a long day.

I get dressed and begin to hide all my many weapons back into my cuirass.

***

Once I'm fully clothed, I take out the map of the continent. According to the temple records, we need to transport our blessed pink flame to the Thatin Cliff Temple, located on the cliffs beyond the Muphion Jungle; the same jungle that Goren and I barely survived a few years ago.

I catch her scent before I even see her. Arysa is no longer bared to me. She wears a clean set of leathers, a shade of black darker than a moonless night. The gear is built for function; slots for daggers and longer blades, more than I can imagine wielding at once.

I catch her eye as another flush of pink crawls up her neck.

I am getting under her skin. I can feel it.

Chapter 41

Arysalia

WE MEET WITH GOREN and Samarra at the entrance of the temple. My uncle is also there, speaking with them. Sam and Goren are holding hands and smiling.

I don't know how I did not see it before. She really does love him.

My body fills with regret and sorrow, and the images of the dream from last night begin to creep into my vision.

"What is our course?" I ask Finox, who is at my side.

"Oh, well, we are stopping in the Bad Lands once we get off the river. We will restock our supplies and spend the night there. Then, we will likely head through the Timbers and into the Muphion Jungle." He looks at me with concern. "Why do you ask?"

"The Bad Lands? What are they? Are they safe?" I have never heard of a place called the Bad Lands. It is not marked on any of my maps in Issalitia.

"Yes, the Bad Lands. There are some markets and villages there that I know well, and that I know we can get supplies from. There are some unsafe areas, but for the most part, it is safe. It is across the river from Valador."

Across the river from Valador? I search my mind for all the maps I can recall.

"That grassy plain near the Azure Beaches?" I suggest, as it's the only place on any of the maps I remember that would make sense.

He nods as we approach our friends. He pulls out a beautifully handcrafted map and points at it, his delicate scrawl running all over it.

"Ary!"

I look up, and Samarra is heading toward me, hands held out. I hope I'm smiling, but I am so nervous. I feel so disconnected from her right now. As she nears, I see it. There is a bandage on her hand.

"Sam! What happened to your hand?" I can't control the concern in my voice.

"Oh, Ary, it's fine. It was part of the ceremony. Goren and I are blood bound now." She looks shy as she shares this with me. I should have been there.

"I'm sorry I wasn't there. I was unwell, and I could not control... Well, you know..." She nods and pulls me into her arms.

Speaking quietly into my hair, she says, "It's okay, Ary, I love you."

I can't help the tears that spring to my eyes.

"Are you sure? I don't know if I'd forgive you for not being at my wedding and acting like a stubborn child," I say, honest as ever.

The laugh that busts out of Samarra is like music to my ears. "You are definitely that, my very own stubborn child!"

I blush. "You wouldn't have it any other way!" I hug her deeply. "How was it? You are really in love with him, aren't you?" I'm not asking to be polite. I need to know this was done for real love and not just for this quest to save our kingdom.

"Ary, I will explain more later, but yes. I have loved him since the moment we met. The first time." She taps the side of her head, indicating that she's *in her dreams*.

I turn toward my uncle. He can't see my face under the heavy cloak I wear, but I bow, nonetheless.

To Finox, he bows and says, "Thank you for visiting our temple, Your Majesty. I hope the ceremony and accommodations were to your liking." Turning on his heel, Lucius drifts back up the mountain and into his temple.

"That guy is weird," I say to Samarra.

"You're telling me. The hot spring blessing was incredibly awkward for everyone." Sam giggles as we head down the mountain toward the Branera Tempest and back into the Ynos Delta.

Chapter 42

Finox

As we head toward the Tempest, Samarra and the princess crush and mix herbs for the sleep tonic they need to produce enough of to get us at least to the edge of the Bad Lands. There, we will be able to travel on foot once Arysa wakes up.

"Are you ready?" I ask Arysa, reaching for her to take my hand. The warmth of her touch always sends a surge of desire through me.

"As I'll ever be." She lets out a self-deprecating laugh. "It would be nice to take in the scenery of our journey, but if my siren wants me to drown, I suppose all I can do is sleep through it."

"We don't want you drowning or falling headfirst into the river on purpose," I repeat. A smile graces her beautiful face this time, and the sight is magnificent.

She doesn't smile often. She's always scowling at me or angry for whatever reason.

Lifting the tonic to her lips, Arysa's eyes immediately turn to disgust. I can smell the tonic from here, and it does not smell pleasant in the least. Handing the bowl off to Samarra, Arysa's eyes begin to cloud, and she starts to tip.

Goren and I catch her simultaneously and get her settled into the massive canoe. "That was definitely easier than last time," I joke. Drugging her will never ever get easier, but it is easier when it is her own choice.

Once we return to the Ynos Delta and head upstream toward the Bad Lands, Samarra clears her throat. "Don't take this the wrong way, but Arysa is not a mind reader. If you want her to know how you feel, you need to tell her already." She gives me a look that says more than her careful words.

"No offense taken. I'm positive she probably already knows how I feel." The image of her perky breasts clouds my vision. Her hands on her hips, all but daring me to take her.

"Well, if she does, you'll have to make the first move then," she shrugs. "She's never had a true relationship, being in the position she is within the locked kingdom. The boys in our kingdom grew into men, and it was like having sex with her siblings at that point." Samarra visibly shivers. "I mean, they aren't obviously, but for us, we always dreamed of finding love outside of our kingdom."

"I know exactly what you mean. I have the opposite problem. No one is forcing me to marry or find a queen. I have been a king since birth. I have had my fun."

Should I tell her my truth?

I look at Goren, who knows me intimately.

"I fell for Arysalia the moment I saw her. The first time we saw you both, it wasn't unlike the first time we met. It was almost identical, really, only that time Umbra didn't expose our snooping." I blush, understanding why Arysalia was so angry with us.

"She looks at you, Finox, when she thinks no one is watching. I think she forgets I'm there, always watching. I am almost an extension of her," she divulges.

Maybe I will make the first move.

"Thank you, Samarra." I bow my head to my best friend's mate.

Behind her, Goren says, "I can smell campfire on the wind. We are near the Bad Lands."

I look down at the slumbering princess, and there is movement behind her eyes.

I can only hope these dreams are better than last night's.

Chapter 43

Xoneas

King Kedron Krel Morbious

IN THE KINGDOM BENEATH the sand, I grow impatient. I have grown wary of the darkness. It has been a few days, and I have not heard from my Forsaken Legion. They must truly be terrified of what will become of them if they fail. I will give them two more days. Once the moon is at its fullest, I will find that disgusting child of a king and his pets. I will take what is rightfully mine and have the entire continent at last!

***

Arysalia

I must still be asleep from the tonic. I can smell the river, but I also smell cherries and citrus. His scent has always been one that truly calms me yet also causes me great irritation. When I think about him in a way that stirs desire, I become very angry with myself.

Why fall for a man who can never be mine? How on earth would we run two separate kingdoms? He has no heir apparent, and neither does my mother. In the end, I will have my heart broken, unable to fall deeply in love with the man I know I could. My fairytale ends here. I will not let his or my own heart get broken during this quest.

The scent of the wind is becoming stronger. I have noticed that we are no longer swaying with the waves. Something warm and firm is under my neck, and my body still will not let me have the reins.

"Arysalia, are you awake?" I hear the soft, singsong voice of my twin flame, my best friend, my soulmate. Well, she was my soulmate until she found her true mate. The realization causes a pang of pain where my heart is. I attempt to move my eyelids or my fingers, but I genuinely have no idea if anything is happening.

"Is she awake?" I hear Goren's warm, low voice. He is never far from her side, so I should not be surprised.

I am jealous of a man with orange hair, a massive scar across his face, and the ability to control the wind... I have reached an all-time low.

I attempt to open my eyes again, this time with great effort, and I see shapes. My eyesight is a bit blotchy. I know this is a side effect of the tonic, but at least I haven't vomited. Nothing prettier than a princess puking up her guts everywhere.

I can smell his magic again. He is close. The king I can't let myself fall for, the king who is paramount in achieving freedom for my kingdom. "Arysalia," he whispers as he edges closer to me, as if I am a frightened animal. "Princess, it is time to wake up. We have made camp, and you need to wake up and eat."

Groggily, I respond with an obscene gesture and groan.

"That was incredibly princessy of you," Finox says, and turns and walks away.

I must have made a face that I didn't mean to make, because now Samarra looks disappointed. "He is really concerned about you. We are still close to the river. I think he wants to protect you as much as possible, but doesn't know how."

"I get that, but I don't need to be coddled," I say sluggishly. My head is pounding, and the shapes are becoming clearer. The siren hasn't stirred since we were in the temple. I feel like I am getting a handle on her, but the herbs may still be at play.

Chapter 44

Finox

I DO NOT UNDERSTAND why she must be so fucking stubborn. I don't wish to make her angry, yet she seems to jump headfirst into anger every time.

As I tend to the fire, Samarra and Goren ensure Arysa eats and gets hydrated. I don't know why I feel the need to be near her; I just want to be around her. Her smile is infectious when it appears, her sass is endearing, and her eyes are an endless green meadow that I find myself completely lost in.

A large form sits beside me near the fire. "Are you alright, Fin?" Goren asks. I almost didn't hear him approach, but when he sat, it pulled my mind out of my thoughts of the princess.

"I truly don't know. I feel a bit lost," I reply, looking over to my closest friend. Goren has been my friend, confidant, and brother for so long that I'm unsure how to feel about everything that has happened on this quest.

"You definitely look lost. I hate that you are feeling this way. What can I do, Your Majesty?" He makes an exaggerated bow with his arms while leaning in toward the fire. The fire reflects against his vermilion hair, and his silver eye sparkles in delight.

"Just having you here is enough, Goren. How does it feel to be married?" I am truly curious.

"It was very uncomfortable to have the blessing in front of every single priest and priestess on the temple island." He cringes. "But truly, Fin, the sealing ceremony was incredible. I felt her pain when he sliced her hand and didn't even feel my own when he did the same to me. Once our blood mixed, it was almost as if the gods and goddesses were there with us." He sounds wistful. I knew he loved her from the moment he saw her all those years ago.

"I bet five years ago, you didn't know you'd have sealed your marriage to that very girl who was braiding the Princess of Issalitia's hair." I remember the day fondly.

"I think I always knew I'd find her. And when I did, I couldn't take my eyes off her," he admits.

"It was incredibly uncomfortable for everyone else in the courtyard." I laugh for the first time in what feels like ages. I have aged more in the last few weeks than I have in the two hundred or so years I've been alive.

"Have you seen her?" he exclaims, turning his bulky form toward the woman in question. "She is light, fire, sunshine, and joy."

"I have. Have you seen her friend?" I raise my eyebrows.

Arysalia is petite, snarky, and beautiful; like the goddesses themselves sculpted her. I feel the burning in my loins for her, and the heat that radiates off me when she is near is too palpable. How does she not know how I feel? How do I show her without downright terrifying her?

"I have. She is lovely. Though she is not my flame," he says firmly.

I put my hands up in surrender.

"Let's try to get some rest before we have to make it through the Bad Lands on foot and survive."

He stands, salutes, and walks away. I watch as he heads over to the ladies, who are curled up together, similar to how we saw them when we would "survey" them in the courtyard. I'd say they were each other's mate if I didn't know better.

Arysalia and Samarra have a bond forged in friendship, sisterhood, and loyalty. They have been each other's person for their entire lives, and their love is more profound than any mere friendship. They are the female equivalent of Goren and me, considering the bond Samarra has with Goren. I know it is just a bond like sisters, fae can't have more than one mate. Once bound as a mate, they are bound in life and death, unable to bond with another.

I've never had a sister or a brother by blood, but I do have one that came in the form of my mother's best friend's child.

Goren of the Wind.

Chapter 45

Arysalia

WE WAKE AND PACK up the makeshift campsite. Finox's magic is still coating the air around me. I don't know if he has illusions in place or if my senses just know that he is near. I attempt to block it out, sniffing the air for another smell or aroma that will distract me.

Why do cherries and citrus smell so divine?

We walk along the narrow path away from the river and toward the Bad Land's markets.

I have been surveying the land around the trail, and I get a sinking feeling that this is the area of the continent where a massive battle occurred, and it fills me with dread. I compensate by growing as many flowers as I can, bringing the tall grass to life and filling the once-dead stalks with lush green. Wildflowers bloom along the trail. It is a defense mechanism I have used throughout my life, transforming what feels scary or bad into something beautiful.

If it doesn't look scary, it can't be.

***

We have finally reached an area that appears to be more used. The grass around us is flattened, and there are old, cold fires.

"We are getting close," Fin tells us over his shoulder. "Just through this next field, there's a lower grassy plain where the markets and villages converge together," he tries to explain, but the exhaustion I feel is overwhelming.

"As long as I can sit down wherever we land, I'll be fine," I say, impressed that I have been walking this long. I am still wearing yesterday's clothes, and the stink I have created on this trek is disgusting.

"Yes, *Princess*. You will be very comfortable once we arrive."

I bristle at the nickname. He looks over his shoulder at me and fucking winks. Clenching my fists and jaw in annoyance, I say nothing. I continue to pepper the land around me with flowers and new grass.

I am a little surprised we haven't run into anyone yet. "Why do they call it the Bad Lands?" As if the goddess Karmana is listening, an arrow whizzes past us and cuts through the tall grass beyond us.

Immediately, the men are on the defensive. I crouch low, ready to attack with my blades. Samarra is blocked between us all; Goren and Finox are large enough to create a wall while I cover the rear.

The scent of cherry and citrus intensifies; it's almost dizzying.

Fin must have a shield illusion up around us.

"Come out!" he yells. "This is King Finox of Valador! You are attacking a royal convoy."

Silence, as if the world has come to a standstill. Then, two figures pop up from the tall grass just within eyesight.

Gods, they are far away! That arrow could have busted right through us even at that distance.

They come out, arms out to their sides, bows hanging in their hands. I can barely make out their form, but I do see... *Are those ears?!*

"We are sorry, Your Majesty!" one of the figures shouts out, moving toward us cautiously. His voice leads me to believe he's male. "We didn't actually see anything on the path, but something did feel off. I loosed an arrow to see if there was an illusion at play or if there were smaller animals in the lower grasses."

"I see," Finox says as his eyes narrow at their approach.

Now they are before us. They aren't merely fae. They are leporis fae. I have never met one in person. These fae aren't unlike others, but they are hybrids. Usually born in pairs or triplets, they are part fae but also part leporids or hares.

"We are Ash and Amber. We are of leporis fae, and we usually survey these plains for possible danger, and well, your group wasn't quite visible to the naked eye," Amber says, her tone calm and kind.

I push to the front of our small group. "It is incredible to meet you," I say, gazing at her.

Amber is tall, with sable brown hair, and her eyes are orange, flecked with brown specks. They were large and quite beautiful. "Do you both mind joining us?" I ask, knowing Finox will whine about it.

She looks back at her brother, seeking his approval. Next to me, Finox shifts on his feet. "I don't feel it's necessary. We can go on our way," he states to the twins, who look up, confused.

"Ignore the king. We'd love to have you with us. You know these lands better than anyone, right?" I argue, with a smirk directed at the king.

The twins look to Finox, who, with a large, drawn-out sigh, says, "Yes, fine." He shrugs. "The more the merrier."

Chapter 46

Finox

I T TAKES ME A few moments to control my anger. The princess has no idea who these leporis fae are, and she just invited them along. We are all closely configured, fae twins in front, Samarra and Goren in the middle, while Arysa and I take up the rear.

"Why would you invite strangers into our party?" I question her once I've placed a silencing shield around us.

"Why the fuck wouldn't I? I've never been to the Bad Lands; they obviously have!" she chastises me, her arms shooting out to her sides in a gesture as if to say, *Why the hell not?*

"Arysa, I've been to the Bad Lands. It's connected to my territory. Goren and I often come here to ensure the civilians are safe and cared for," I explain, and her face scrunches.

"Oh. Well, I didn't think you actually knew," she admits sheepishly.

Why does she make it so hard?

"I need you to trust me." I take her hand as we walk. "I have your and Samarra's best interests at heart. I want Issalitia to be free," I explain. "I want to keep us all safe."

She doesn't say anything. She just looks at her hand in mine and then back up into my eyes. My mind immediately goes to the memory of her, topless and angry. Her eyes have dilated, and I can smell her magic.

She seems to realize this and rips her hand from my grasp.

"Princess," I say as she strides up to Samarra, taking her hand and saying something to Goren.

Samarra kisses him, and he heads in my direction. "What was that about?" Goren asks. "We didn't even hear you guys fighting."

"Illusion shield," I wave my hand around. "I wanted to inform her I do indeed know the Bad Lands, and we don't need any guides to lead us to the market."

He nods.

"She is so infuriating, I have so many feelings for her, and she just continues to distrust and hate me." I replace the shield so my words are not overheard.

"Have you told her how you feel, or are you just being bossy?" he replies.

I scoff. "I am a king. I am not bossy." I take a breath. "She can smell my magic." I haven't told him this fact yet.

He stills. "Can you smell her magic?"

I nod, not saying another word.

"Finox, that's incredible. Do you understand how rare that is?"

I stare at him, growing impatient. "Yes, Goren! I understand that! That is my point!"

"Well, does she understand the significance?"

"No. She doesn't know." I look away from my best friend. "She did ask why my magic smells the way it does, but I was so caught off guard by the comment, I just brushed it off as a coincidence. Nothing more."

"Fin, I love you. You're my king and my best friend, but you must tell her. She needs to know."

He's right. She does need to know. But how do I tell Arysalia Beck Creighton, heir to the throne of Issalitia, that she is my mate?

***

Arysalia

As I walk hand in hand with my best friend, we remain quiet. I can't stop thinking about the way he makes me feel when we're together, his touch shoots right through me. I just can't trust him, and I don't think I really want to.

As if reading my thoughts, Samarra speaks up. "Arysa, what is going on? You have been acting very differently since we left the kingdom."

"I just feel uneasy. All the spying and secrecy have really thrown me. I mean you're married for goddess's sake!" It spills out of me in exasperation. "I don't know how so much has changed in such a short period of time." My shoulders sag, my face falls, and tears threaten to follow.

"I think you need to forget about the spying. I know it may be hard, but they weren't trying to harm us; they were only looking for knowledge, a way to save our kingdom," she tries to reason, but it only makes me feel like a cornered animal.

I bristle. "I can't just forget. They were watching us for *years*. How can you just look past it?"

"Because, Arysa, there is no way we can change the past. We can't go back; we can only move forward with what we know now. I know I want to save our kingdom, my father, your mother. Our kingdom deserves better, and Finox is risking his own life, his own kingdom, to rescue ours," she whispers, knowing full well that the raising of voices only makes my anger flare.

"I will try, but Sam... He makes me feel things. I can smell his mag—"

Samarra sucks in a gasp before I can even finish my sentence.

"Arysalia, you can smell his magic? Are you sure?" Her eyes are wide and wild. "Does he know?"

"I don't understand why you're so surprised. Can't you smell it whenever he creates an illusion or shields a conversation? He is using it now as we walk. I feel like I am walking through a cross between a citrus orchard and a cherry orchard." I look at her with confusion.

"I see. Well, no love, I don't smell it." Her face relaxes. "It is important that you don't tell anyone else about what his magic smells like."

"Why?"

"Oh look! I can see the tents! We must be at the markets." She immediately changes the subject, and the topic is forgotten, for now.

Chapter 47

Finox

AFTER MY CHAT WITH Goren, I realize I need to tell her. I just can't do it tonight. We have arrived at the market village, secured a campsite, and are finally settling in for the night. Amber and silent Ash went their own way when we arrived. *I am beyond happy with that. We no longer have to deal with people knowing our business and what these ladies are, well, who they really are.*

"Arysa, you need to eat," I compel her. "We have an even longer journey ahead of us tomorrow."

She rolls her eyes at me and shoves bread and cheese into her mouth.

Hot.

Watching her eat, even when acting like a child, is an experience to behold.

She loves food, so I'm not sure why she is being so stubborn at the moment.

With her mouth full, she chokes out, "Better?" She smiles with her mouth full of food.

"Sure. At least you're eating." I roll my eyes now. "That tonic is going to take it out of you. We need to make a river crossing tomorrow, and we need to do it without your siren trying to kill you, or us."

That seems to have gotten her attention, because her cheeks flush, and she deflates a bit. "I know." She is done with the conversation. She turns herself away from me and gets into the warmth of Umbra's wings and soft, feathery fur.

Across the fire, I see Samarra making eye contact with me. Her eyes are wild, she looks from me to Arysa, then back again. I mouth "What?" to her, and she pretends to smell a flower.

What the fuck is that flame doing? She is making no sense... Wait, I've got an idea...

I place a shield around Umbra and the princess. I hear Umbra growl and look over her shoulder at me.

Sorry, girl, it's essential. I try to convey my thoughts to the sassy beast.

"I have blocked her listening, Samarra. What are you saying?" I shout across the fire, not worried about the sleeping princess beside me.

"You can smell her magic!" Samarra screeches. She has probably been holding in that secret all day. The color drains from my face, then anger surges.

"You *told* her?!" I shout at my best friend. "Goren? Why would you do that?"

"I have disclosed no such thing, Your Majesty. I would never have told her something so intimate." He looks to his wife. "I did, however, hear from her lips that Arysa told her. She said that she could smell your magic, seemingly having no idea what that means," he explains, looking at me knowingly.

I deflate. "I will tell her. I just can't do it tonight."

Whoosh! Screech! Bang!

Seconds later, the village around us is in flames. Arysa doesn't stir, but Umbra knows something is wrong. In a moment, the three of us are on our feet and getting Arysa up.

Chapter 48

Arysalia

THERE IS FIRE EVERYWHERE, and I can't breathe. All I can smell is his magic and smoke. He is hiding us, but that's not what I want. We need to save these villagers; they are our people, everyone in this kingdom. Those who no longer wanted to be part of it, or those who were locked out five hundred years ago.

"The Forsaken Legion is here. They have found us," Finox says beside me. "We need to protect the flame and you, Arysalia." He's not asking; he's telling me.

I look at Goren. "You're her husband. Protect her with your life, or your life is mine to take." I grit my teeth. "Stay here, Samarra. I love you." With that, I turn on my heel and sprint as far from them as I can. Umbra's wings flap above me high enough in the dark that she cannot be seen.

"Arysa!" Finox shouts as he chases after me. I am actively accumulating all the molecules of water around me, in me, and even from the air. I need to put these fires out. Away from his shields, I can barely smell his magic.

The air is full of the scent of burning flesh, roasted herbs, and death. It lingers in the air as I run to where the flames are the highest. Someone grabs my wrist and stops me. I turn hard and am about to drown whoever is touching me when his yellow amber eyes flash. Finox has managed to catch up with me. "No! You need to protect Sam!" I scream at him.

"Arysa, I am! I am holding a shield around them, but you need someone at your back. I need to be here to help you." His eyes are wild, searching my face. He is acting like I am his property or a child; I just don't know which.

"Fine, help me get these people to safety. I need to put out these fires!" I yell over the din of screams.

Slowly, we work to get everyone out. After putting out fire after fire, the water in my veins is dwindling. The water in the air is evaporating faster than I can absorb it. I am beginning to fatigue.

I hear sounds like wolf howls coming from the edge of the village, and a shiver of unease rakes down my senses. The zorag... Those disgusting beasts are here to find me, I can only assume, and get the dagger from Samarra. That must be the reason we are being hunted.

"Fin, the zorag!" I shout, pointing toward the edge of the village. As if reading my mind, Umbra comes shooting from the sky. She pounces on the hellhound, ripping its flesh, then teleports away. Over and over, she attacks like a bird of prey, not a panther.

Finox and I stand in stunned silence, watching as Umbra tears apart the terrifying beasts. The air reeks of death from her kills.

Do not throw up, do not throw up. It is all I can manage to think as the smell hits me. The zorag is not of this earth; there is nothing natural about it.

"We need to get to safety. Get out of here!" Finox shouts. He is right, of course. My elemental magic is depleted, and we need to get Samarra and the dagger out of here.

"Fine! Let's go!" We are off again, sprinting back toward our illusioned campsite, where I hope Sam and Goren are safe from the evil that is pouring through the Bad Lands. We need to get back to them. They must be okay. I can't imagine a world without Samarra. My thoughts are racing as we sprint through the Bad Lands that, at this exact moment, have earned their name.

Chapter 49

I AM HUNCHED WITHIN a more minor illusion, shielded and sheltered with Goren. We have been inseparable, and at this moment, I wouldn't have it any other way. The only issue is that my best friend, my soul sister, is on the other side of the market, saving civilians.

She is so brave and strong, while I am so weak.

"Samarra, she is going to be okay." My husband looks down at me with his warm forest green eye and silver eye that looks directly into my soul.

His scars don't scare me. He is my savior. He has kept me alive when I didn't want to hide my truths any longer. The secrets I was keeping from Arysa were killing me, and then the dreams started.

"I know she will, she is strong. I just worry that she will burn out if she uses all her elements," I try to explain while my voice cracks. "The spring magic is easy for her to control, but the water... She has never truly played with that magic. We were so scared to tell anyone about it or to practice. The Mad King would have killed her. He will kill her if we return."

Goren pulls me in tighter, whispering and praying to the goddesses. He can't help them; the dagger at my hip is too important. He would say he's here to protect me, but I know. I am aware of the need for this dagger and the urgency with which we must destroy it.

We married and sealed in the Temple of Gera for goddess's sake. It was the most magical thing ever. Arysalia and I both have scars on our right hands to show the blood oath we took for each other, but this blood oath was different, my left hand was punctured and marked, sealing our blood together in a ceremony that can never be undone. I was petrified, but I felt safe at the same time. From soul sisters vowing an oath to each other as children to sealing my life with another; two hands, two scars, two people I would give my life to save.

Please be okay, Arysalia, please.

Chapter 50

Arysalia

"T HERE THEY ARE!" I can sense her magic anywhere. Samarra and I are bonded by blood and friendship, and I will never not be able to spot her, illusions be damned.

"Almost there, don't slow down!" he shouts over the din. The screams coming from the hellhounds are disturbing, but Umbra is a queen and will protect what she loves.

"Samarra! Goren!" I shout, and their illusion dissipates. He's holding her tightly, but when she sees me, it's as if she can finally breathe. The expression on her face changes, and they turn and run.

"Are you okay?!" Sam shouts over her shoulder. Fin has illusioned us from the danger around us, but we aren't out of the woods yet. We need to make it to the coast, to the river. My stomach sinks because I still can't control my siren. It is much easier to put her to sleep than to let her rule my emotions.

"The river," I say to Fin. "What are we going to do?" I have a stitch in my ribs, but we can't stop. We need to keep going.

"I have an idea, but you might not like it."

"What is it?" I need to know his plan. The screams of the zorag have ceased, and I can hear the familiar beat of Umbra's wings. In response to my question, he points up, right at Umbra.

"There's no way she can carry me." I'm a full-grown fae woman, and she's still a baby. "How are we going to make that work?"

"We only need to get you over the water. She doesn't need to fly for extended periods of time; just long enough so you don't attempt to drown yourself." He shrugs. "We can tie you to her, so you don't jump off to your death in the depths of your kingdom's noble river."

So sarcastic, this one.

"Fine, we'll do it!" I concede. "What are you three going to do? Please don't say swim."

"That's the only option, unless a bridge magically materializes."

"What if you drown?" I ask as we slow our approach to the riverbanks. A prickle of awareness climbs up my spine.

"*The water is cool, the water is quick, come play with me, we'll make it quick. The water is fun, the water is grand, come play with me, and find a new land.*"

I stop abruptly in my tracks, startling Fin beside me.

"Arysa, are you alright?"

I most certainly am not. The siren is awake, and we aren't even on the water yet.

"I–I... She's awake, Fin." I can't breathe. "She's calling me down." I struggle to get the words out, writhing in place, trying to fight the pull I have to the water's depths.

"Shit. Goren! Samarra! Come back here," Fin shouts to our friends who are a few hundred yards ahead of us, almost at the banks.

"Umbra!" he shouts, but nothing happens.

She does not come for you; only me.

"Umbra, I need you," I choke out, gritting my teeth. With a whoosh of wings, the oracat lands gracefully next to me. I smile at Fin. I don't win humbly.

"Very nice, though it would be nicer if you came when I called, Umbra. What if she were injured?" he asks the cat, as if she cares about what his majesty has to say.

In response, she growls low and deep and whooshes her tail from side to side.

"Easy girl, he's just a sore loser." I unleash a strangled laugh. "How do you feel about a ride, girl?"

In response, Umbra cocks her head to the side and lies down flat for me. "I just need you to get me over the water, okay?" She bows her head lower so I can climb onto her shoulders.

"Goren, I need the rope," Fin demands. "We have to tie this around your waist and hands." While we were in the forest, I had made a collar from ropes and vines for Umbra. I had a feeling it would eventually come down to me riding her. Fin adjusts his ropes so they link easily to the rope collar around her neck.

"Great, now I won't try to kill myself," I shrug.

"*The water is cool, the water is quick, come play with me, we'll make it quick. The water is fun, the water is grand, come play with me, and find a new land.*"

I go still, because the voice singing in my head is so familiar, but I just can't place it.

"Arysa, you will be fine," Samarra says, coming to my side and hugging me tightly. "I'll see you on the other side," she whispers and kisses my forehead. I love her so much it hurts. I hope we make it through this fucking quest and get home safe.

The siren's song plays on repeat in my head as we get closer to the water.

"All right, Arysa, you ready?" Fin looks me in the eyes, and there is something there I can't quite place.

Sadness? Anxiety? Love even? I shake off the thought.

"Hold on tight, okay."

I nod in response.

"Let's go, Umbra! Show me what you can do!" I shout at my oracat. She crouches low on her haunches and launches us skyward. I let out a squeak of terror and hold onto her feathers and fur, probably squeezing her neck harder than I should.

"The water is cool, the water is quick, come play with me, we'll make it quick. The water is fun and grand, come play with me, and find a new land."

I start to lean on the edge of Umbra's side, looking down at the water that is calling for me.

It looks so calm, so still for a river.

Then I see them, my friends are moving through the water rather quickly. I can only assume Goren is guiding them toward the edge with his wind, and Fin is using his illusions to mask their likely distress in the freezing water.

Gods, I hope they make it safely, is my last thought before everything fades to darkness.

Chapter 51

Finox

I HAVE HIDDEN US from anyone who could possibly see us struggling to cross the water. I keep the water calm around us, but don't block our figures. The water is moving too much to do both. I am sapped of my strength from the minor scuffle we just got in.

I laugh to myself. Princess Arysalia is nuts. She went full bore toward the villagers without even a second thought. It was endearing and utterly stupid.

Samarra and Goren are ahead of me. Samarra is sucking in water as she tries to keep up with Goren. It is likely a one-hundred-yard swim, but it feels like miles. I am out of breath and exhausted. Looking skyward, I can see Arysa on Umbra's back; they seem to be attempting to keep track of us. Arysa looks completely transfixed by the water, as if she doesn't even see us down here.

I do not understand this siren magic, but once we complete the mission, we need to figure out how to silence it or teach her more control near large bodies of water.

I attempt to keep my own head above water. We are getting closer to the bank. Only a few more yards, and we'll be back on dry land.

Samarra and Goren have just made it up the embankment when Umbra lands just beyond them. Arysa is still transfixed on the river, and I don't know what we're going to do. I climb up the bank, sucking in air and trying to get to the princess. Umbra lies down gently, and Samarra stumbles to Arysa.

"No!" I shout. "We need to get her further from the water!"

Samarra looks up at me with concern. "But she's bound. Her wrists are raw already." Her tone is quivering with desperation. Goren takes Samarra's hands in his, effectively keeping her together while I orient myself. Goren raises his hand, and a gust of wind blows through my clothing, hair, and soul.

"We need to get her closer to the forest before we can untie her," I explain.

"Arysa," Samarra says, trying to make eye contact with the hypnotized princess. She does not speak or react to any of us. She watches as the water continues to flow downriver toward the Ynos Delta.

"There isn't much time. We were able to evade the legion, but who knows how many they had with them?" I try to keep my voice calm. "Let's go."

I create an illusion around us, making sure to keep Umbra and Arysalia out of sight.

I will never let her drown, not while I can stop it.

We move quickly to the Wild Timber Forest.

***

Arysalia

I wake from what could only be a nightmare. "Umbra, what is happening?" She startles beside me and begins to purr loudly.

"You missed me, huh? How long was I out? Why were we flying and everyone else hoofing it?" She doesn't respond to my question; she merely adjusts her position next to me.

I can smell his magic all around me. He has us illusioned. We must have had to cross over water. I can't remember anything but making it to the markets and losing sight of Ash and Amber. I look back into my memory. I must have tried something with the water to end up bound to Umbra.

"Arysa!" I hear my best friend rush to my side from where she was cradled in Goren's arms. Sam is shaking as she reaches for me. She looks concerned but excited at the same time. "Are you okay!?"

"Yes," I say, a bit groggily. "What happened?"

"You don't remember?" I hear Fin's voice, low and controlled, with a hint of worry in his tone.

My wrists and abdomen are sore, and the skin there is red and raw.

They must have bound me to Umbra.

Goren isn't far behind. "I am very good with knots," he shrugs. "Thankfully, they kept you seated. I'm sorry for the marks they left. At least we didn't have to go princess fishing tonight."

Did Goren just crack a joke? Laughter bursts out of me immediately.

"Are you okay?" Sam looks concerned. I don't think I have laughed or smiled much since we started this journey, and apparently, it shows.

As I attempt to control my cackles, I wheeze, "It was so funny. I literally would have dove headfirst into the Issalitian River without them!"

I sit up and Sam immediately gathers me into a full, loving hug I didn't know I needed so badly. I feel at home in her arms. The tension in my body releases in the embrace.

The scent of cherries and citrus gently fills my nostrils and senses once more; he must have changed the illusion. Immediately, my gaze searches for him, but he seems to be trying to stay out of the way. I try not to take it personally, since he doesn't owe me anything.

"I am glad you're okay," he says, stepping closer. "You scared us. You weren't coming back to us once we made it to the other side of the river. We decided to keep you on Umbra's back to make sure you came out of whatever state you were in." He is matter-of-fact, but I can hear the concern in his voice.

"I thought we were staying in the markets of the Bad Lands?" The three of them look back at me with utter confusion on their faces.

"You don't remember the attack?" Finox asks. "You ran toward the markets and the flames. You saved many lives, Arysa."

I am taken aback by this information. I don't remember wielding at all, and I don't remember the fire or the attack.

"The Forsaken Legion?" I question, already knowing I am correct.

"Yes, the zorag, too. We were able to make it out of there because Umbra completely annihilated the beasts," Fin explains. "She teleported in and out of sight, taking pieces of them over and over." I look over to my cunning oracat. She looks back at me as if to say, "What? It was just a disgusting dog."

"Well, that sounds gruesome. Where are we headed now?" I don't even know how far into the forest we are, but I am a bit uneasy about all that has transpired.

"We need to make it to the Thatin Cliff temple to destroy the dagger, so we need to cross this smaller area of the Wild Timber Forest, then head into the Muphion Jungle," Goren says. "It won't be for fun this time, unfortunately. Whatever tried to eat his majesty and me that last time we were there is hopefully asleep or dead."

I can't help but giggle.

"Were you always this funny? Or was I dropped at some point?"

The unmoving face of Goren, the wind wielder, twitches a bit before immediately returning to its mask of indifference.

I am not even sure any of this is real. *There are chunks of time missing from my memory...*

We continue into the dark and rather eerie forest around us.

Chapter 52

Arysalia

I'M NOT SURE WHY the siren has taken my memories of what happened in the Bad Lands. I'm torn between whether it's meant to protect me or harm me. All I know for certain is that Samarra is okay, and Goren and Finox are too. We need to survive whatever lurks in this massive forest and make it to the murder jungle, where apparently Fin and Goren played in for shits and giggles. I remember them going on about all the places they explored while Sam and I were trapped within the walls of Issalitia.

***

It feels as though we have been walking for miles, and the forest is endless. We find a crop of trees against a large rocky area that provides cover to our backs. With Umbra and Fin creating illusions and watching for anything that spots us, I feel a bit safer. I need to talk to Sam to make sure we're okay. I can survive her finding her soulmate, but I can't survive losing our lifelong friendship. Looking down at my scarred palm, I think back to the day we gave them to each other.

"Arysa, we're going to get in trouble. We aren't supposed to use blood magic," Samarra chastises me. "I want to, but we shouldn't," she tells me.

I look over at her with false annoyance and hand her the blade. "Sam, wasn't it your idea?"

"Yeah! But it's a bad one. I was only joking," she says, trying her best to weasel her way out of it.

"You are my best friend, the sister I never had, and my twin flame," I explain. "It's just you and me trapped in here. If we can't get out or if something ever happened to you, I would be devastated. This blood oath will keep us from ever having to turn on the other or harm the other."

"Fine, but you can never leave me, Arysalia. If you marry and need to leave the kingdom, I will go with you! You are my best friend, and I can't imagine a life without you by my side."

I lift my blade, and she forfeits her hand. The blade glides across her porcelain palm, leaving a straight cut.

As blood begins to pool on her hand, I do the same on my hand. Once the blood has pooled, we take each other's hands and repeat the words, "With a slice to me and a slice to you, we merge our blood in an oath so true. With friendship and courage, we will guard our lives, a blood oath never dies."

We repeat these words five times in the courtyard. There is rarely any wind here, but it has picked up and begins to blow. Almost as fast as it came, the wind disappears.

"Did you feel that?" she asks me.

"It definitely got windy there for a shake, but I don't feel any different," I admit. I don't feel any change, but I hope that one day, when the time comes, the bond will protect us and keep us safe.

"Yeah, me either." Her eyebrows furrow in confusion. "I guess I thought maybe it would feel like a bond snapped into place? Or would we feel a bit different?"

"Welp, we could go fight some people and try to die and see what happens," I say, sarcastically.

"Absolutely not!" she cackles, as we sit in the courtyard under the stars, dreaming of what life would be like outside these walls.

"Are you comfortable?" I hear Finox's voice bursting the bubble of the memory. I look into his amber eyes, and the warmth that only seems to appear for me is present there.

I cough. "Yes, this is fine." I fidget under his gaze.

With a nod of his head, he turns and goes to the other side of the fire.

I whisper to Umbra, "Why does he focus all his attention on me? It is very unnerving."

Umbra responds with a huff and adjusts herself beside me, the warmth of her feathered fur and large wings blanket me into sleep.

Chapter 53

The Dungeon of Issalitia

Queen Zandra

I HAVE BEEN LYING on this stone dungeon floor for longer than I can truly comprehend. I have lost all aspects of time, days, and self. I have not had a visit from Maggard or Jerix. I close my eyes, wishing to have another moment in my mind with him. To feel him, smell him, and hear his gentle voice coax life back into me.

Where has Arysalia gone? How is it possible that she left? I know the dagger holds the magic used to lock down the kingdom and enslave its people, but I still can't figure out how she did it.

Maggard knows she has Jerix's water magic and is likely his siren. I remember how hard it was for him to keep her at bay, especially when we would escape to the Azure beach where she would call, but he would resist. It was the only time we could truly be alone and free in this world of kings and queens. I can only hope Arysalia learns how to resist the call; and quickly. There is so much depending on it.

Arysalia

We survive the first night in the Wild Timber Forest and have another half-day's travel on foot to the mouth of the Muphion Jungle. Umbra has disappeared into the shadows provided by the forest. Finox and Goren seem on high alert; hopefully, the Dryad witch they fear doesn't appear.

"How much further?" I ask with a toothy grin.

He rolls his eyes dramatically. "Forty-five more minutes," he lies.

"You said that over an hour ago!" I whine, giving a pouty face that could save the continent from mass destruction.

"I will tell you the same thing again; when you ask *again.*" He shrugs.

I ignore him and turn back to Sam. Goren gives him a look that seems to tell me he knows something I don't, but I'm not sure what exactly is going on in their weird brotherly language.

✳✳✳

As night begins to fall, the forest truly comes alive. We finally reach its edge. The jungle has never been officially mapped; the cartographers who entered either went mad or were never seen again. The jungle really has only one proper entrance, which is flanked by passive stone pillars with the face of a jungle cat. Not an ordinary jungle cat, but a dogla, which is a panther–tiger hybrid fae. Stealthy like a panther, lethal as a tiger. It is white, with thick black stripes. Unlike the traditional tiger's uniform stripes, the dogla's stripes are chaotic and dense.

The massive doglas are carved into the giant stones; the stripes appear to be gouged into the surface. It is said that a dogla gains its thick stripes over time and is not born with them. No one knows what causes the stripes to appear, but many believe it is because when each fae is killed, it absorbs its magic. A shiver runs down my spine.

Umbra appears beside me. She moves with grace and silence. I hope that will protect us from the dogla. She purrs and rubs her soft head against me, as if she can feel the anxiety roiling inside.

I feel Sam's hand squeeze mine. "Are you alright?" she asks me, concern written all over her face.

She has been so relaxed since her sealing ceremony. She doesn't seem to have an ounce of anxiety. I'm over here stressing that she will die during this mission, that the dark magic will create a gap between us. I will likely lose the closest thing I have to my family besides my mother. If we even survive this fucking jungle.

With a huff beside me, Umbra nudges me again.

"I'm not. I am worried about this mission," I respond, without going into detail about all my fears.

"We will survive, Arysa. The men have made it out of the jungle before, and they will do it again!" Her positive attitude is genuine; she believes it to be true.

"If you say so, Sam." I kiss her on the cheek and turn toward the men. "We should stay here for the rest of the day and into the evening. We need as much daylight as we can get for the jungle tomorrow."

"It doesn't matter if it's day or night. The canopy acts like a ceiling, blocking out the sun," Finox tells me, eyebrows raised. "Why don't you want to start today? The sooner we get in there, the sooner we get out."

"I can't tell you why, Fin. All I know is everything in my body is telling me not to go in tonight," I affirm. "I don't care if you think it doesn't make a difference."

"Well, Princess, I think we need to go in today. We need to complete this mission."

"Your Majesty, this mission is to free *my* kingdom. And I am telling you, I will not set foot in that jungle until tomorrow morning." I stand firm, my face a shuttered mask. The blood in my veins is humming.

"Are you sure?" Samarra interrupts. "We will be okay, Arysa."

"Sam, I love you. I'm trying to tell you that something is off." Frustrated, I breathe out. "I don't want to argue; I just do not want to go in there today."

"I agree with the princess." Goren's level-headed, stern voice cuts into the conversation. "I believe we should listen to whatever is telling her not to enter."

I raise my eyebrows in surprise.

He is gaining some points from me now.

I look over at Finox and smirk.

Take that, Kingling.

His surprise at Goren taking my side has put him off guard. "Fine," was all he replied and turned on his heel to do whatever he could to escape me.

Win for Arysa, check!

Chapter 54

Finox

I WALK AWAY FROM my friends to find solace beneath the massive timbers around me. I suck in breath after breath of forest air. I need to calm down. I cannot control her. I don't want to control her, but why can't she just trust me? I continue to pace. I need to gain her trust. The bond between us is driving me crazy. I just want to touch her and make her mine.

Once I finally get my emotions under control, I hear the crack of a stick in the distance.

Almost instantaneously, Umbra is at my side. Her growl is not something anyone should tamper with; the feathers along her spine flare in a display of aggression.

"What is it?" The princess comes running up beside me.

"I heard something, and so did your oracat," I reply. "There is something out there," I whisper low. "Seek, Umbra. Bring whatever is stalking us here."

Without another growl, Umbra shoots into the sky, hiding in the shade of the clouds above. Moments later, I hear a shrill scream, like a dying animal. It's so familiar, like a small creature...like a rabbit.

Oh no! The thought hits me harder than I imagined. *Once the fires were out, Amber and Ash must have followed us into the forest.*

"Arysa, it's Ash and Amber!" I shouted to her, and she came running up toward me after Umbra took off into the sky. "Call her off!"

Arysa's eyes are wild as she screams for Umbra to return. The screaming stops, and only a low whine is heard. We are moving now, Arysa and me, through the timber trees. We are jumping over roots, trying to avoid low limbs until we see them. Ash is on the ground, and Umbra is over him, growling.

"Umbra, off!" The princess shouts while waving her hands at the beast. The oracat listens and shoots back up into the sky. Amber is kneeling next to her twin; he seems to have something wrong with his shoulder, but there is no blood.

"Ash, oh my gods, Ash," Amber cries next to him.

"Let me look at you," I insist, and help the fae sit up. His left shoulder appears to be fine, but the right one is definitely hanging a bit low. "I think your shoulder is out of its joint." I cringe. "We will need to reset it."

"No, let's get him back to camp before we do that. We have a tonic for the pain," Arysa insists. With his good arm, Ash grabs my arm and looks me dead in the eyes.

"King, you will set my shoulder here. Now," he pleads. "Please, Your Majesty."

"Of course. Though I've only done it once before," I warn.

Ash nods, closes his eyes, and lies flat on the ground.

With a steady hand, I take his right arm by the wrist and shake it up and down like I'm shaking his hand. He winces in pain but does not stop me. I bring his arm up to shoulder level and shake it a bit more. Lastly, I lift it above his head and shake. With a loud click and some foul language, his shoulder is set.

I look over my shoulder at the very silent princess. Her face is a shade of white I have never seen before, and it's now turning a shade of green that one would not call pretty. "Are you—"

She takes off into the trees.

***

Arysalia

I have seen some disgusting things, but that was on a new level. I can handle blood, guts, and gore, but the sound that came from that man's shoulder was fucking disgusting. After retching up the last bit of bread and cheese I ate, I wipe my mouth and head back toward Samarra and our camp.

Once I reach the small clearing where we have set up camp for the night, I see Amber hovering over Ash, and Samarra mixing a tonic for his pain. The dark dagger hanging from her belt is mocking me. Finox is over by the fire, speaking in hushed tones with Goren, and Umbra is nowhere to be seen. The sun is slowly drifting toward the horizon, and I am utterly exhausted.

The anxiety of the jungle, the siren song, and this mission have truly worn me out. The new muscles of my magic are changing, and the pull of water and spring in my blood is growing rapidly. The desire to wield it becomes stronger every day. I don't know what has changed, but if I don't get it under control soon, I might explode in a rage of vines, flowers, and rapids. I suppress the thoughts along with all the other unsettling ones I've had over the past week.

I find a spot close enough to the fire but out of range, where I can't hear what the boys are saying. The scent of his magic drifts through my senses, and I know he has an illusion around us; the illusions that keep us safe and the illusions that kept them out of sight for years.

I thought I was going crazy over the years when I would randomly smell cherries and citrus. I would chalk it up to the kitchen or the seasons. Never in my wildest dreams had I thought the king of the closest kingdom would be stalking us in Issalitia. Had I known sooner than the five-year gap he supposedly had been surveying us in, maybe I wouldn't feel this way. I curl in on myself, and there is a rustle of feathers behind me. I know it is my oracat coming to snuggle in and bring down my anxiety.

Umbra, my protector, even when she was a tiny kitten guarding our courtyard garden. I think about the day I met the King of Valador and Goren.

I wish it could go back to the way it was; no dagger, no Forsaken Legion tracking us, none of it. I wish I didn't want to escape Issalitia so badly.

Part Three

Chapter 55

Xoneas

King Kedron Krel Morbious

I SIT IN MY underground desert in wait for news of the Rythorin Dagger that I have been searching for centuries. That despicable king took what should have been mine to take. I should own this continent. He wasted its dragon-imbued power to lock his kingdom away. Why stop there? I could have an entire army of enslaved Nedonian's to help me conquer this continent, maybe even the planet.

None of my Forsaken Legion dares to enter my keep. They do not even dare to touch the sands I own. They send messengers in their stead.

Your Majesty,

We have failed you. Our enemies have dispatched the zorag, and the dagger, the princess, and the others are in the wind. They escaped the Bad Lands in the flames. We lost their scent when we lost the zorag. We will not return until we have the dagger and the princess.

Captain Wesson

Forsaken Legion

"Fuck!" I scream into the ether.

If they can't get it done, I suppose I'll have to do it myself.

I contemplate how I will reach those disgusting royals without being burned by my own sun.

***

Arysalia

We rise with the sun and pack everything up from the camp. Ash and Amber are going to accompany us on our trip through the jungle, and no one has mentioned that Umbra almost disfigured one of them.

They really shouldn't sneak up on an oracat, especially one so protective of her people.

Fin and Goren take up the front of our party, Ash and Amber take up the rear, leaving me and Samarra in the middle. We are surrounded by the tallest vine-covered trees I have ever seen.

The trees are as tall as stone towers. There is sparse sunlight and what appears to be very little animal life. It's a bit too quiet in this jungle for my liking; it's too dark, too wet, and downright uncomfortable. We are all drenched in sweat. We have been walking for hours. I haven't heard a bird call or a stick crack since leaving the Wild Timber Forest.

"Does anyone find it unnerving how quiet it is here?" I question the obviously exhausted group.

Samarra looks over at me, eyebrows furrowing. "It is bizarre that we haven't even heard a carow bird."

A shiver runs down my back. The carow bird has wings as black as pitch. The color is an absence of color;

in Umbra's feathers, there is nearly a twinkle of the rainbow. The carow bird eats death, death it usually doesn't cause, but eats it, nonetheless. Anything left over from another kill goes to the carow bird. They are loud and typically call to each other. They were common in Issalitia, particularly in the pastures and some of the more rundown areas.

"That is true. I haven't even smelled the scent of death yet. No leftover kills, signs of a struggle, or tracks of any kind," I say as I look around the trails beside ours.

Finox looks over his shoulder, and his gaze singes mine. It is hard to look away from him when his eyes meet mine so fully. "I have masked us well. I would have thought the creatures would carry on like they did when we were in the forest."

"It's just weird," I tell him. "What do you think is going on? Was it like this when you came in before?"

Goren responds, "We were so quickly in and out of this terrifying place that we didn't take the time to notice the greenery and creatures that could possibly be lurking."

"Should we find somewhere safe to camp then? Make a big fire to keep everything at bay?" I ask no one in particular.

It does feel like we are being watched, but I don't see or hear anything. Umbra hasn't growled or alerted us to danger since we were in the forest.

"I agree. We do not know what hour it is, but from the darkness around us, I do believe we would benefit from a fire," Ash says.

I glance over at him. He has his arm in a sling made from torn cloth. He looks as exhausted as we do, if not more. He and his sister managed to catch up with us, and he barely survived an encounter with Umbra. A rest would do him good.

Chapter 56

Finox

I STILL CAN'T GET the look on the princess's face out of my thoughts as we make camp. When I looked back at her, it was as if the entire planet stopped spinning, and it was only us at that moment. Her face was so open, surprised, almost happy. Then, in an instant, it was gone; her mask returned.

I don't know how she can do it. How can she feel our connection, but mask it? Can she not feel the pull between us?

"This rock formation will work well to shield us from the back. What do you think, Arysa?" Using her name gets her attention. Her gaze snaps up to meet mine again.

Yes, look at me, Princess...

"Oh, that...that should work great," she rushes to respond. "I'll take the first watch with Umbra." She turns on her heel and whistles for the cat. Umbra stalks out from the shadows around us and takes up guard next to Arysa.

"Okay, then," I say under my breath as I begin to set up our camp, trying not to throw and slam everything in sight. Goren looks over to me and simply shrugs. It is a gesture I am beginning to hate.

"Your Majesty, would you like us to help get the fire started or gather food?" Amber comes up beside me. She is tall, lean, and beautiful. Her sable fur weaves itself into long braids, beginning at her lepus brow and flowing back between her tall, graceful ears. They extend straight up; one has a slight curve to it, causing it to fall to the side. She has yellow eyes, almost shades of daffodils, and her demeanor is soft spoken and kind.

"Ah, yes, Amber, that would be wonderful. If you'd like, Samarra would probably love to help with the fire. She can start it herself, but she would love the company and some extra wood." Amber nods and heads over to Samarra, who is already leaning over a tripod of sticks, getting ready to start the fire.

I look around our small campsite, taking in its boundaries and create an illusion that no one is here. I look over to Arysa. As if she can feel me watching, she looks over her shoulder. Her nostrils flare.

She can smell my magic.

I look away first. The pain I am beginning to feel regarding her rejection is something I never thought I would experience, not even as the King of Valador.

***

Arysalia

I ponder why he looks at me like that, as I watch him look away first this time. Umbra brushes her soft self against me. I know she wants to tell me something, but I can't understand her, not in the way she needs me to.

We have the first watch, and it's hard to tell the time while we're deep in the jungle. The sun doesn't even try to peek through the canopy. When it sinks behind the horizon, the jungle seems to get even darker, if that is even possible. I look up at my oracat, who sits statuesque next to me, her eyes shining with a green gleam in the firelight. She can see anything in the dark, and I know she will keep me safe.

While her eyes are trained on the perimeter, I play with the water in my water skin, pulling it out and making circles in the night. Not a single drop hits the ground, and I am able to make tiny water creatures that play in the air. I work on my control because it is the only way I can release the tension inside me.

With this new ability to access my water magic, I have to release it in small bursts of energy, or it feels like I may explode. I genuinely don't know if I will survive the magic coursing through me.

I wish I had truly known my father. He would have taught me control, love, happiness, and strength.

I wipe a lone tear from my cheek. Maggard robbed me of the chance of ever knowing my true father, and robbed me of the ability to control the magic I wield.

***

We survive our shift with no incident, and Goren takes over for us. He never really says a lot to me, but I know he wants to. Samarra probably told him not to add more to my plate because she knows this is so hard for me.

"Goodnight, Arysa," he says to me in his soft, kind voice, the voice I know my best friend fell in love with immediately.

"Goodnight, Goren. Be safe," I say. With a nod, he turns and takes up the post we left.

Umbra and I find another unoccupied corner of the camp. I sit first so she can do the circling she needs to get comfy. Once she is settled, her massive wings fold down and cradle me tightly.

My oracat, my protector, my Umbra, my shadow.

I drift off into a deep sleep.

Chapter 57

Arysalia

"JERIX!" I HEAR MY mother's voice calling. I sit up immediately, but I am alone. The jungle is still surrounding me, but I can hear her calling for him. "Jerix! Where did you go?!" There is a slight hint of angst in her voice, but she appears happy and youthful.

"I'm over here, my darling flower," my father calls from the shadows. I spin around, but I don't see him either.

Where are they, and why are they running around the Muphion Jungle?

I slowly walk through the towering trunks, ducking between vines and massive palm leaves. I hear my mother scream at the top of her lungs, and I stop breathing altogether, waiting for the pain to crush me.

"Oh, my gods, Jerix ha-ha-ha. No, no, no, don't. Ha-ha-ha, tickle me!" My mother is cackling. I release the breath I was holding.

My mother is laughing with my father in the jungle, which is known for killing people. People who enter this jungle never survive, or the ones who do, do so missing a body part.

The laughter grows louder. I peer around a crop of palms; the sound is coming from my mother, who is in my father's arms. He is holding her and adoring her. They are alone in the jungle. Except, they aren't. I can sense someone else here, watching...

Pulling back from where I was hiding, I survey the area as Brandon, my guard, once taught me: "Know where you are, know your surroundings, and find the cause of the unease you feel." I can hear him as if he is right beside me.

I begin surveying low between the trees and shrubs, then high, making sure I take in the long limbs of the giant, ancient trees. A black-and-white blur catches my eye; it does not belong in a massive jungle tree.

I edge ever closer to the tree with the creature perched on its long limb, and I suck in a breath. There's a dogla watching my parents; it's lying lazily up in the tree, its tail swishing back and forth. The creature watches my parents as they nuzzle and snuggle among the dark shadows of the jungle, creating their own light and love.

The dogla slowly lifts its head and makes eye contact with me. Standing, the dogla leaps from her perch, down to the lowest limb. My parents don't even seem to notice her arrival or departure.

Why is it coming toward me? Is this real? I am not truly here in this time, am I?

"Arysalia," the dogla's feminine voice purrs. I take a step back. *How the fuck does this thing know my name?*

"I–I... How do you know my name?" I am shaking, sword drawn, as if it will protect me from the stealthy killer, this dogla of the Muphion Jungle.

"Shh, child, I do not wish you harm at this time," she purrs. "I only wish to show you something." The dogla looks over her shoulder at my parents, now almost asleep in each other's arms.

"Why am I here? Why am I dreaming this?"

Because I am dreaming, I know this can't be real. I have never seen my mother this young or this content. My father is so young and in love with his princess.

"You, my child, are here because I knew your parents." She sits before me, her prominent haunches curving to allow for the position. She is stunning, all black feline with thick white streaks. She bears an incredible resemblance to Umbra, minus the feathers and wings.

She has a panther-esque build and face. Though her eyes are almost fae in shape, they are green emeralds that twinkle without any added light.

"You knew them? How?"

"Yes, Zandra has been a sort of friend to me for centuries," she explains while licking between her large, sharp paws. "Jerix was a new addition in the last few decades, and I had grown fond of him."

"I wish I had known him," I admit, not realizing I said it out loud.

"I know you do. When they got pregnant, I didn't find out until news of Jerix's demise reached me. When I met them, they were so young. This was before your mother was forced to marry that despicable, power-hungry beast of a man." She almost gags on the words, like a cat choking on a hairball.

"So, you knew them, but why bring me here?" I ask again.

"Because, Princess, you are safe in my jungle."

I am taken aback by what she has just said.

"Your jungle?" Instead of an answer, I watch the creature in front of me transform, her legs elongate, her head changes shape, her paws turn into hands and feet, and lastly, her eyes stay the same. The fae eyes I saw were, in fact, fae eyes.

Her eyes are wide-set, large, and green. Her luminous onyx skin is beautiful, with no blemishes or scars to be seen. Her hair is a shock of white; it flows down her back like a waterfall. The stark contrast is stunning. She is dressed in what appears to be a combination of traditional and modern clothing: cargo trousers and a cut-off tunic that hugs her body. She is armed with knives with a dogla face carved into their hilts.

"Why, yes, I am Dezmelda, a dogla shifter fae." She gestures to herself, as if I missed the transformation. "I have reigned over this jungle for millennia, back farther than even you could imag—"

"Were you here when the last flame lived?" I interrupt her. "I mean Seraphina Zinnia?"

"Yes," is her only reply.

"So, you know how we can destroy the curse of our kingdom?"

Dezmelda puts a finger up to silence me.

"You are asking the wrong questions."

"What questions should I ask? That is why we are in your jungle. We need to reach the Thatin Cliffs and perform the ritual to destroy the blood magic to destroy the dagger," I explain, exasperated.

"Yes, child. I know why you have come. That is not why I have brought you into this beautiful memory of mine." I look up at the stunning fae.

"Okay, why have you brought me here...?"

"Because Arysalia, Princess of Issalitia, this was your past, and it can be your future."

Riddles... These fucking fae and their riddles.

"Yes, yes, history repeats itself." I shrug and look past her to my mother and father. They are snoozing peacefully beneath the largest tree trunk I have ever seen. AZ&JB is carved deep into the trunk above their heads.

"No. History does not repeat itself. It's people who make the same mistakes, expecting a different outcome. It is the definition of insanity," she preaches to me. "You have the opportunity to have this," she gestures to my parents, *"their love."*

"I do not have the luxury of falling in love. Not with my mother and kingdom at stake," I push back.

"No, Princess. It is in front of you. You smell it and see it, but you do not expect it," she riddles some more.

"I don't understand what that even means, Dezmelda..."

"When you open your heart, your eyes will tell you."

I look away from her and her confusing verses, and instead look toward my parents, who are gone. Immediately, I look back at the jungle witch, but she is gone too.

Chapter 58

Arysalia

"**A**RYSA," AMBER WHISPERS. "PRINCESS Arysalia," she says again.

My eyes pop open one at a time. "Yes?"

"We are all getting ready to leave. You have slept the whole time," she states, not out of rudeness but more out of fact. "We are ready to move forward. We will sleep once more, and the next day we should reach the cliffs."

I take her hand, and she helps me up. Even Umbra has disappeared into the shadows.

That was a wild fucking dream, and it didn't answer any of my questions. But at least she will keep us safe. Well, me at least.

"Thank you, Amber." I dismiss her to go ahead while I clean up and grab my stuff.

"Not a problem at all." She bows and turns on her heel to head toward her brother, Samarra, and Goren. On instinct, I look around for Finox. I survey around us, but I don't see him. I can smell him, so he must be here.

"Looking for something?" His voice breathes across my senses. Apparently, I need to look behind myself before I search in front of myself for this pain-in-the-ass Kingling.

"Oh no, Your Majesty. Just making sure Umbra is nearby," I lie.

"Ahh, yes. Well, she left you this morning. I assume it's to hunt the animals that do not exist in this jungle." He shrugs and heads toward our friends.

I can feel the blush running up my neck to my ears; I hate the reactions he gives me.

✳✳✳

My mind constantly drifts back and forth between the dreams of my mother and father. I cannot seem to get them out of my mind. *What would it be like if my father survived? Would my mother have known happiness then?* I think, the sadness engulfs my thoughts and emotions.

Samarra grabs my hand gently. "Arysa, you're growing and killing flowers as we have been walking."

She tilts her head in the direction behind us. She isn't wrong. It looks like a meadow threw up all over the jungle trail. There are dead and decaying flowers everywhere I have stepped.

"Oh goddess, I hadn't even realized." I cover my face with my free hand, feeling a bit dizzy and confused all at once. How do I even come close to explaining what is happening with me when Samarra could die trying to save our kingdom? The guilt is consuming me, the fear is drowning me, and I don't know how to cope anymore.

"Arysalia, I love you deeply. Please tell me what is going on." She takes my other hand from my head, and we stop. As if sensing Sam has stopped walking, Goren stops and looks at Fin, who is staring at me.

"I–I don't know how to explain what is happening, Sam." My tears are betraying me as they run down my cheeks. "I can't lose you."

"Oh, Arysa, you will not lose me!" She is so sure when she says this, but I don't know how to believe her.

She is the new last flame, and we don't know what releasing her full magic will do to her. Will it burn her alive? Will it kill us all? Will it even break the blood magic locking our kingdom?

"How do you know that, Sam? How can you possibly know that?" I wipe my hand across my wretched tears. "What if we do not succeed?"

"We have no other choice, my dear friend. We must succeed. Your mother and our people are counting on us to save them from the Mad King." She stands a bit taller now, with more confidence than I have ever seen her have before.

Goren has been rubbing off on her. She looks every bit like the fire queen I know lurks within.

"Okay. I will try to have more confidence in us, but if I'm right and you die during this ritual…" I can't even handle the words leaving my mouth. "I will have you resurrected and kill you myself."

"Ha–ha, very funny," she mimics my tone and pulls me in for a hug. I grip her tall, slender body so hard and cry into her rosy locks of hair.

Please be right, Samarra. Don't let me lose you.

***

Finox

I look back at Samarra and the princess, now embracing each other. I have no idea what they were talking about, so I throw a sound shield around them to give them privacy. Though looking at the trail of decaying meadow left in our wake, I can only assume that it is the cause. I did wonder why I was smelling her magic so much today, and more than before. She was wielding water creatures and practicing last night, and I fell asleep to her scent filling my senses.

I can't wait until this quest is over. But what will I do without the spicy spring princess mouthing off to me on a daily basis?

I watch her cry into her best friend's hair. Both seem to be crying now. Their shoulders and arms shake as they clutch tightly to one another. Arysalia pulls back and kisses her friend on the cheek gently, wipes the tears from her own face, and straightens up. The two nod and turn toward us. I haven't put the shield down yet, but I see her mouth something in our direction.

I drop the shield.

"What are you staring at, Finox?" the princess says flatly.

"Well, you. I did shield you from all of our ears." I extend my arms to encompass the group as a whole and say, "You're welcome."

She rolls her eyes, bows, and says, "Thank you, Your Majesty. You're so kind for not eavesdropping on our conversation."

That mouth. I swear she will be my undoing. I have never wanted to kiss someone so hard in my life. My body fills with warmth, and the blush on my neck betrays me.

"Let's go a few more hours, then we will break for the evening," I decide, turning on my heel and heading deeper into the jungle.

The dogla has not shown itself yet. I am unsure if that is a good thing or a bad thing. She tormented Goren and me when we were in these trees. Maybe having the two most powerful females on the planet at my back is the reason she keeps her distance.

Chapter 59

Arysalia

W E SURVIVED ANOTHER DAY in the Muphion Jungle, but there was no sign of the dogla or Dezmelda. We have been traveling for most of the day, and according to the maps we have, we should reach the cliff tomorrow by early afternoon.

The trek in this jungle has been moist, to say the least. We have sweated through all of our belongings. There is a small creek that runs along the edge of the path that we have used for water and nothing else. We wipe our faces with it, but submerging ourselves doesn't look like it'll happen any time soon.

Samarra and I haven't talked much because doing so uses too much energy, and I have been attempting not to kill every flower I summon. We have reached a section of the jungle trail that appears to flatten out; there are no rocky formations, only gigantic tree trunks surrounding us. We have stepped off the main path.

"I think we should probably reduce our camp size significantly, or we will have to have two on watch tonight," Fin tells us as a group. No one seems to disagree. The group nods and we begin to place our belongings in a circle beneath the largest trunk we can find.

The tree has an alcove at its base large enough for two to sleep, but there are six of us and a massive oracat. It doesn't really matter where I end up sleeping because I will be tucked into Umbra's side the entire time. She takes up an edge of our circle, leaving only a smaller area that needs to be monitored for danger.

Goren and Samarra take the base of the trunk, Umbra and I take the right edge, and Fin takes up the left side of the trunk along the circle, placing his belongings next to Goren, leaving Ash and Amber to take up the front of our circle. We will likely build a large protection fire, not so much for heat because it is blazing hot here, but to keep predators at bay. Though it is unlikely there is anything that will keep the witch of this jungle from us.

Umbra and I take the first watch again, leaving the rest of the camp to settle in and get some rest. We have no idea how complicated this process will be or if Samarra will survive, let alone if it will be successful.

Seated in front of the circle containing most of the people I love, I lean into Umbra while braiding and weaving jungle vines, creating them from the soil. I pull at the spring magic in my veins, creating intricate weaving patterns. When I was young and anxious, I would weave any flower combination known to this continent; daisy chain necklaces and lilies of the valley crowns interwoven with berries and twigs. I would pretend to be the Spring Queen of Issalitia, even with my mother on the throne. The idea of ruling a kingdom was exciting for me until I turned one hundred and sixteen years old. Those years led to a deep-seated desire to never rule in my life.

My mother gave her happiness to rule her kingdom, and it was taken from her anyway. Zandra, Spring Queen of Issalitia, has become a skeleton of the majestic queen she once was.

That's why we're here, right? To save our kingdom and free my mother from the Mad King who sits on our throne, bearing our name.

"Arysa." Fin's voice comes from behind me. Turning on the log I'm perched on, I see his eyes first, the amber yellow eyes that haunt my waking daydreams and my nights.

"Yes?" I reply, questioning why he isn't asleep and talking to me in single words.

"I haven't had the chance to talk to you and explain some things," he admits. His cheeks are red already, and I haven't said anything remotely inappropriate or rude yet.

"Sure, sit down, what do you need to talk to me about?" My tone is indicative of my frustration and lack of eagerness to speak to him at all.

He sits down next to me. He turns his entire body on the log, so our knees are barely touching, his gloved hands are in his lap, fingers laced.

"Have you been able to smell my magic?" The words rush out of him so quickly that I almost didn't hear them at first.

"Yes. Why does that matter?" I don't understand why this is so important; everyone can smell magic.

"Well, that is a sign of something bigger. No one else can smell my magic." He takes a breath. "Arysa, no one else can smell your magic but me." He speaks clearly, slowly, and in a way that I still don't get why any of this matters.

"And? Spit it out."

"Arysalia, has no one ever told you why some people can smell each other's magic?" he questions gently, his voice probing, almost as if he's testing to see what I know.

"It has never come up before, Fin."

It really hasn't, and I still can't figure out where this conversation is going.

"Why are you telling me this?" My impatience is propelling the words out of my mouth.

Fin reaches into my lap now and takes my hand in his. I look down at our hands, my eyebrows knitting together.

"Arysalia Beck Creighton."

I stop breathing.

"You *are* my *mate*."

That…was absolutely *not* what I thought he was about to say. I don't even know where I thought this was going, but *his mate?*

"What?" I throw his hands out of my lap and scooch back as far from him as I possibly can.

This can't be true. Can it?

I almost fall off the log, and would have if Umbra hadn't been behind me.

A low growl emanates from her, and I reach behind me to grab hold of her.

"That can't be possible," I ramble. "I can't stand you. You're the king of another kingdom."

My chest heaves. *I'm lying to him.*

"You can't be my...my...*mate.*" My ears are ringing now. I can see he is speaking, but my world is starting to spin, and I can't hear what he is saying.

He can't be my mate, he just can't.

Chapter 60

Finox

THAT DID NOT GO as planned.

"Arysa! Arysalia! Talk to me."

I try to draw her out of her panicked state. Her face has gone a ghostly shade of white. It's as if she can't hear me. I reach for her hand again, but she holds it firmly at her side.

"Princess, I did not mean to upset you. I thought you knew what was happening."

She doesn't respond. She just sits there, unseeing. I decide she needs some space from me. As I retreat, I see Umbra adjust her position, wrapping a protective wing around her princess. Even though it is their watch, I plan to stay up until Ash and Amber take over in a few hours.

I take in the camp around me. Soft snores, loud snores, and crackling from the fire echo around the small space.

How could I have gotten this so wrong? She definitely keeps her distance from me, and her anger could be considered justified, but I just thought maybe... maybe she reciprocated my feelings.

I sit next to the fire and think about all the signs that Arysalia may have been accepting of our match. She walked out of our bathing chamber naked from the waist up. I close my eyes and can still see the blush of her skin and the perkiness of her breasts as she stood, hands on hips, chest heaving with frustration. I think of the way our eyes always seem to meet. She is my true north, the magnet to my compass.

As the hours go by, Ash and Amber wake and relieve Arysa. She leans heavily on Umbra as they make their way over to their side of the camp. I can see the usual color of her skin has returned, but she does not attempt to speak to me or make eye contact. The loss I feel in this moment is momentous. When a fae's love or connection has been rejected, the strength that usually runs through them diminishes. In some cases, it can lead to madness, depression, and, in extreme cases, insanity.

The casualties from insanity are not singular; they come in masses, affecting small towns, villages, and even a kingdom, which is not safe from the insanity that can become of a rejected bond.

She did not reject you. She was unaware of what was happening between the two of you. She has never left her kingdom, let alone her mother. How would she know that a mating bond is something so delicate and strange?

I try to quell the longing I feel deep inside. Knowing that she has seemingly recovered, I allow myself to relax and fall asleep until it's my turn to take watch.

Chapter 61

Arysalia

I AM THE ONLY person here, waking from the absolute nightmare that was my shift on watch. Umbra, Samarra, Goren, Ash, Amber, and Fin are nowhere to be seen. Standing from where I lay on the jungle floor, I notice I was not where we made our camp, I am somewhere else altogether in this terrifying jungle. There is a large pool of water, not big enough to be considered a pond or lake, but more of a pool like the ones in the castle.

As I ease toward the water, my siren does not seem to call to me. "You don't want to kill me today, siren?" I say out loud.

There is no scent of salt in the air and no steam emitting from the surface, leading me to believe this is just a typical freshwater spring. Using my elemental wielding, I lift the water in a stream to my lips, tasting the moisture.

"Fresh water. But why am I here?" I spin around, dropping the water I had called up to my lips. I felt her presence before I saw her.

"Why are you here with me?" Dezmelda purrs from somewhere in the near distance. I search through the larger branches of the canopy for her distinct black-and-white silhouette.

"I am not surprised to see you this time, Dezmelda," I respond, turning in place. I see her now. She leaps down from her perch to land beside me.

"Well, I am glad I did not scare you this time," she says, lying down next to me in the flattened area surrounding the pool. "I need to tell you a story."

I look into her green eyes. "What kind of story?" Confusion is taking up residence almost permanently on my face lately.

"One I don't think you have heard before." She no longer shifts, having found a comfortable position. "It is a story of the first time I met your mother."

"I know you knew her. I just can't figure out how you could have possibly *known* her," I comment.

"You should sit down, Princess. It isn't a happy story, but it isn't a sad one either," the witch confesses to me as I make my way to the ground next to her. Crossing my legs, I rest my impatient hands in my lap, twisting and untwisting my fingers.

"It was a very warm summer over five hundred years ago. Your mother entered the jungle. She was in a way that concerned me, even without knowing her." She takes a breath as if it is hard to speak, "Your mother came into the jungle hoping never to leave again—"

I interrupt her abruptly. "That cannot be true. She has survived over five hundred years living with the Mad King."

"Yes, but she was a person before the Mad King came into her life. She had love before the king ever came to your kingdom. Your mother was deeply in love with the man I showed you in the previous dream. A nobleman's son, a water wielder, but he wasn't of royal blood. The law states that the heir to the Issalitian throne must wed a person of royal blood, lineage, or, by marriage, be a royal.

"Seeing no possible way of getting out of the betrothal forced upon her by the kingdom's counsel, she entered my jungle looking for me, hoping I would take her life upon entering." She gives me a sly smirk. "What she did not know is that I am a fair and honorable witch. I only take the minds and souls of those who deserve it. Those who enter my jungle searching for the lost treasures of old, the treasures that were given to me by gods, kings, and queens over the millennia." She wags her finger at me. "Your mother was not that. Your mother was lost, heartbroken, and terrified."

I lean in with rapt attention as she tells me the story of my mother's heartbreak.

"Zandra was so witty, smart, clever, and kind. She did not deserve her fate. I explained to her that she had a love worth living for. Jerix could be her consort, and she could have the marriage in name only, saving her heart and soul for the nobleman. She agreed and saw reason once I explained that she could have it all with mild discomfort."

Knitting my eyebrows together, I interrupt her story once more. "Did she know he possessed such evil? Was the King Brontos of Ramman aware of his youngest son's intentions?"

I need to know...

"From what we knew of her betrothed, the King and Queen of Ramman were known for being kind, understanding, and gentle rulers. No one could have guessed Maggard would do such a thing to such a prosperous and safe kingdom. But unfortunately, Zandra lost her lover, her kingdom, and now her daughter," she admits with great sadness, lining the curves of her muzzle.

"But I'm not gone. I am still here. Fighting to rescue our kingdom from him," I murmur, my heart filling with sadness all over again for my mother and the situation she was put in. A problem not so dissimilar to Finox and losing his mother and father at such a young age. However, his court did not enforce archaic laws that required him to marry a royal female at a certain age. The King of Valador can marry at any time in his life, if he secures an heir to succeed him. If in the time of his ruling, he does not produce an heir, he may name an heir to take his line to the throne, leaving room for a less incestuous royal bloodline.

"Yes, my child, you are still here, but you are not by her side at this moment in time," she reminds me. "You will complete your mission and save your kingdom. I will make sure of that."

Looking up into her bright green eyes, I can see her assurance, her strength, and her truth. She will not allow us to fail this mission; she has kept us safe thus far.

"How much farther to the cliffs? Do you know the ritual we need to perform to make the dagger's blood oath fail?" I inquire, praying she can help us.

"I know the ritual that will be performed, it is an unbinding ritual, but it is dangerous. Any imbued object forged in dragon fire can only be destroyed with dragon fire." She looks at me knowingly. "I do know that the pink-haired girl in your party is her."

"How do you know that?" I ask, mildly terrified but more curious.

"She dreams as you do, my child. The power of a dogla fae is to enter someone's psyche and either learn from them or scare the absolute sanity out of them." The evil grin that grows across her feline features is somewhat unnerving. "But in her case, I want to understand her. There are very few who use runes to cover their appearance. Your man's illusions cannot hide everything from sight."

"He is not my man," I say firmly, no longer interested in what else she has to say. I look away and into the jungle beyond, a stray tear making its way down my cheek.

"You do not return the feelings of your mate?" she questions sternly.

"That is not important," is all I respond. "How did you know of Sam's power?"

"She dreams of fire, dragons, pink scales, and battle. It was not difficult to piece together." She seems to shrug in her dogla form. "She is usually guarded by the fire-haired one, who seems to be a conduit of power for her. The Clode boy has strong wind elemental magic."

My mouth sits agape. How could she possibly get all of that from dreams?! "How do you do it? How do you get into others' dreams and souls?"

"Dogla's are dream walkers. We can step in and out of your reality. We can create dreams and destroy them, we can warp and scare, but we can also give hope and happiness. It isn't all I can do, but that is a secret for another dream."

She stands up, adjusting on all fours and crouches low. "Stay out of trouble, my child, and love that boy. He has loved you for an age now." Without letting me respond, she pounces up into the canopy, out of sight.

Grumbling under my breath, I say, "He is not my love, he doesn't love me."

Or does he?

I was so taken aback by his admission this evening that I forgot all about it until now.

What am I going to do about him?

Chapter 62

Arysalia

THE FOLLOWING DAY, I woke up feeling less exhausted and distracted. The dream of walking with Dezmelda was both insightful and confusing. I still do not understand why she told me the story of the darkest day on the planet for my mother. I'm not sure if I should share these dreams with the group. Did she tell me about it to push me not to let my mother down? Or did she do it to push me toward Finox? I am so distracted by my circling thoughts that I don't notice Samarra standing beside me until she touches my shoulder.

"Arysa, I need to talk to you." Her voice breaks the fog of my thoughts. Looking at her now, I can see the concern on her face.

"What's going on, Sam? Are you okay?" I sit up abruptly, taking her hands in mine, looking down and evaluating them for injury. There is only our shared scar and a fresh pink scar on her other hand.

"It's not about me, Arysa, it's about you." She gestures to the bedroll I was working on rolling up. I look around the camp, and it's practically deserted. The men aren't here, just Amber, putting the fire out and packing her belongings.

"What about me? I am fine. We're almost there." I gesture to the jungle around us.

"No, it's about you and Finox."

I interrupt her before she can continue. "No. There is nothing between us. I don't know why everyone is so obsessed with this topic," I say sharply.

"Well, that's because it is important. If you reject or deny the mating bond, Arysalia, you could lead Fin to insanity."

Lead him to insanity?

"Mates are incredibly sacred and hold a lot of importance when it comes to fae lineage and bonds. If a mate rejects the bond, it could leave irreparable damage."

Her words don't make any sense. We are not mates. Why would I be damaging Fin? I would know if he were my mate. "Finox is not my mate, Samarra," I say flatly, losing all sense of sweetness in my tone.

"Arysalia Beck, that is where you are wrong. Finox *is* your mate." Samarra has never been this firm with me before. It's hard not to believe her, but we can't be mates because we are both heirs to two entirely different kingdoms.

"I don't understand how that can be possible," I rush to say. "We are from two different kingdoms! How can we possibly be mates? We could never truly be together."

"It doesn't matter if you're from Xandelar and he was from another planet. You are mates." Sam isn't holding anything back. "Finox is Goren's best friend. He is practically his only family, and not to mention, he is his king. We cannot let Fin fall into insanity and possibly hurt himself or others because you are too stubborn to welcome the match."

I am at a loss for words. My best friend is standing up to me like a general standing against a battalion of troops. Her face shows no sign of being a shy girl any longer. The fire in her has grown, and she isn't holding back anymore.

Goren really has helped her blossom and grow into a stronger woman, something I could never do for my friend.

"Okay, Sam. I will consider him. I will consider the bond." I fold quickly. "But I am not ready to bond and seal ourselves like you and Goren."

"No one is asking you to seal the match; just accept the fact that you are his mate. Let him court you, let him love you. You need to open up a bit to the possibility that this could be destined."

Content that she has reached me, she deflates a bit. The energy it took to stand strong against me must have been exhausting, because my friend is back to her normal, shy self, the one I have loved since we met in the halls of my castle.

Later that day, we finally reach the end of the jungle. We did not run into any creatures that would kill us or anything that could remotely drive us insane. I should probably tell everyone about Dezmelda, but I want to make sure we make it through destroying the dagger first.

The early afternoon sun begins to pour through the canopy, and a collective exhaling of breath takes over the sounds of nature.

"Well, we survived," Finox exclaims as he walks out of the jungle, arms outstretched, taking in the warm sun. The way the sun shines on his auburn hair and his tanned arms causes a not-so-unpleasant stirring inside me. I need to try to let the idea of us being bonded not completely throw me into a spiral.

"That we did," I respond, coming up beside him. "I am sorry for earlier. It scared me." I look up into his amber eyes that glow yellow in the sun's rays.

"I know it did. I have been wanting to talk to you about it for a while. I just wasn't sure how to do that without upsetting you further," he admits, releasing a chuckle. "Do not take this the wrong way, but you are headstrong, stubborn, hardheaded, frustrating, and beautiful. You are so compassionate, it makes it hard not to fall in love with you."

I can feel the blush climb my neck and cover my face. No one has ever said anything like that to me before.

"I am not stubborn or hardheaded." I cross my arms in front of my chest to prove the point. In return, he lifts one eyebrow in challenge and winks.

Ugh, that wink.

"Let's agree to disagree on that one, Princess," he says with an earnestness I haven't come to appreciate until now.

I want to correct him about using my name, but part of me truly missed him saying it.

We stand in silence, basking in the sun we haven't seen in days, waiting for everyone to join us on the cliff tops.

"It is absolutely stunning here." Samarra comes up beside me, taking in the magical view around us. Few have ever made it to this side of the Muphion Jungle, let alone survived its queen.

The steamy, dark jungle abruptly ends at a flat expanse of grey stone where stairs are carved from the earth. As if grown entirely from the earth itself, there are no joints or tool marks to be seen.

We climb the stairs, and at the top, a large temple stands, with columns that appear to grow straight into the sky. It is topped with an open-air style ceiling, and you can see the blue sky between the rafters. The once-magnificent tapestries that hung here long ago have faded into strips of fabric lost to time. There are runes, magic markings, and depictions of the gods carved into the temple's floor.

"It's really incredible here," I say aloud to no one in particular. As we walk around the temple, I see all the elemental magic in a circle, with the gods and goddesses representing the different elements and seasons.

"When do you think was the last time anyone has been here?" I ask Fin over my shoulder.

"I have no idea. It is incredible, though. They are all here: fire, water, earth, wind, illusions, light, dark, and all the seasonal magic." There is a whimsical quality to his tone as he lists different magics that have not been seen in a millennium. Fire magic disappeared over five hundred years ago, and earth magic has not been seen for even longer.

"When do we get started?" I question the group. "Do we wait until nightfall or before dusk?

"The texts were unclear, but the strength of the moon should come in handy with what we will be wielding," Samarra says. "We are almost at a full moon now, and all the elemental magic will be at peak strength. It would be ideal to wait a few more days 'til the moon cycle has matured."

She isn't wrong. I am intrigued to see how strong my water magic will become now that it is free from the walls of Issalitia.

"We don't have that kind of time. The Forsaken Legion will likely be here before we know it," Ash and Amber say in unison, like only twins can.

It makes me uneasy.

"They aren't wrong," Goren interjects. "We need to perform the ritual in the temple along the cliff. The podium at the edge of the temple appears to be the site where most rituals have been performed. By the sheer number of runes present in the stones..." he gestures to the podium.

That is what scares me. We don't know how to interpret these ancient runes or what power they hold. For all we know, it could be runed against the very ritual we need to perform. I look over at my best friend, the *Pink Flame, Last Flame.*

It's now or never.

"There is something I need to tell you all." Immediately after the words leave my mouth, the group stops what they are doing to look at me. "Yeah...so...I have been having dreams."

Fin immediately takes a step toward me. His magic is still concealing us, and it is intoxicating. "I have been dreaming of the dogla...the Muphion Jungle's witch."

"What?"

"How?"

"When?"

"What did she say?"

The group bombards me with questions that I will answer. One at a time.

I put my hands up in front of me, palms facing out, a sign that I need them to shut the fuck up.

"Okay, just listen." I tell them about Dezmelda, her hybrid form as a dogla, her dream walking, and insanity-inducing magic. I tell them of her connection to my parents and their love, but most of all, her hatred toward Maggard.

They all stare at me with confusion, then Goren speaks. "So, is that why we have not encountered anything terrifying the entire time we were in the jungle? She has been protecting us, to uncurse your kingdom?"

His questions are valid.

"Yes and no. She knows what we need to do, she knows what Samarra can do, she knows that the Mad King will die. She doesn't want to hinder us." I shrug my shoulders. "Now, will she let us survive the trek out of the jungle…that I genuinely don't know."

"Well, thank you, Dezmelda," Finox shouts back to the jungle. "It was a much better experience than our last trip in there."

Yeah, that's my mate. Sometimes I don't know what the universe has planned, but that goober is apparently part of it.

Chapter 63

Samarra

THERE'S A TENSE ENERGY surrounding us all this evening, but I can't blame anyone for it. I'm about to use all of the magic inside myself to destroy a dagger that has taken an entire kingdom hostage.

No big deal, Sam. You've got this.

As we prepare for this evening, everyone seems to be walking on eggshells around me, except for my husband. He knows what I must do and he knows what will happen, probably more than I can ever know. Tonight is the night.

Arysalia comes up and sits beside me on the stone steps at the base of the temple. "Are you ready?" she asks.

She sounds so afraid for me. My heart squeezes, knowing that I may not survive this change, but I will do anything to save my people and the queen who will one day rule them all.

"As I'll ever be," I shrug, taking her hand in mine. "No matter how scared you get, how in pain or terrified I seem, you cannot interfere this time, Arysa." I am stern with her because I know she will interfere. She would give her life for mine in an instant.

"I will try very hard to let you do this, Samarra. I don't know how I will survive if you don't. The oath we took all those years ago would have been for nothing. I'm meant to protect you and you me. In this, though, I cannot save you." Tears begin to stream down the loyal princess's face; her strength not only lies in her ability to defeat any foe but also in her heart. She loves fiercely, and this will be one fight she cannot fight; *she cannot win.*

"Thank you, now go prepare. We will begin shortly." I squeeze her hand one last time.

I am strength, I am flame, I will destroy this piece of shit, and the blood will stain.

There is no true spell to destroy this dagger; just dragon flame and intent. I have been working on the rune words I will use, and this is as close as I have come to perfection. Goren has given me a lot of help finding the words, but the strength to complete the task will lie solely with me.

***

Finox

My best friend is a wreck; he looks like he's keeping it together for Samarra, but I know this man as well as I know myself. He is terrified; she has never shifted before or used her flame to the extent that she will need to use it tonight.

Will she turn into a full-blown dragon? Or will she look similar to her maker, Seraphina?

I don't know if she will survive this, and neither does he. He will become her conduit, giving her the oxygen she will need to create a strong burn. I will be on princess duty, keeping Arysalia from interfering. The twins will guard the temple in case the legion gets here before we have completed the mission. I still don't know what their magic is; they have skills they earned in the Bad Lands, but they have never wielded any magic while among us.

I look up at the temple. Samarra and Goren are there, and Arysalia is by my side. This is the second time she has ever let me hold her hand for longer than a few seconds. It isn't her bare hand, though; we are both gloved and ready for anything.

"Are you ready?" I ask her. The green in her eyes has dimmed. The sadness dwelling within her is palpable.

"No." She releases my hand and heads up into the temple.

Gods help us if this goes poorly.

I look up to the cloudless sky filled with stars and an almost full moon. *Please keep us safe, Seraphina, if you're watching over us. Please keep us safe.* I pray to the goddess of fire. She will be the only one who can save us.

As I reach the temple and look out onto the ritual stone surface where Sam, Goren, and Arysa are circled, I see the dagger. The onyx blade, with dragon scales etched into its hilt, extends down into the blade. This is the first time I've actually taken the time to examine it. There is an onyx stone that glows in the moonlight. How can a blade so deadly hold so much power? How can blood magic be that powerful?

Taking a seat on the stones yards from Sam and Goren, Arysa pats the surface next to her. A part of my heart swells a bit, knowing that she may be giving us a chance. She doesn't shy away from me as I take a seat, probably a little too close, but I need her warmth. There is a bite to the air this evening as the extreme nature of what is about to happen settles over us.

I hear Samarra begin to speak softly. She speaks in circles, repeating the verse repeatedly. "I am strength, I am flame, I will destroy this piece of shit, and the blood will stain." As she speaks, she slowly removes one arm at a time from her long cloak that has covered her arms, chest, and legs during our entire journey. I never quite noticed how much it covered her body until it slowly slid down her spine.

Samarra is magnificent, with fuchsia scales running up her spine, over her shoulders, and down the front of her chest and arms. The scales vary in shades of pink, from bright to dark, and they seem to glow in the moonlight, much like the blade she holds.

"I am strength, I am flame, I will destroy this piece of shit, and the blood will stain," Samarra chants. "I am strength, I am flame, I will destroy this piece of shit, and the blood will stain."

She's done a wonderful job with the wording. As she continues to chant, her scales begin to glow even brighter, and we can feel the heat coming off her.

Goren fills her with his wind, igniting the flames at her fingertips. Doing so engulfs the dagger in a magenta pink ball of fire. The glowing scales down her spine also ignite, just above her trousers, and a long, tail-shaped flame begins to extend. It is incredible. She isn't shifting into a dragon, but rather starting to appear the way Seraphina once did. She does not have the wings of the great flame goddess, but she is just as incredible.

As Samarra continues to chant, the flames grow brighter, and her eyes start to glow. The air around me crackles with tension, causing a shiver to run down my spine. There's a loud crack near the edge of the cliff further down the ridge. A growl shatters through the air around us; Umbra has landed at the edge of the temple.

"We've got company!" Ash shouts from where he and Amber stand at the ready. Arysa looks at me with terror; she doesn't want to leave Samarra.

"You and I are their only hope. Use what your royal guard has taught you!" I try to pump her up.

"Fine, but if she dies, I'm going to kill all of you!" she screams, standing with a huff.

Dammit. She is sexy when she's angry.

"That's fine, I will die on my own sword for you, Princess." I know these words will just irritate her further, but a blush runs up her neck, and she turns away abruptly.

We begin our descent down to the twins.

Chapter 64

*A*RE YOU FUCKING KIDDING *me?!*

I am making my way down to Ash and Amber. *I knew we couldn't just get this shit taken care of without being interrupted.*

The anger inside me flares, and I begin to gather in all the moisture around me. The cliff drops down to the sea, and for once, I am not being dragged down by the siren.

We will kill these little assholes, and I will be there for Sam if she needs me.

"I'll go left," I tell Fin as he nods and moves toward the cliffs on the right. I take one last look over my shoulder and at my best friend; the flames she is creating to destroy that fucking dagger are incredible. It's the most beautiful shade of pink I have ever seen.

I am so proud of you, Samarra. I look to see what exactly has come to attack.

I survey the cliff. There are three ashen, scarred men. They wear black metal uniforms for their protection, but their arms and calves are bare. They have terrifying helmets that resemble the beast created by the King of Xoneas. His most recent creation, the zorag, was destroyed by Umbra in the Bad Lands, but their helmets don't look like anything from this land.

They have jagged blades and are accompanied by hellhounds. The hounds are similar to the zorag, but not nearly as large; they resemble emaciated dogs, although they are extremely strong and vicious.

"Little princess, it's nice to see you." The man in front sneers at me. "Give us the dagger and we will go on our way. There is no need for more destruction and bloodshed."

I doubt he speaks a lick of truth. Likely, he would get the dagger and kill us all for good measure.

"Absolutely not," Finox shouts. "If you care to live, I suggest you get the fuck out of here now." His tone is angry, deep. He sounds ready to kill. I can scent his magic as he seems to be creating illusions to hide Samarra and Goren from their sight.

It is incredibly attractive when he just does things, protects our friends, and has our backs.

"Oh, the king of illusions. I forgot you were here," the leader of the Forsaken Legion says with an air of boredom. He waves his hand around. "Give me the dagger, or I will release the hounds."

Wrong answer.

I whistle as loudly as I possibly can, and Umbra shoots into the sky behind me and launches her own attack on the hellhounds. The men surrounding them must know what is about to happen because they all dive to the ground away from the hounds.

Immediately after they hit the ground, they seem to bounce back up, leaving the dogs to their demise, and rush toward us. Ash and Amber take up the middle with their bows and arrows, attempting to pick them off before they get too close.

Using the water that flows inside me, I attempt to encapsulate the man before me. He is trying his best to slice through the pod of water that is slowly attempting to drown him.

Fuck, this is exhausting. I should have just fought him hand-to-hand.

I slowly push the water into his nostrils and throat. I have never intentionally killed a person before. I know he is trying to do the same to us, but it is so hard.

I hear Fin, to my far right, pass the twins. He grunts as he uses his sword against a forsaken. He has a gash on his shoulder, and the forsaken has blood running down both of his arms and the visible portion of his leg. I turn back to my own forsaken, and he is clutching his neck now; all his weapons are on the ground, and he is slowly fading. I can feel it in the cool water; his temperature is dropping, and the color has drained fully from his face.

Finally, with a loud thud and a whoosh, the water dissipates. The man is left for dead, drowned on the cliff before me. I make a break for it and jump behind Ash, then Amber, as they continue to loose arrows into the hounds that Umbra hasn't killed yet and the last of the legion, who are moving in our direction. The disgusting hellhound is peppered with arrows but continues forward.

What are these beasts and fae fuckers made of?!

I move around the twins to head off the attack on Fin. Lifting my palm, I will the vines from the jungle to climb the cliffs. They begin to twine up the legs of the forsaken, and Fin finally gets his footing again. With a hard crunch, Fin lops the man's head square off from his shoulders; the rest of his body stays rooted to the spot where the vines hold him, and his head tumbles down.

With nothing left to lose, the last of the Forsaken charge toward the twins. I don't know if they hold any magic, but they only have bows and arrows as weapons. I watch them curiously as I move cautiously toward them. They make eye contact with each other, seeming to come to an agreement.

All at once, the twins lift their hands to the stars, and the ground begins to shake.

What the fuck are they doing?!

I look over my shoulder and see that Fin has stopped running. He is looking at the twins with wide eyes.

Looking back at the twins, I see that the ground is cracking and shifting. There is movement within the cliffs. I drop to the ground, so I don't lose my balance and get injured. Fin follows suit. We are within his bubble of the illusion, and I can still see Sam and Goren.

Stay strong, Sam.

Samarra is standing now, with the dagger out in front of her, and it is blazing. There is inky blackness dripping from the tip of the blade.

There's a loud manly scream that echoes over the cliffs, and before me, the twins have opened a chasm.

Holy shit! Earth wielders!

The screams of the final assassin begin to quiet, then stop altogether. After the Forsaken has been dropped to his death, the twins slowly piece together the cliffs again so no one else falls. I look away from the gaping hole.

Umbra has destroyed all of the hounds and is lying on her side, patiently waiting for what, I am unsure.

Fin stands and makes his way toward me, "They are earth wielders, Arysalia. Earth wielder fae have not been seen on Nedona from even before Seraphina disappeared."

Holy shit, the lost magic of this continent is resurfacing in a big way. If anyone finds out about the twins and their dual ability, they will be taken and enslaved to do the bidding of whoever holds their lives.

The twins turn once they have completed their tasks and shrug sheepishly. "Sorry, we didn't tell you sooner. It would have endangered us if the wrong people found out," Amber explains.

"No, we get it! That's how I feel about Samarra. She is the last flame..." The descendant of Seraphina, the only soul left alive who can save Issalitia.

An earth-shattering screech rips through the night, and I whip around. Samarra is on the ground. Her flames are completely out, and Goren is gathering her in his arms. He is ripping fabric and wiping furiously. His gaze is wild as he lifts her to his chest and rushes toward me.

"Arysal—"

I am running to him before he can even finish my name.

Chapter 65

Samarra

During The Ritual

IT'S JUST ME AND Goren now; we are going to destroy this blade if it is the last thing I do. The flames that I have held deep in my body for the previous two centuries come to life. The small number of dragon scales I once had has now doubled. My corset armor feels too tight, and my leather trousers, meant to keep me safe, are suffocating me now.

The dagger is heavy in my hands as I begin to melt it from the inside out. "I am strength, I am flame, I will destroy this piece of shit, and the blood will stain. I am strength, I am flame, I will destroy this piece of shit, and the blood will stain. I am strength, I am flame, I will destroy this piece of shit, and the blood will stain." Again, I pulse my heat into the metal.

I cannot take my concentration away from the dagger, but I can hear Arysa and Finox running to help Ash and Amber. My mind is racing. How did the Forsaken Legion find us? How did they know to come to this temple? The anger that we have found fills me even more, until I am exploding with flame.

Goren is at my side, breathing life into my body; his oxygen not only grows my flames, but it keeps me from overheating and burning out. We can't stop, though, even if I get to that point. We need to destroy these runes and break the curse.

The ground begins to shake beneath us, and the tip of the dagger is bleeding now. The blood magic is being dismantled and melting into the flames I have created around it. I stand to my full height. "I am strength, I am flame, I will destroy this piece of shit, and the blood will stain."

And with that last chant, the blade fractures in my hands. It shatters and melts all at once, exploding in my hands. It happens so fast I can't stop it.

I let out a scream so powerful it could stop the world in its tracks, or send it spinning off into the galaxy. I am covered in the inky, boiling black liquid. I fall to the ground, *I can do nothing, I may have burnt out completely.* Goren screams for my twin flame, and then the world goes completely black.

I am in a void of utter nothing.

Part Four

Chapter 66

Arysalia

THE DUST SETTLES AROUND the temple along the edge of the Muphion Jungle. Goren has not left Samarra's side; she still hasn't woken up. I don't know what I'll do if she doesn't. I have tried everything to get the black, inky substance off her hands. The black droplets are everywhere, along her hands and arms, even her chest. She is almost completely naked at this point. The leather she was wearing had all but melted off her body during the ritual. Her once barely noticeable scales have become more transparent, no longer something we can cover.

She didn't shift into a dragon, but her scales won't go away. We can't hide her anymore, and I'm not sure what scares me more: her secret being out or the fact that my best friend is now visibly the last flame. I think about all of this on repeat, causing myself more anxiety than is necessary.

My best friend is the last flame; she has the same fuchsia scales as Seraphina. She was the most powerful fire-wielding goddess this continent has ever seen. Now, my best friend has become just that; she is a goddess who walks among us. She is alive, but still hasn't awoken, and it has been hours.

Ash and Amber have taken up post again to watch for any lingering forsaken. I don't know how they found out where we were, and I don't know how they survived the climb up the Orcus Avala Mountains. The terrain alone should have killed them; they are something more than fae to be able to scale the edge of the cliffs. They must have known they would never survive the jungle.

I survey what is left of the pile of burnt, forsaken corpses, of the demonic fae experiments created by Morbious. Finox and Goren built a pyre and burned each one of them for good measure. Who knows what King Morbious has in store or if he has a necromancer in his keep? I shiver at the thought; necromancers have not been seen in Nedona in millennia.

I need to figure out the best way to help Samarra, so I have taken to looking through the herbs, spices, magic tonics, and manuals she brought on our journey. I need to know she can survive this.

***

Queen Zandra

I have no idea how long I have been down here. The darkness has completely taken over my psyche. I don't know the time, the day, or the season at this point. All I know is my daughter is in danger, and there is nothing I can do about it. I lay here thinking, constantly. No one has come to visit me. Food appears in my cell often when I wake. They must come when I am unconscious.

The sound of chains moves toward me, down the long dungeon corridor. *Clang, jingle, jingle, clang, jingle, jingle;* until it stops right outside my cell.

The guard whispers, "Your Majesty, the king wishes to have you brought to the throne room."

I don't respond. I don't understand why he would want me there. I am filthy and haven't eaten in gods knows how long. Has something happened to Arysalia? She must be dead.

"Your Majesty, are you awake? I don't want to bring you to him, but I must." The familiar guard whispers, then slowly unlatches the heavy–duty lock on the cell door.

I slowly pick my head up; he carries a torch in one hand and the keys on a long chain in the other.

"What is happening?"

"I don't know what he's planning." He doesn't explain further as he moves into the cell to unlatch the heavy chains that have been eating at my ankle for what feels like an eternity.

"Is Arysalia okay? How long have I been down here?" I question him, still groggy.

"Weeks, Your Majesty, and there has still been no sign of her in a few days. We have gotten reports of sightings in the Bad Lands and by the river." He gestures to the open cell door, letting the chain fall to his side, and helps me to my feet. I know this guard, he trained Arysalia to be the weapon she is today.

"Thank you, Brandon." I remember when his mother named him Brandon the Bold. Brandon means sword in the old language. A fitting name for the leader of the princess's guard. Many of the fae in our kingdom have unique abilities, along with their craft or position in the castle.

"It is my pleasure. I have been waiting for the right moment to check on you. It was not safe for me to show any favor toward you and the princess." The side of his mouth quirks up in a small grin. The gesture makes me think of Jerix, the fun we used to have when he was the head of my guard. My heart twinges in pain from the memory, but I live with the loss now, as it is part of me.

"Bring me to that beast. Let's find out what the fuck he wants." He offers me his arm and leads me out of the lowest level of the dungeon.

Brandon helps me walk up the many stairs to the main floor of the castle. The chill has been present in my bones for so long. I feel as though I can breathe again, the iron in the dungeons suffocating any strength or power I could muster. We edge closer to the throne room, to the large, beautiful doors that, for as long as I can remember, have stood shut and guarded by my own knights. My wrists are still shackled as the knights open the doors, and a loud creak echoes around me. Behind them, I can hear a frenzy of what I can only assume are the nobles.

I do not hesitate to glance at any of them as the room erupts into the loudest silence. "There is my treasonous wife," the king spits in our direction from my father's throne, my throne.

"Nothing to say?" he bellows again as we approach. I don't even lift my head to meet his eyes. I want to kill him. I want him dead, but I can't touch him, not with the entire castle in this room. "Speak, you bitch." He stands abruptly, spittle leaving his lips.

Brandon stops us at the edge of the dais. I lift my chin and say, "Fuck you, you disgusting pig." I spit at his feet with the last of the moisture I have in my mouth.

"How dare you!" He leers over me. I hold my head high now.

"Do it, Maggard." I will for him to lay a hand on this kingdom's queen. "Do it."

He doesn't. He rights himself, sitting back down into my throne, the smug bastard. "Where is Arysalia? Where is she going? How did she get the dagger?" He gets angrier and angrier with every question.

"I told you, I don't know where she has gone, and I don't know how she got the dagger. You found me unconscious in my chamber the next day." I shrug. "I haven't seen my daughter since dinner the night she knocked out the entire castle and stole your beloved dagger."

Ahh, that hit its mark. The dagger is a massive issue for everyone in the kingdom, including me. He won't be able to gain sympathy from the castle. His treasonous wife is just as trapped as they are. The kingdom doesn't know the royals can leave. Maybe I should inform them.

"I don't believe you, Zandra. You had something to do with this!" He's vibrating with anger, nostrils flared, sweat running down his brow, and it takes everything inside me not to smile.

He reaches for his goblet, taking massive gulps. He wipes his face with his silk-robed arm.

"Believe what you want. Why have you brought me up here?"

"We are going to find out exactly what you know. Gods, is it boiling in here? Who has stoked the hearth?" Maggard looks around wildly, beginning to cough uncontrollably. "Poison! Someone has poisoned my goblet!" He stares daggers right through me. "You did this!"

"How, Maggard? How could I possibly have poisoned you?" I shout this time.

He coughs into his clenched fist. He begins to turn bright red, then slowly more purple. I have no idea what is happening, but I can't help the grin that crosses my face.

"What is happening?" I ask Brandon, and he can't help but grin when he looks down at me.

"Your Majesty, I have nothing to do with it, but I am truly loving every second of it," he admits; and *I believe him.*

"Zandra!" the Mad King bellows. The sound echoes around the room. My eyes jump to his face again; the once purple hue has now turned almost black under his pasty flesh. I have no words. I am completely enthralled by what is happening to him.

His eyes are beginning to bulge and seep black goo. His hands are shaking, and he isn't speaking anymore. The whites of his eyes are darkening, slowly filling with black until they match the inky shade of his irises; *fitting, he has no soul anyway.* His nostrils begin to fill and well over with the inky black ooze. His ears are hidden beneath a mane of long black hair. They are probably oozing as well.

He begins coughing again. Black ink pours out of his foul maw; *die, my darling, die.*

During the commotion, a younger courtier bustles up to the throne with a rag to pad the sweaty brow of the king, but it's too late. The room erupts in screams. There is chaos everywhere, women are fainting and men are bellowing, all are terrified of what is happening to the king.

"We're next!" one woman screams.

"We're all going to die!" a portly man bellows.

But I know exactly what has happened. My girl has done it. The king could have been poisoned, but I don't know a poison on this planet that makes someone implode with inky black, dark magic like this. His blood runes have been destroyed.

***

Later that evening, when all the nobles were back in their homes, the castle finally quieted. Brandon comes to check on me. "Your Majesty, would you like to come to the dungeon and see the damage?"

I give him the evilest grin I can muster. "*Yes!* Bring me to that disgusting bastard!" I reply with gusto.

The king has been placed in a fully sealable iron cell in the dungeon. No magic can be used within. He is still dressed in his throne-room garb, now splattered with the black goo and wine. He is so still, so quiet, and I think this is the only time I have ever liked the man.

I give myself a long moment to gaze into his dead eyes. The youngest son of the King of Ramman is finally dead. His face is sunken, and where his eyes, mouth, nose, and ears used to be, thick inky black goo now drips. It's utterly disgusting but so incredible.

I don't know how much time passes while I stand here in the dim light of Brandon's torch, but I am finally free.

She did it, Jerix. Our girl did it.

Chapter 67

Arysalia

I HAVE BEEN WORKING on her for hours. The sun is slowly making its way up into the sky again on this new day. We are all exhausted, scattered around the fire. Goren has not left Sam's side since the ritual. She has been asleep but breathing. I don't know what happened while she was up there destroying the dagger, but I knew it would cause some damage.

Why didn't you let me help you? I stroke her hair repeatedly.

"How long do you think it will be?" I whisper to Goren, who is lying next to her, holding her hand tight in his own. His eyes remain closed. I know he isn't asleep; the crease between his brows shows a man who cannot even begin to relax.

"I do not know. She has been down for hours. It can't be much longer." The pleading in his tone breaks my heart.

She has to wake up. There isn't a world in which I can't have Samarra.

"Should we secure her to Umbra? Maybe she can carry her out of the jungle?" I am trying to think of any way to help her.

The scent of cherries and citrus pierces my nose. I don't have to look up to know that Finox is nearby. He doesn't even have to use magic anymore and I can still scent him. "Hello, Princess. How is she doing?"

"She still hasn't woken. I think we should try to start the journey back to Issalitia."

His eyebrows rise, and he looks down at his best friend.

"What do you think, Clode?" Finox asks Goren.

Goren raises on an elbow, leaning toward Samarra. He gently brushes the hair from her face. "I think we can't just stay here. We need to get her seen by a healer." He looks physically pained as he speaks.

I can't believe that Umbra can't even seem to wake her.

"Okay then, let's get everything packed up. Hopefully, we can make good time in the jungle," I command. We need to get back to the kingdom. The fallout from this curse may have had dire consequences.

No one argues as we pack up the camp. Samarra still does not stir as we get her onto Umbra's back, securing her similarly to how I was secured during our escape from the Bad Lands.

"I'll follow you anywhere," a quiet whisper hits my ear. His scent hasn't left me since we began this trip, and I am finding it harder and harder to resist him.

I need to stop thinking this could never work and just let it happen. I need to let myself finally live.

∗∗∗

Finox

As we re-enter the dark jungle, it feels almost light. The darkness has a shine that it didn't have before, as if the blood curse that plagued Issalitia plagued this place as well. As we parade through the jungle, Umbra stays in sight, Samarra on her back, and Goren at both of their sides. He has not left his wife's side, and I commend him for that. I would be absolutely losing my mind if this happened to Arysalia, and she isn't even mine.

We proceed in much the same formation as when we first entered, the twins take up the front of the party, Umbra and Goren in the middle, and Arysa next to me. She seems to be lost in thought, but at least she seems to be giving in to the fact that there is something between us.

I have no idea how things will work in the future, between the heir of one kingdom and the king of another. The thought has come to my mind more than once, so I can only imagine how many times it has entered hers. Could her mother stay as Queen of Issalitia?

"Do you think the dogla will keep us safe this time?" I ask, trying to get a reaction out of the princess.

"I think she will keep us safe. She is now free to see my mother if she so chooses," she shrugs. "I want to know if they have another connection. How did they become so close?" She takes a breath. "How did she feel when my mother fell in love with my father?" They are all fair questions to ask.

"You'll be able to ask her soon enough," I say lightly, hoping to bring up her spirits.

"Fin, we don't even know if my mother survived the wrath of the king after we escaped. We have been gone long enough for her to be slaughtered, and the kingdom be none the wiser."

Arysalia trembles with the words, and without a second thought, I take her hand. Immediately, we stop dead in the trail. Her eyes are swimming with emotion. She hasn't let herself believe those words until now. I can see the anguish all over her beautiful face.

All at once, Arysa rushes into my arms, dropping my hand and wrapping her arms around my midsection. Squeezing her back tightly, I revel in the feel of her body against mine as her floral scent with hints of the sea envelops me.

I could live in this moment forever.

"We don't know what has happened in the castle, but we do know that if the queen has come to any harm, there will be consequences."

"I'll kill him," is all she says before she lets herself fully erupt.

The tears come hard and fast, as the anguish she has been containing for this entire mission boils over. We embrace as we stand in the Muphion Jungle, the jungle that claims almost every life that enters. Dezmelda, the queen of this jungle, has a soft spot in her heart for Arysalia and her mother.

She is the only reason we are the only people ever to survive a night here, let alone an entire trip.

Chapter 68

Arysalia

I HAVE FINALLY BEEN able to calm down. The sun must have gone down by now. The jungle is so dark, the only light coming from the fire in the middle of our group. Umbra and Goren surround Samarra, and I find myself wrapped in Finox's arms.

I don't hate this, but I feel like I should pull away.

I just want to be alone, but the warmth he is giving me is making the ache in my chest just that much lighter. He held me while I finally let my world crumble.

Soft noises, snores? They are rhythmically coming from Fin now. His grip has lessened, and he is fully asleep. I am slowly able to pry his arms from around my body and roll onto the jungle floor.

Ash and Amber are awake and are on watch. I hear Amber humming a tune and leaning into her brother. They are so incredible, brother and sister, twins. Twins are uncommon in non-hybrid fae, but in hybrids, depending on the type, can happen more often. They could be the last of the earth elementals to walk Nedona, and they are on our side.

I make my way around the fire to check on Samarra.

"Sam, it's me. I know you're in there. Please come back to me, you made an oath..." I whisper to my friend, my twin flame.

I pray to all the gods and goddesses I can. *Please let her live. She is the light of this world.*

Looking down at her beautiful pink scales that are dotted with black, my heart breaks. My beautiful best friend gave everything to save our kingdom, and I don't know if I will be able to save her.

I pat Umbra on the head, and she gives me a low purr in response. Taking up refuge beside the fire, watching the flame dance across the darkness, I hope to fall asleep and slip into a dream with Dezmelda.

I need answers, and we need help.

***

Being sucked into a dream walking will never get easy. I am standing beneath a canopy of massive trees, ferns, vines, and roots. The jungle's expanse still amazes me, and we have spent days here.

"You have done it, my child," I hear Dezmelda purr into the eerie green.

"We did, but Samarra... She still hasn't awoken. She still breathes, but she cannot regain consciousness."

I still don't see her. She is likely stalking me, as if I am prey, from the large limbs that create the ceiling of the canopy above us.

"Oh, my darling, she needs time. Your twin flame has never expelled as much elemental magic as she did during that ritual. She destroyed a dagger that was forged by dragon fire and imbued with blood magic." She tsks. "Did you truly believe she would walk away unharmed?"

It was as if she, too, had access to my thoughts during this entire journey. My biggest fear is happening, and I don't know when it will end.

"Well, I hoped she would be okay. I hoped she'd survive, but she looks smaller and more delicate than I have ever seen her." I picture my once–tall, thin, elegant best friend. "The once barely noticeable scales on her limbs, shoulder, back, and chest are more pronounced now. We won't be able to rune those away. Everyone will know she is a descendant of Seraphina," my voice shakes.

"Arysalia, you are stronger than this. You must give her body time to heal. Your oracat will attempt to heal her, and if you make it back to the castle... There is a spring that runs through it that is known to have healing magic properties in its molecules."

She hops down and transforms back into her beautiful fae form. Her ebony skin shines, and her shock of white hair is such a contrast. She is beautiful and so, so dangerous. She walks like a predator, but she doesn't scare me.

"I will *try* to be patient, but will you come back to the castle with us? Will you come see my mother, make sure she is safe?" I ask, knowing she won't come.

"My child, I cannot leave this jungle. Without me, anyone could walk in here." She gives me a wink. "When your mother is ready, she will know exactly how to find me."

She steps closer, pulling me into her strong arms. She is only a few inches taller than me and has barely aged for someone who is older than a millennium; she looks not a few years older than I. My mother has aged gracefully, but she has still aged. Dezmelda seems to be stuck in time.

"I will tell her of all that you have done for me." Just then, I let myself feel again. I haven't cried this much since I was a child. I do so now in the arms of the maleficent witch queen of the Muphion Jungle. I cry for all the time I have wasted holding it all in. I cry and cry, being soothed and rocked back and forth.

"Shh, Arysalia," she croons into my hair. "You survived, you saved your kingdom, you led this mission," she reassures me. "Your friends followed you and fought by your side."

I choke on a sob. "But Sam..." I cry even harder. I can't lose her. I will feel more lost if I lose her than if I lost my own mother. Samarra and I have a blood oath bond, a bond that can only be severed in death. How will it feel to have that piece of myself gone forever?

"Shh, she will live, my child. She will live." Dezmelda's voice grows quiet, and the arms that surround me are no longer muscular in a feminine way. The scent of cherries and citrus crests my senses, and the arms around me are strong and toned. He pulls me from my sleep and drags me into his lap.

I don't have the energy to fight you, Kingling.

"Arysalia," he whispers into my hair. "She's awake."

Chapter 69

Samarra

I HAVE BEEN FLOATING in darkness for such a long time. The last thing I remember is the blade exploding in my hands. The inky black magic soaking into my flesh felt wrong. It was entirely evil, but I felt calm. Where it landed on my hands and arms burned for only an instant, the scales that were once so small grew and protected the surface of my skin.

I remember hearing Goren screaming for Arysalia. My best friend, my twin flame... Life is going to be so different now, but we did it. We conquered a curse that has ravaged our kingdom for half a millennium.

Arysalia pretends she is the strong one because of my delicate nature, but what she doesn't see is the power that thunders in my bones, that burns just below the surface of my skin.

Seraphina gifted me her magic, her soul's fire, and her dragon. Our oath is still intact, and I am still sealed with Goren.

I need to wake up. I can feel the anxiousness of everyone surrounding me. I cannot hear what they are saying, but I can feel them.

***

Finox

"Arysalia," I whisper into the princess's hair again as she sobs in her sleep. "She's awake." As if I flipped a lever, Arysa is scrambling out of my arms to get to her friend.

"Samarra," she shrieks, running full bore toward her friend. Samarra lies in Goren's arms, as she has finally opened her eyes. I am right behind Arysa when she lands on her knees in front of the couple.

"I told you she'd be okay," I say delicately. Arysa looks over her shoulder and gives me a look that promises pain. Lifting my hands in surrender, she turns back to Samarra. I really need to work on my timing.

"I have been so worried. Are you okay?" Arysa asks, her voice quaking.

"Yes, Arysa, I am okay," Samarra sighs.

"Are you sure? You're so pale, and you were asleep for so, so long." Tears stream down Arysa's beautiful face as she reaches out her hands, holding tightly to her friend.

"Yes, I was just drained. I was very close to burning out when the dagger finally imploded. It was very dark for a while, as if I were floating on the breeze on a moonless night." She closes her eyes as if recalling the feeling. "Then I could hear you all calling for me. I could hear your voices but not your words. I just couldn't reach you. When I finally gave up and relaxed, I was released."

What she's saying makes sense, but it sounds terrifying; a sensation of being wildly claustrophobic in that space, not knowing where you are or when you will wake, sounds incredibly unsettling.

"Well, we are glad you made it back to us," I exclaim. "Please don't do that again, *ever*." I discreetly point to the princess. "Some of us were *very* emotional." Again, Arysalia shoots daggers at me with her beautiful green eyes.

At least she's looking at me, even with murder in her eyes. I chuckle at my own joke.

"Well, I am glad to be back. Waking up surrounded by my husband and Umbra was quite comforting." She reaches up to scratch under the massive feline's chin. "I'd rather not do that again, either, if it is at all possible."

Goren just sits there, unspeaking, holding her tight. The terror he has been feeling for the past twenty–seven hours has been palpable. He hasn't let go of her, eaten, or even moved once we arrived and set up camp.

"Well, flaming one, you made it out!" Amber comes over with Ash, who is not too far behind her.

Samarra smiles, but I interrupt whatever she was about to say. "They are earth wielders!"

I'm sure I turn a shade of red that isn't attractive at all.

"Oh, my gods!" Samarra's eyes glitter. "There hasn't been an earth wielder in centuries."

"Yes, it isn't something we advertise, but you all were in danger, and we had to help," Ash explains. Amber shrugs, as if opening a massive hole in Nedona and watching it swallow our enemies and then stitching it back together like an open wound is an everyday thing.

"Well, thank you for saving the people I love," Samarra says, her voice cracking. "I'm sorry I missed the show."

"You'll see it soon! We still need to make it back to my mother," Arysalia says.

"Samarra has just woken up. We should let her heal some before we go," I gently tell Arysa.

She looks up at me with eyes still freshly damp with tears. She nods and doesn't argue for once. I miss the sass in her tone, but I understand the sorrow she is feeling.

"Okay, we will leave tomorrow," she agrees, looking up into the dark canopy.

I'm not sure how we will know it's tomorrow, but when Samarra is ready, we will all get the hell out of here.

Chapter 70

Arysalia

I HAVE FOUND MYSELF spiraling again, even though I know Sam is okay and that we have destroyed the dagger. However, my mother is still not safe. With the wards from the dagger destroyed, anyone can enter the castle, and anyone can leave. What will happen? Will the Forsaken Legion try to take the kingdom now that it is unlocked? How many experiments did Morbious create for his league of assassins?

I need to get a grip.

Samarra has sipped from the water skin and has kept down small bits of bread and berries that the twins foraged. The inky black markings are still on her arms, but the once barely visible pink scales have completely come in, even more pronounced now than they were hours before. They are darker and raised; her once pale arms, shoulders, chest, and back are now layered with them. She looks magnificent, but we can no longer hide the fire within her. The fear of the future is weighing heavily.

***

I have grown increasingly restless. Once Samarra is up and moving around, we finally decide to move forward. I haven't felt such relief to be leaving this place as I did when we exited out onto the cliffs just a day ago.

Umbra stays close beside Sam, not leaving her alone with Goren. The trail seems to be shrinking in size, with the heft of Umbra taking up the darkness with her own shadow. Sam and Goren are again in the middle, making it impossible for Finox and me to see Ash and Amber. We are in the same orientation as when we entered the jungle, when Samarra was still unconscious. The jungle still feels uneasy. I know Dezmelda means no harm to us, but still, my hackles are raised, and I am buzzing with anxiety.

"We're going to be all right," Fin whispers next to me, taking my hand in his again.

The rough surface of his thumb glides across the soft part of the back of my hand. I really want to hold his hand, and he did what I needed without me having to ask or initiate. The confusion coursing through me about this bond is causing more problems than my worries about Samarra, I think, nodding to him in response.

I don't have words for him right now.

***

Queen Zandra

The castle is buzzing, and whispers of "The Mad King is dead" keep flitting past my ears. It sounds more like music than buzzing, but that's neither here nor there. Now, to reclaim my castle and free my kingdom, I must inform the kingdom of what has happened and that freedom is now imminent. I contemplate how to go about this as I pace back and forth in my chamber.

I need Arysalia to be safe and back in the kingdom before we announce the curse has been dissolved with the death of that creature dressed as king.

There is a soft knock at my chamber door. "Your Majesty." I hear the steady tone of Arysalia's head guard, Brandon. "The counsel is requesting your presence. What would you like me to tell them?"

"Come in for a moment."

He enters cautiously, closing the heavy wooden door behind him.

I gesture for him to take a seat in front of my massive windows that overlook the kingdom. "We are in an odd situation, if I am honest."

"Very odd. If I had my way, I'd kill the lot of them that allowed you to be kept down in the dungeon," he grumbles. Rage emanates from him in waves. His hands were tied, he had no sway, no way to pull me out except to wait for the end. I monitor him, looking more closely at his kind, handsome face.

"I know if you could have saved me, you would have. Unfortunately, these council members also represent the kingdom and its people. We need to let them know what is happening, but I was hoping Arysalia would have returned before I would have to face them," I admit, feeling resigned and worried about her and Samarra.

"Yes, this is the truth, Your Majesty. I will remember it in the future." He heads toward the door. "I will let them know that you will convene them when you have recovered your health. Let them stew," he says with a wink and an exaggerated bow before he turns on his heel and exits.

I'm not quite sure how I would have recovered if it wasn't for Arysalia's head guard. I look out onto the kingdom that is mine once again.

***

Arysalia

I still haven't seen or heard from Dezmelda since the evening when I wasn't sure if Sam would survive the night. She has not come back. She hasn't even had me dream walk or show me the precious memories of my parents' past. It is an odd feeling to miss something you never truly had. I never really thought I'd ever experience or witness those intimate moments. Dezmelda and my mother were friends, and they haven't seen each other since before the curse.

"Do you think Dezmelda will leave the jungle to see my mother? Do you think she will continue to be on our side?" I ask Fin as we continue through the humid, dark, and green jungle.

"I think she should see her, but she is also the guardian of this jungle. There are many hidden places within this jungle that need to be protected from groups like the Forsaken Legion," he explains. "Maybe she can dream walk to her?"

Yes, I hope that is the case. I don't want her to continue to live alone anymore.

We walk in an uncomfortable silence. I don't really have anything else to say. The excitement I thought I would feel at destroying the dagger and freeing my kingdom has left me with more questions.

Umbra has taken off into the jungle without us. She has left me, again. I don't understand why I have had such anxiety about loss recently. The visions of my father have opened a wound within me that I didn't know was a source of pain until now. I know Umbra hasn't truly left me, but also, hasn't she?

I hope she is just out hunting in the darker parts of the jungle and hasn't indeed left.

Chapter 71

Finox

As we edge closer to the jungle's exit, Arysalia seems to grow increasingly anxious. I noticed it once Umbra disappeared into the shadows and still hasn't returned. She has become more open to holding my hand and attempting to accept the bond we share. I know her hesitation. The kingdoms have never had two heirs of two kingdoms be fated mates. I am willing to do the research and make compromises for this union of kingdom and hearts. The idea of her mother staying queen until we have a way to appoint a regent or consort to aid in her rule is a good one.

I feel a prickle of unease come over me, the always too silent jungle seems even quieter. Ash and Amber have stopped up ahead. Their ears are visible now that Umbra is no longer a boulder of shadow. Their ears seem to be turning and adjusting to whatever sound we can't hear. Goren pushes Sam behind him as Arysalia and I take up a defensive stance.

My gods, it's super hot when she is about to kick someone's ass.

Her blades are slim and sharp, making them easy to wield and slice through air and flesh.

"What do you hear, Ash?" I question the leporis fae.

"We do not hear anything. It is the silence, Your Majesty; it is most deafening," Ash proclaims, his ears twitching in a way that demonstrates he is listening intently.

I don't fully understand what he is trying to say, but I do think the silence is ominous.

"What could be the cause of the lack of sound?" Arysalia looks over to me, dagger raised in the direction of the jungle's exit. We are so close to getting out of the dark, I can feel the breeze that blows through the Timbers from the Issalitian River.

"I'm not quite sure. It could be something coming from the Wild Timber Forest. With my illusions in place while we slept, I doubt anything knew we were camped out," I try to reason; not just with Arysa but with myself too.

There is a significant crunch, a sound of bones breaking. The sickening sound is coming from the direction of the jungle's exit. We are close enough to see the pillars but not to see what is beyond. The sound has caused the entire party to freeze in place. My illusions are in place, and they are strong, but I was thwarted before with Umbra...

Next to me, the princess shifts. "What the fuck was that?" she whispers desperately.

Before I can begin to answer, a mutilated body lands in the center of the trail between the pillars, blocking our only way out of this fucking jungle.

The gasp that leaves her lips surprises me more than I thought it would.

"Who's there?" Goren shouts at the figure that has appeared over the body; a grotesquely large thing with a massive head and horns coming out from its sides.

Whatever it is, the darkness seeping from it is unnatural. It feels similar to the zorag and the fae of the Forsaken Legion.

"That is one of the Dark Minotaurs, Fin. Morbious created them. Dezmelda must have warned me about them. I don't know how I know this." Arysalia's voice sounds so small.

"Ah, yes, the king of illusions." The shadowy figure's voice is dark and ominous as it echoes through the air. "I can see past your silly tricks."

"What do you want from us?" the princess yells.

I wish she had stayed silent. If this dark fae can see through illusions, he can likely smell her lineage.

And with that thought, an audible sniff echoes through the darkness. "Mmmm, you smell quite delicious. I can taste your fear and smell your blood," he responds in a deep, unsettling tone.

"You're wrong! I taste disgusting!"

I cannot even handle this girl.

"Oh no, Princess, you taste divine. I am going to eat you up, bring you back to life, and eat you all over again."

I must hold every muscle still in my body, or I am going to die, because he has threatened to touch what is mine.

"You will do no such thing!" Ash shouts and begins to shift the earth beneath the dark fae's feet.

"Come to play, earth bender?" The minotaur dives away from the tilting earth.

"I don't play with filth such as yourself, minotaur of the dead," Amber shouts. The shifting earth takes out his footing and rumbles beneath us.

"We need a plan," I whisper to Arysalia.

"We do. The twins are providing a great distraction, but where is Umbra?" she whispers back to me.

The air around us changes, and the trees begin to sway. We both look to Goren this time. He is blowing high winds toward the darkness emanating from the minotaur. Samarra is safely tucked behind his hulking frame. There is no way she is strong enough to wield, but if she were, she could fry him up like an egg.

✳✳✳

Arysalia

Goren and the twins are fighting off the dark minotaur, and Fin and I are at the back of the pack, ready to come down on him with whatever force necessary. Samarra looks like she wants to help, but she isn't even glowing with heat.

"Do we sneak around through the trunks of the trees? Should I call for Umbra?" I ask Fin.

"I say call for the oracat and hope she decapitates him, and then we can get to Issalitia with no other issue."

He's not wrong. Umbra is fearsome.

I place my forefinger and middle finger to my lips. Samarra's father taught me how to whistle this way. I have never tried it with Umbra, but I don't know how far away she is; the whistle I release is shrill and high-pitched. I follow that up with a scream for my oracat. "Umbra!"

"Oh yes, Umbra! Come and rescue your beloved princess," the minotaur shouts while mimicking me as he rights himself on the uneven ground.

"Continue to be unafraid, pathetic dark fae," Goren shouts over his own wind. "She hasn't had a good meal in days."

"You think I'm scared of whatever creature you have coming to handle me?" His laugh is so sinister that the hair on the back of my neck stands on end.

Come on, Umbra...

"Ash, Amber, drop him!" I shout over the wind, and his laughter is still coming from the darkness.

They look at each other and smile. "Yes, Your Majesty."

The two lift their hands above their heads simultaneously, facing the dark creature. Their fingers go from a clenched fist to an open hand, fingers splaying into the air, and the ground around the minotaur's feet shudders. We finally see him, as he has made it past the pillars. His eyes begin to bulge as the ground begins to let go beneath him.

"Fuck!" he bellows, looking as though he may fall to his death without laying a hand on any of us, until his hands reach out and stop his fall. He grips the edge of the earth that the twins have opened.

"Shit, can he climb out of that?" I yell over to Amber. Her eyes are wide as they meet mine. I have no idea what powers a dark fae minotaur has or what he can do when his life is truly in danger.

A loud whooshing, snapping, and flapping sound can be heard. And then a loud growl sounds above us, along with the shrill screech of what, I have no fucking idea.

Next to me, Finox starts to move. "Sasha!" he shouts. The screech sounds again, and for fuck's sake, Umbra went and got the hippogriffs.

"Greta," Goren shouts, followed by another screech.

"Great, a family fucking reunion," the minotaur shouts from the hole he is dangling in, for now.

Umbra does exactly what I think she's going to do.

She lands right in front of the disgusting creature, and a low, ominous growl releases from her as she places her sharp claws into his large hands. She hisses down at him. It's interesting how he suddenly has nothing else to say.

Umbra bends down and grabs his scalp with her long, sharp, deadly incisors, carefully avoiding the massive horns, effectively ripping him from the end of the hole to hell.

"Well, Umbra, that was creative." I am both disgusted and pleased with her at the same time.

Moving back from the hole, Umbra and the two hippogriffs stand together. Ash and Amber lift their hands to the sky again and close the earth over the dark minotaur. A screech echoes from one of the hippogriffs as the earth shudders beneath our feet.

Screechy little beasts, but at least we don't have to walk.

This thought brings me so much more joy than I could have ever imagined.

Chapter 72

Arysalia

GOREN AND FINOX ARE over the moon. Their hippogriffs have been absent from our journey for their own safety, but it seems that Umbra wanted a faster way out of this mission. The only issue is we don't have a way to transport the twins without weighing down the beasts. Umbra could barely carry me while I was incapacitated, and walked with Samarra when she was in her long sleep. I can see the cogs in Samarra's mind moving as well.

"What are you thinking about?" I step up beside my best friend. I haven't spoken to her much. I don't know what to say, *you saved the kingdom and almost died, and why are you so stubborn?*

"Probably the same as you. We need to find a way to get Ash and Amber safely into Issalitia. Umbra can't carry them..." She has come to the same conclusion.

"Princess," Amber strides up behind us. "Ash and I can continue on foot. We know the forest well and have survived many years just the two of us."

"We could not have saved the kingdom without you. We can't just leave you here," I try to convince her. "We can find another way."

"You know our secret. We can protect ourselves very easily with the earth around us. It's a two-day journey to the gates on foot, and you will get there in a day," she reasons. "We will meet you there."

"If that is what you choose, we will honor your wishes," I concede, hoping we don't regret this decision. A cool breeze sends a chill down my spine.

"Let me get the rest of the supplies we have!" Samarra shuffles around through her satchel, which is filled with anything you can find in the forest to survive on. Sam ate the last of the bread and cheese, so we're down to berries, mushrooms, and roots. If the twins can hunt some small game, they should make it.

"Thank you, Samarra." Ash stops her rifling and pulls my best friend into a warm hug. I'm not as jealous of their kinship as I was of Goren when they first became attached. I need to learn to let go. I have never been betrayed or hurt by Samarra, so I don't know why that would change.

Looking away from my friends, I head toward Umbra, Sasha, and Greta. The hippogriffs are stomping and chomping their beaks with excitement. The golden-feathered beasts have not been without their riders for long periods.

"I forgot how beautiful they are," I say to no one in particular.

"They really are," Finox says fondly, as I watch his expressions change and how he interacts with Sasha. I'm a bit lost for words. She nuzzles him and bends down to be on his level. He whispers to her and pats her lovingly. I find I'd like him to look at me that way. It seems like the Valadorian King is growing on me, much like a stray cat or a fungus.

✳✳✳

Finox

Relief flooded my body when I heard Sasha and Greta's screech echo over the jungle.

"Sasha, my beautiful friend! I am so glad to see you!" I croon into her gilded neck.

The minotaur is dead, and now we don't have to walk for two days to return to Issalitia. I think, gratefully. We can even make a more thrilling entrance, avoiding the front gate at all costs. If the curse did not take out the king, as we believed it would, the element of surprise would be ideal.

Looking over at the girls discussing travel plans, my heart squeezes a bit at the sight of Arysalia. She seems to unknowingly consume my vision, my mind, and my senses. I hope that she can one day see that this was not decided by fae but by the gods. We are mates and we will make this continent stronger together. We just need to find a way to make that work.

As if she can hear my thoughts, she looks up, her light green eyes meeting my own; a flash of pink creeps up her beautiful neck.

"Sire, we should ready the women for the flight. If we leave soon, we should reach the kingdom by nightfall." Goren ruins the moment as soon as he starts to speak, Arysa looks away immediately.

"Yes," I say on a sigh. "Let's do that. Sasha and Greta are probably tired, so let's get this over with." I try not to come off annoyed, but where do we go once this mission is over?

I don't know what will become of my mind or soul if I am rejected and sent back to Valador without my mate...

"Your majesty?" I hear Ash approaching.

"Yes, Ash. Also, you can call me Fin or Finox." I shrug. We have been through battle together, it's the least I can offer.

"Absolutely not. You are the King of Valador, and that is how I will address you," he says, bowing in respect. "I did want to let you know Amber and I will be making the journey on foot. We will hopefully make it back to the castle by tomorrow evening."

"I'm sure there is another alternative." This fae saved us, we should at least find a way to give him a lift.

"There is no need, Amber and I have survived the woods and land for our entire lives. Samarra and the princess have made sure we have enough snacks, herbs, and healing tonics to survive another week alone." He looks over to his twin fondly. "We will survive and be reunited with you all soon."

"If that is what you choose, we will support you and await your arrival in Issalitia," I reassure him.

I do wonder what their plans are for the future. Will they want to go back to the Bad Lands, or would they like to be a part of one of the kingdoms again? An earth elemental fae would greatly be of benefit to either kingdom, mine or Arysalia's.

Chapter 73

Arysalia

THERE REALLY ISN'T ANYTHING else in the world that feels like flying. When you are atop a hippogriff and soaring through the sky, the trees resemble small vegetables, and the small shacks and cabins that are almost completely hidden in the Wild Timber Forest look like playhouse toys from up here.

"Are you okay back there?" Finox asks from in front of me. We do not ride with a saddle, but she does have a harness around her beak. She doesn't need it, though; she can pretty much sense what Fin needs.

"I'm great. I forgot how incredible this was," I say into the back of his neck.

I am incredibly aware of the fact that my body is pressed against his and my arms are wrapped around his waist. I thought there was nothing here, that the idea of us being mates was a delusion, but maybe it was me who was delusional. I think to myself, waiting for his response.

"Me too. I haven't gone that long without her," he admits with a tone of sadness in his voice.

I wonder if he will miss me when he goes. Will the distance between us drive him mad, like all the legends claim?

"I can't imagine. I know that I rode Umbra, but I couldn't imagine flying with her, then being without her for so long," I tell him. "I thought she had left me, and it made me feel a bit lost."

"I had a feeling her absence was affecting you more than you were letting on." The King of Valador noticed the change in me when I didn't respond. I take a deep breath in through my nose, filling my senses with his scent. He smells like spring when the cherry blossoms bloom, with citrus notes all over. I devour his scent and think; *maybe, just maybe, everyone else is right.* He smells like the future.

***

Finox

As we soar ever closer to Issalitia, I try my best not to get under her skin or push her too far. I hear her take a deep breath through her nose, and part of me hopes she is taking in my magic, letting it will her to enjoy the sensations. I have been breathing in her magic this entire journey, and it hopefully will not cause my own detriment.

Sasha and Greta are having a good time, flying like they haven't flown before. I think they want to get home as soon as possible, and the faster this mission is over, the faster that can happen. However, I don't see Greta coming home with me and Sasha if Samarra chooses to stay in Issalitia with Arysalia. I ponder while we continue our course, flying further and further from the Muphion Jungle.

The Wild Timber Forest is finally thinning out as we reach the tall white stone walls of Issalitia. The contrast between my kingdom and this one is apparent. From the drier climate and darker stone, the building structures are quite different.

The estates, houses, cabins, and even the castle are all carefully crafted from the beautiful white stone, and the roofs are thatched with what looks like long, coarse hay. The trees that are dotted around the kingdom are stunning; they have long curling branches, beautiful budding leaves, and some of them are even fruiting. The fragrance in the air, filled with the scent of all the blooming flowers, is intoxicating. A true spring evening is upon us.

"It's just as beautiful as the last time we were here," Arysalia says into my neck, her breath caressing me, her grip getting tighter around my waist. Her anxiety seems to be getting the better of her at this moment, and I am perfectly okay with it. Her toned arms feel like heaven on my body, and even with leathers, cloaks, and underthings between us, I can still feel her heat.

"It is much prettier when you are there," I admit, with a blush building up my neck and onto my cheeks. She can't see it, and I can't see hers, but she doesn't respond, instead burying her head into my back between my shoulders.

From this height, we can see the courtyards of all the suites and chambers along the outskirts of the castle. There is a large gathering area at the center of the castle that lends itself to being where the royals address the citizens and nobles. There is a large stage that seems to be covered in flowers, candles, and paintings. We are too high to see exactly what is going on down there, but

I have a feeling that the king is indeed dead, and the citizens are mourning his loss.

If only they knew the monster behind the crown.

***

Arysalia

The kingdom is just as I left it. There is no rebellion, and no one is hurt or suffering. The commoners' courtyard is filled with what looks like a massive shrine. My heart sinks. *Please don't be for my mother,* I pray to whichever goddess is listening.

As we glide closer to home, I can see my people. I know everything will be okay now that he is gone. Holding on tightly to Finox seems to be the only thing keeping me grounded in reality. I can't keep sinking back into that place of loss, loneliness, and terror. I have survived, Samarra has survived, Finox has survived.

I catch myself when his name comes to the forefront of my mind. Finox, he has survived, and I am happy about it. We have spent so much time pushing and pulling against each other, and I never imagined I would end up thinking about the King of Valador in any other way than with disdain, annoyance, and frustration.

"We have made it," I whisper into his neck.

"We have, Princess."

I don't bristle at the nickname anymore, because it is what I am, is it not?

"Let's get down there and find out what has happened. The stables are on the western edge of the castle." I point, and without a word, Sasha knows the way.

Chapter 74

Queen Zandra

THERE IS COMMOTION OUTSIDE my study, a clinking of steel and rattling of chainmail. I jump to my feet. *Please don't let us be under attack.* We are not prepared for an invasion; we are only just now training the fae men and women who chose to be in the military.

"Your Majesty!" A shout comes from beyond the door, and without knocking, Brandon comes rushing in. "She's back, Zandra. She is back." He has tears in his eyes, and I know he is telling the truth. Arysalia has survived and is finally home.

Without a second thought, we're moving. I have my skirts in one hand and Brandon's hand in the other as we make our way outside. "Where are they?"

"They have just landed in the stables."

I stop short.

"They flew in on the king's hippogriffs, with an oracat in tow."

With a huge sigh, we pick up the pace. My study is on the eastern side of the castle, up quite a few flights of stairs. The exhaustion is worth it; we are going to see her soon.

"I can't believe she's okay. Are they sure it's her? Are they sure she is with him?" I ask breathlessly.

"The servants who alerted the knights claimed it was the princess, the king, his general, and Samarra," he explains. "Her father has been informed."

That poor man was brought down to the dungeons when I was. He did not fare well. When the king finally expired, he was then released. Unfortunately, the toll on his body was tremendous; we do not know how long he has left, but he will get to see Samarra, the *Last Flame*.

***

Arysalia

Umbra disappears into the shadows of the stable, and we wait while Sasha and Greta eat. I don't want to move from this spot. The servants who were in the stable when we arrived ran to inform the knights, and likely my mother, if she has survived.

Finox comes up beside me, and I welcome his warmth. I don't think I have taken a full breath since we left the castle all those weeks ago. Across the stable is the entrance to the commoner courtyard, where the massive vigil has been erected. The massive wooden gates are shut, but there's a loud commotion coming from the other side.

"Open the gate!" I hear my mentor shout. I could place his voice anywhere. Brandon, the sword, is on his way.

"They are coming." I look up to Fin, taking his hand in mine. "I want to introduce you to the queen, but we may need some time first," I urge.

I think I may be falling harder than I thought when I was up in the sky, wrapped around him.

"Take all the time you need." He winks at me. My heart melts a little bit more, which would once feel unsettling but now feels perfect.

Samarra and Goren are waiting next to us, holding each other. I think we are both overwhelmed; she to see her father, and I for my mother.

"Arysalia, darling flower!" I hear a feminine voice as the gates open at the speed of a garden snail.

"Mother!" I cry, and then I'm moving, not walking or running. There is no holding back the tears now. My composure has broken, and I don't give a fuck because my mother is alive!

"Oh, my *gods*, I have been so worried." She wraps her arms around me, pulling me in so closely that it's impossible to stand. Sliding down to the ground, we sob, holding each other in front of the entire kingdom. Mother and daughter are together at last.

"We are so proud of you," Brandon says, standing above us, always on guard. I don't have the strength to say another word, nodding my head thank you.

"Samarra!" A gruff, sickly male voice echoes across the expanse.

"Papa!" The crack in Samarra's voice scares me.

Her father is so frail. He looks as though a strong breeze will drop him.

Whispering into my hair, my mother says, "Maggard placed him in the dungeon. We were both down there since the day you left."

My eyes are wide, and my tears grow heavier as they fall from my cheeks.

"I am okay, my darling flower. I have survived, but her father's magic isn't as strong as ours," she explains.

My heart is breaking for my best friend.

"Oh, Papa, I have missed you so much," Samarra tells her father. "What has happened to you? Are you sick?" It's hard to understand her through the tears.

"Oh, Samarra, my flame. I am fine. I will be okay."

He lies; he looks incredibly ill. I don't know how long he has. I must stop myself from thinking those thoughts, but at least he got to see her. It may be the last time they are together.

"Mother," I lean back, wiping the last few tears from my face, taking her hands in mine. We rise together. "This is the King of Valador," I gesture to the auburn-haired, amber-eyed man standing behind me.

"Your Majesty, it is a pleasure." Finox takes her hand and places a kiss upon it. A surge of jealousy zips down my spine.

He has never kissed my hand.

"The pleasure is all mine. I believe you are the reason this kingdom had a chance of being free." She doesn't ask, only states the obvious. "Sneaking into a locked kingdom was very dangerous." She delivers a rather devious look.

"She was worth the risk," he admits, looking down at me with eyes that sparkle like the brightest of suns, with no hesitation in his tone.

My mother winks. "She really is."

If everyone loves the guy, why have I been so reluctant?

Behind us, Samarra is introducing Goren to her father. He takes her father up in his arms, giving him the gentlest hug I have ever witnessed. It seems he approves of their sealing and the fact that they are mates.

"Can we go inside, please?" I beg. "I need a shower and the largest leg of whatever bird the cook has in that kitchen."

The crowd around us breaks into laughter.

"I'm with her. Can we eat something?" The Kingling agrees, giving me the brightest smile I think I have ever seen.

Chapter 75

Arysalia

WE ENTER THE MASSIVE dining room, which is brimming with flowers.

"The kingdom is mourning *his* death, then?" I ask my mother, who is seated at the head of the table. She has finally taken back the seat she always deserved as the true ruler of our kingdom.

"Oh, I do believe they are confused and a bit shaken up about the whole ordeal, but to tell you the truth, I think the flowers are for me. This kingdom has seen me grow from a girl into the woman I am today. I wilted like a daisy in the cold when Jerix died, and they are just happy to see his killer taken." She shrugs.

"I mean, it makes sense. I am just so glad you're safe," I admit. "What happened in the dungeons? Did he have you tortured?"

"Oh no, my darling flower. He only questioned me about where you were. For the most part, I was alone with my thoughts." She sighs. "Your father came to visit me in the haze of unconsciousness."

This doesn't surprise me because he came to see me, too.

"What did he say?" I ask.

Finox's firm, warm hand stops my bouncing knee, grounding me.

"To stay strong and that you would not fail us." A lone tear falls down her cheek.

"He came to see me too," I admit, my eyes starting to pool.

"Oh, Arysalia, I bet that was wonderful. I wish you could have known him. He was an incredible man."

"He was amazing. He told me of my heritage on his side. He told me how dangerous the siren in my blood could be. He told me he loved you. Oh, mother, it was amazing."

"I know it was," she whispers, taking a sip from her golden chalice.

We eat in comfortable silence for the rest of the meal. No more memories, no more questions; just food.

***

Finox

Goren and I are shown to separate chambers on the same floor below Arysalia's tower. It feels as though we are guards of her tower, but if I am honest, I'd guard her with my life any day. My heart twinges with pain, listening to her and her mother speak of their time apart. It brought me back to when my parents did not return.

I need to speak with her alone, but I don't want to upset her or the queen. There is a gentle knock at my door. "Come in," I shout.

"Your Majesty, there is a note for you." The young male servant bows and hands me the rolled note. Reaching into the pocket of my trousers, I retrieve a gold coin.

Flipping it off my thumb, the boy catches it. "Thank you!"

"You're welcome," I reply as he shuts the door behind himself. I untie the green ribbon around the note. There is handwriting that curves and moves almost the same way Arysalia moves, with flourishing bold points.

Kingling,

Come to my tower in two hours' time. I need to speak with my mother a bit more, but we need to speak as well. There are things I haven't had the courage to admit.

Love,

Princess

***

Arysalia

"Mother, can you please explain what happened when the king died? Samarra has blotches of black all over her arms and part of her chest from destroying the dagger."

"Well, surprisingly enough, I was there to witness it. It was the only time I was brought out of the dungeon that I can clearly remember." She leans over in her seat and rings the servant's bell.

Moments later, there is a soft knock. "Come in," my mother commands gently.

"Yes, Your Majesty." The beautiful young woman, with slightly pointed ears and a green hue to her hair, curtsies and bows her head.

I wonder what her magic is. I don't remember her from before I left.

"Please fetch the princess's head guard."

Without a word, the servant bows and departs.

"Why do we need him?"

"Because he is a memory recall fae," she says in a way that makes me feel stupid.

How could I have forgotten?

"Well, that is handy. Was he there as well?"

"Yes, he was the guard to retrieve me and hold my chains during the entire event," she admits with a look I can't quite place.

It's not long before there is another soft knock on the door. "Come in."

"Your Majesty, what can I do for you this evening?" Brandon bows. His gaze contains a familiarity I don't recall from before I left. I will analyze that another time.

"I need you to recall the memory of the king's death for me. I need Arysalia to see."

I suck in a breath and almost choke on the air. "No, no, that's okay. I don't need to see it." A sickening feeling washes over me.

"Don't you want to see how incredible it was?" Her eyes light up with joy, and I'm just a tiny bit afraid of her in this moment.

"No, Mother. I watched it happen on our end, and that was terrifying enough. I don't need to see what could have possibly happened to Samarra if she didn't succeed the way she did." I stand abruptly.

"I'm sorry, Arysa, I didn't realize." She dims a bit, and her voice loses its joy. "We can have Brandon show you whenever you want, should you change your mind."

Brandon gives an almost imperceptible nod.

I need to get out of here; the room is suffocating me. I need to see Finox; he will be able to bring me back to Xandelar, to make me feel grounded. I am almost vibrating with anxiety.

"I'm going to go up to bed if that's okay, Mother?" I question, with a little more confidence than what I am feeling inside.

"Yes, of course, darling flower. Go. Sleep," she commands. I lean in and kiss her on the forehead.

"Brandon," she says, "I need you to stay here for a moment. There are things we need to discuss about the safety of the kingdom."

There is my exit.

I love her, but I can't relive the events of what just happened. He was an awful king, but I do not wish to watch the death of anyone else; this journey has taken its toll... Samarra's decline after destroying the dagger was enough. I console my anxious mind as I make my way back to my tower.

Chapter 76

Finox

I GIVE A GENTLE knock on the chamber door at the top of the tower. There is no answer, so I knock again and wait.

"Sneaking around in the dark, Kingling?" Arysalia steps out from the shadows of the stairs behind me, scaring me more than I care to admit.

"Absolutely," I say with a tiny bit of confidence.

"Oh really? You know it's creepy to sneak around a castle at night." She reminds me of what I have been guilty of for the last five years. I can't tell if it bothers her anymore or if she has changed her mind.

"Well, Princess, I could not resist your beauty." I wink, because I know how much it affects her. The dark pools of her eyes widen almost completely, hiding the lovely green that has enchanted me from day one.

"Open the door, King," she commands.

I push the door open, and she ducks in under my arm. She opens her arms wide in the center of the room, spinning a bit. "Welcome to my humble abode."

The room is very much Arysalia. Weapons are hanging carefully along one wall, bookshelves as tall as the ceiling line another, and lastly, the last two walls are covered in beautiful windows. Hanging vine plants surround the windows, and the windowsill is hidden beneath more plants that I can't even attempt to name.

"It is quite lovely," I admit, because it is. It smells just like her: spring flowers and sea salt.

"Now, since you have kissed my mother, I think it's time for you to kiss me." She is not pulling her punches in here, apparently.

A thrill runs up my spine in anticipation.

"Kiss your mother? I did no such thing, Princess."

Did I? I find myself searching for my own memory, confused.

"When I introduced you, you placed a kiss atop her hand. I have not once received a kiss from you."

Is she serious right now? I have kissed her more times than she knows.

"Well, I did kiss you on the head when you were upset, when you slept, and when you were drugged asleep in the canoe."

Her eyes go wide.

I have said too much.

"You didn't!" Her voice gets a little squeaky and high-pitched. She doesn't look angry or upset; she looks surprised, and there's an expression I can't quite place.

"I might have." I shrink back a little bit; she can be quite terrifying.

"Fix it then," she demands, her chin lifted with the slightest bit of defiance, the green of her eyes completely gone.

I am now even more confused. "Fix what, Arysalia?"

"Kiss me," she says. "Don't make me beg, because I won't ask you again."

Before she can change her mind, I pounce.

Arysalia, the Princess of Issalitia, has finally given in to the fact that I am indeed her mate. She kisses me hard and deep. Her hands roam through my hair, almost scratching into my scalp. I love every second of it. Working my hands down her body, I slowly unlace, untie, and unbutton all her clothing. As I do so, her blades and other weapons begin to fall to the ground.

With a hand I didn't know was no longer in my hair, she pushes me back hard.

"What—"

"Take off your clothes." Her eyes are feral. "Now."

While I begin to undress myself, she steps out of her own clothing. My goddess is stunning. I knew she was beautiful, sexy even, but this is a whole new level. Her petite frame is toned, with muscles and soft curves.

My mouth is dry. I have seen those nipples before, and I need them in my mouth. I move with unnatural speed and lift her up by her thighs and pin her up onto the cold stone wall beside the chamber's door. She smiles down at me with a smirk that does things to my heart I can't even begin to explain.

I kiss the smirk right off her face, adjusting her head back to get a deeper kiss. She melts fully in my arms. I feel her heat against my *still-on* trousers. I moved too quickly to have her against the wall. My cock strains against the blasted fabric.

Slowly, she begins to move from side to side around me, legs laced and pelvis creating perfect figure eights over my cock.

The feel of her in my hands drives me to the edge of reality. My mind is fighting to give in completely, wanting this pleasure to last longer. As I explore her body pinned against mine, her soft flesh begins to turn to gooseflesh.

"Fuck," I accidentally say out loud. She smirks, slow and knowing, and suddenly she's on my lips.

She is finally mine.

The room around us seems to have dropped a few degrees. We went from flames nearly melting us from the inside to being able to see our breath in the air.

Arysalia pulls back and looks around. "What the fuck is happening? It's freezing in here." She shivers in my arms.

Before I can respond to her, the candles in the room snuff out, leaving the room completely pitch black. A cool breeze blows through the room. I go still when I hear it. The scratchy ancient voice of what can only be the Dryad.

A voice echoes through our chamber. "King of illusions, king of stealth, King of Valador, remember our bargain. You will return as promised, or your health will suffer. If you have not returned in two days' time, a curse will follow in kind. The land of illusions may suffer through time."

"What the fuck is happening? What bargain?" Arysalia looks to me, eyes filled with confusion. "Who was that?"

How do I explain this to her without making her anger flare?

"It's hard to explain, but the Dryad was in the forest after we met for the first time. We were trying to find a way to save Issalitia." I take a breath and lower her gently to the floor. The cold that had once filled the space dissipates, and heat falters between us. "She told us a riddle and said the payment for the riddle was a favor."

Her eyebrows knit together. "Royals don't make bargains," she tells me, as if I don't already know this. "You should not have done that!"

"How could I not? I couldn't let you be trapped in a kingdom for the rest of your life, I couldn't not have you, Arysalia."

"You could have! You could come and go, and no one would have known." Her eyes shut, and she lets out a long breath. "You should not have done that for me."

"I didn't have a choice. I love you, Arysalia. You are my mate, the other half of my heart," I admit to her. "I want to make you my queen and I want you to have everything you have always wanted; freedom, love, happiness."

I scoop her back up into my arms, and she doesn't push me away.

"Well, I guess we have another quest on our hands, Your Majesty," she hums, a twinkle in her eye.

"I wouldn't want to save the continent with anyone else."

I kiss her hard and deep, so she never forgets she is mine.

To be continued...

401

Epilogue

Dryad

THE FOREST AROUND ME is changing, and the darkness that once lurked here has also changed. There is a sickness that is claiming my Wild Timber Forest. The king beneath the desert's beasts are moving into the shadows. They are infecting and killing my creatures. The shrubbles are gone, the green meadow sprites are dead. What looks like dried or dead grass to a regular fae looks like murdered flowerful creatures.

Their once vibrant colors and brilliant stalks of grass, which jumped and played in the meadows and along the banks of the stream, have all been drained of their color. I knew there would be retaliation from the desert king if I helped Issalitia. However, I did not expect his beasts and monsters to destroy the creatures of peace and joy.

The knots in my ancient stomach are twisting, the agony of losing just one of my creatures of magic is too much. The forest's only hope is in the hands of the king of illusions and his spring princess...

Glossary

Characters – (Difficult Pronunciations)

- Arysalia - AR-IS-AH-LEE-AH

- Dryad - DRY-AD - Wood/tree nymph, protectors of the forest.

- Finox - FIN-OX

- Goren - GO-R-N

- Muphion Jungle Witch - DEZ-MEL-DA - Is a dogla shifter named Dezmelda

- Samarra - SAH-M-AR-AH

- Seraphina Zinnia - SARE-AH-F-EEN-AH Z-IN-EE-AH - The last fire goddess.

- Zandra - Z-AN-DER-AH

Locations/Regions

- Agen Springs - AA-GEN - Named for the God of

Destiny.

- Azure Beach - AZ-SURE - Blue Beach.

- Eastern/Western Branera Tempest— as seen on the map

- Geras - GAAR-AS - Temple of the Geras (Gifts)

- Haemah - HAY-MAH - Temple of Haemah (Blood) - Where the enchanted dagger was kept, created by Haeman God of Blood.

- Issalitia - IZ-AL-EET-YAH - Kingdom of the Goddess

- Issalitian River - River of the Goddess

- Muphion Jungle - MOO-F-EE-ON - For the Goddess of the Lost (Lost Minds).

- Nedona - NEH-DOE-NAH - Continent - God of Birth - The Continent is said to be created as a gift to the fae, a gift from their gods who once roamed Xandelar.

- Northern/Southern Branera Tempest— as seen on the map

- Orcus Avala Mountain Range -

ORE-KUS-AVA-LA - Deadly snow people/avalanches.

- Phymis Desert - FEE-MIS - For the God of the Sun.

- Ramman - RAH-MAN - Kingdom of Lightning

- Thatin Cliffs - THAT-IN - For the God of Miracles (if you survive the Muphion Jungle, that is).

- Valador - VAH-LAH-DORE - Kingdom of Valor

- Wild Timber Forest - Forest between Issalitia and Valador.

- Xandelar - Z-AND-EL-AHR - A planet.

- Xoneas - ZON-YS - Kingdom of the Dark (desert kingdom beneath the sand) (Note: Bring Nedona under control using the enchanted blade of Rythorin).

- Ynos Delta - EE-NOSE - For the Goddess of Rivers.

Creatures/Objects

- Carow - CAR–ROW - Black carrion bird, eats leftovers from other predators, they are considered a nuisance bird, but are incredibly intelligent

- Dagger of Rythorin - RYE–TH–ORE–IN - An enchanted dagger made from dragon–forged metal, with onyx enchanted gems.

- Dark fae - Like normal fae beings, but they use their elemental magic for dark, sinister acts. Most are found in the kingdom beneath the sand and the Muphion Jungle.

- Death dingo - The wild dog of the desert, it hunts in packs but can also be domesticated by the evilest sort. They can be found in dens within the Kingdom of Xoneas.

- Dogla - DOE–G–LA - Tiger/panther hybrid, with thick back stripes that are chaotic, not uniform.

- Enigma Assassins - The worst of the worst fae, who use their talents to kill and are contracted to do whatever is necessary by the buyer.

- Grog draft - A caffeinated, hot beverage.

- Hippogriff - HIP-AH-GRIFF - Part griffin, part horse. The hippogriff is a creature of myth on some continents, but on Nedona, they are the favored pet of Valador. The king keeps the only pair of twins ever to have been born. Hippogriffs are known only to conceive one foal per cycle. Sasha and Greta are a mystical, magical beast of a mystery on Nedona.

- Leporis fae - LEP-OR-IS - Humanoid with hare features and fae elemental magic.

- Naiads - NAY-AD - Rivers/waterways, guardians of the water.

- Oracat - ORA-CAT - As a kitten, they stand no taller than one foot, have ears with points, and have an eight-pointed star on their forehead. This type of magical feline is exclusively female; it can mate with any large feline, but the resulting females will be born as an oracat with feathered fur and owl-like eyes. As they mature, they grow into a massive panther creature.

- Pumar - PUM-ARR - Puma and a humanoid that plays with their food and kills for sport, not dinner.

- Sand Wyrm - WUR-M - No eyes, only a nose, it cannot hear where you are or see you, but it can smell you. From one hundred miles away, it can scent the sweat running down your back. If there is food between you and the sand wyrm, you will stay alive.

- Spinspiders - The size of a large human, spinspiders spin a web around you while you sleep, and eat you right then and there.

- Zorag - ZORE-AG - A hell hound created by the king of Xoneas. Like the death dingo but larger, more aggressive, and more despicable, as it is a succubus of emotion, power, and feeling.

- Zink - ZI-INK - Big, unintelligent beast, with a plated back to protect it from attack and the sun's heat. They wander the desert looking for food and companionship.

Goren, Samarra, Arysalia, Finox

Acknowledgements

I WOULD LIKE TO take a moment of your time to acknowledge the people who have supported me throughout this journey. *The Kingdom Rescue* is my first-ever fantasy novel, and also my second published work. I have grown a lot as an author. I wrote *Beneath the Willows* about an experience that was very similar to one I have lived myself. A lot of the details are real, but about twenty-five percent is dramatized fiction. *The Kingdom Rescue* is an entirely different work; I created a world, characters, plot, and relationships based on a dream that I had. Book two will follow. In it, we will find out what happens to Nedona and what the Dryad has in store for Arysalia and Finox.

Now down to the actual acknowledgements. First, my husband, Brandon, has been with me through all the words, edits, and drawings. He has helped me in more ways than even he can imagine, and I wouldn't have been able to create this novel without him. Next, my son told me, "Write me a story about dragons, Mommy." It may not be about dragons specifically, but I did it for you, buddy. To all my friends and family who have been supporters, my best friend Niki, and the girls from my traveling annotating book club (you, the 'Unhinged

Belles'). To Amy, my editor at Plotwise Editorial, who took the time (and my money) to help me fine-tune and create the best piece of work I could. She helped me with plot holes, spelling, and tenses (God, I suck at keeping to one tense) for all of that, I am thankful for you. I hope we can work together on book two and beyond!

Lastly, to my outstanding author-friend E.S. Portman for doing the final proofread before it went off to Audible. Thank you so much for always being here for me when I need you the most. You were one of my first-ever bookish friends, and now we are authors together. I don't think I can say thank you enough; words can't express the depth of my appreciation for you.

Stay tuned for what happens next on Nedona! Follow my Instagram @author_k.l.blake for updates on the story and other works in progress I am cooking up!

Thank you again,

Love,

K.L. Blake